Until The Rescue Ship Arrives

D. E. Miller

Published by D. E. Miller, 2024.

This is a work of fiction. Similarities to real people, places, or events are entirely coincidental.

UNTIL THE RESCUE SHIP ARRIVES

First edition. October 26, 2024.

Copyright © 2024 D. E. Miller.

ISBN: 979-8227070128

Written by D. E. Miller.

Also by D. E. Miller

The Road and Other Liars
Until The Rescue Ship Arrives

Chapter 1

Father Gerald Hughes folded his eyeglasses and tucked them into his jacket pocket, and then, with his walking stick in hand to assist his aging knees, he hiked down the steep trail to the beach as Buster, his old yellow Labrador retriever, led the way. Father Hughes enjoyed visiting this narrow stretch of beach on cool, misty mornings during the middle of the week. Here, he could fill his lungs and savor the ocean air as the rhythm of the waves cleared and quieted his mind. Here, he could escape into a little piece of the world still untouched by the troubles in the larger world surrounding it. Here, on this beach, remained a remnant of that world where he needn't pretend he was free. Here, he could think, wander, and do as he pleased, and what pleased him were the simple things that no sensible society could regard as revolutionary. Here was a remnant of that old world that now existed only in the scattered, ignored oases where the reign of human pride and folly had not yet spread its darkness. Here, in the company of the waves, the aromas, and the solitude of this little strip of sand, rocks, and driftwood, he could briefly return to an undefiled vestige of life as it once was. And as he strolled at the edge of the defiant, unyielding, unconquerable Pacific Ocean, he could hope life would be so again.

There was nothing exceptional about this less-frequented beach. Other beaches north and south of this spot were more spacious, picturesque, and popular, so Father Hughes and Buster often had this beach to themselves. Here, free and unleashed, Buster could meander to and fro, sniffing all the mingling scents and scrutinizing all the items of dog interest that the ocean had tossed onto the shore. At the same time, Father Hughes could permit his thoughts to roam and allow the sea air and "the chorus of the waves," as he called it, to clear and rest his mind.

Buster discovered half of a Dungeness crab shell lying near the surf's edge and began carrying it in his mouth. "So, Buster, you've found yourself a trophy to take home, have you?" said Father Hughes. "Don't strut too proudly with it, or the seagulls will think you have something worth stealing."

Suddenly, Buster halted, dropped the crab shell, and gazed at an object farther down the beach.

"What do you see there, boy?" said Father Hughes as he paused. He put on his glasses, but the object was three hundred yards or more down the beach, and he could not tell whether it was a sea animal or a piece of debris that had drifted to shore. Then he saw the object stretch out and try to crawl onto the beach.

"Oh, Lord! It's a person! It's a person! Come, Buster, come!"

Buster bolted down the beach as Father Hughes trotted at a pace as near to running as his worn knees allowed. Buster halted about ten feet from the person who barely left marks in the sand with their fingertips as they feebly attempted to pull themself from the surf. As Father Hughes caught up to Buster, he heard Buster's short, low growls followed by a few quick puffs of stifled barks.

"I'm here to help you, my friend," Father Hughes shouted as he approached the person who lay facing away from him. "Can you hear me, friend?" he asked.

The person gave no reply and did not move. Using his walking stick for support, he knelt and lightly rested his hand on their shoulder. They wore a tan uniform with a hood that had shifted and obscured their face. Father Hughes gently rolled the person toward him and pushed the jacket hood away from their face.

UNTIL THE RESCUE SHIP ARRIVES

"Oh, Lord! Oh, Lord! What have we found? "Father Hughes gasped as he lurched backward. He knew this could not be a human. For a moment, he wrestled with the urge to run. He could not predict how the being would react under stress and fear if touched. But for Father Hughes, such concerns had to be shoved aside. Compassion had to prevail over his fear of the consequences. He leaned in and lifted the being's head, resting it in his hands."Who are you, child? Wherever are you from?" he asked as he gently stroked the alien's cheek. As he did so, the alien exhaled with a faint, almost musical sigh.

The alien was tall, around six feet, Father Hughes guessed. Its head and limbs were proportionally similar to a human's. It had light brown hair, clipped short, very soft, and thick in texture. Its facial features, while vaguely Asian in appearance, did not match those of any earthly race. Its eyes were closed. It had a petite nose, a wide mouth, and full lips—complementary features forming a proportionally attractive face. Its ears were somewhat smaller than a human ear, with contours similar to those of a human; its neck was noticeably fuller and thicker than a human's, and the being had five delicately tapered fingers on each hand.

Father Hughes gently felt its arms and legs for broken bones. As he did so, he realized the being was shivering.

"We must get you out of here, child." He pulled his cell phone from his pocket and was about to call the emergency services, but then he paused. His "little voice," as he often called his intuition, rebelled against the idea. He had long ago learned to trust his little voice and decided to try a different option.

"Hello, Mother Catherine, this is Father Hughes. I'm in a bit of a situation here, Mother, so I must be brief. I have a critical matter for which I need your help."

"Well . . . yes, Father. What is it?"

"Is your little guest cottage available?"

"Yes, it's available."

"I recall that a few of your sisters have nursing skills. Is that correct?"

"Yes, two of them were studying to become nurses before discovering they had a vocation to the religious life. What's this all about, Father?"

"Which of them do you know to be the most discreet, unshakeable, and absolutely reliable?"

"I have complete confidence in all of our sisters, Father, from the youngest to the oldest. Again, I must ask, what's this all about?"

"Mother Catherine, this is most important. I can't go into details now, but you will understand. I have someone—an exceptional someone—who needs care and refuge, which I'll explain later, and this person's presence must be entirely confidential. I ask you to assist me in helping them."

"Father, I'm beginning to feel uncomfortable with this. I don't think what you are requesting is something we can provide."

"Mother, I'm sure you and your sisters are the best option for helping the person I hope to bring to you. I'm familiar enough with all of you to know that each of you is of high character, but please, choose the sister with nursing skills who you are sure is an absolute rock of reliability and discretion. And please make the little cottage available for this guest, if you would. I hate to impose upon you, Mother, but I promise you will understand my urgency when we arrive. With your permission, we will be coming to you shortly. We shall drive directly to the cottage and meet you there. Please be there and have the bed ready for the guest, and please, whichever sister you select, have her bring whatever first aid items you may have on hand in case we need them. I hope to be there in about an hour."

Mother Catherine paused and then replied, "Father, I must say, I am not comfortable at all with this idea, but if this is for someone in great need, I cannot refuse. I will trust your judgment on this, Father, but I hope this will not be a mistake."

"Thank you, Mother. You will understand when we arrive, I assure you."

The alien's shivering worsened, and it momentarily half-opened its emerald-colored eyes and uttered a weak moan as it looked at Father Hughes before closing its eyes again. Father Hughes patted the alien's hand, "I'll do what I can for you, my friend," he said softly. "If you can understand me, please do not be afraid."

Father Hughes removed his jacket and lifted the alien's upper body enough to drape the jacket around the being's shoulders and torso. As he did so, the alien feebly attempted to help raise itself but fell limp.

During this time, Buster never displayed aggression toward the being but behaved with cautious curiosity. He hesitantly stepped up to sniff the alien, then jerked away as Father Hughes struggled to cradle the being in his arms. With painful effort, Father Hughes lifted the alien and stood upright. He wobbled and shifted his stance several times before feeling sure of his balance. "I'm glad you are slender, child," he whispered as he caught his breath. "Come, Buster, let's take our friend to Mother Catherine."

With steady, deliberate steps, he plodded down the beach toward the path leading up to his car as his walking stick, tethered around his wrist, left a narrow drag trail in the sand behind him.

The mist covered his eyeglasses, which he had forgotten to remove before carrying the alien back toward the car. Twice, he almost tripped over pieces of driftwood, but he dared not set down the unconscious being to remove his eyeglasses because he knew he'd never be able to lift the alien again. He lowered his head, chin to his chest, to see over the top of his eyeglasses and trudged on, ignoring the burning fatigue in his arms. Buster trotted alongside him, occasionally sniffing the being's dangling hand, otherwise, paying barely more attention to the alien than if the being were an armload of driftwood that Father Hughes was carrying.

When he reached the base of the trail leading up to his car, Father Hughes grimaced as he squatted, slumped rearward, and rolled onto his back in a controlled collapse onto the sand, landing with the alien on his chest. Then, as gently as possible, he pulled himself out from under the still-shivering being.

"I'm sorry, my friend, I have to pause," he said as he leaned back onto the sand and tried to catch his breath and rest the muscles in his arms that now, unladen, continued to contract as if they were still resisting the weight of the alien. Buster rushed over to him. "It's all right, my good dog," he said as he reached up, stroked Buster's cheek, and patted his head, "we'll be up and going again in a moment, boy."

But how would he do it, he wondered? He could never climb the trail while carrying the alien. Even if the strength in his arms didn't fail him, he couldn't avoid losing his balance on the steep, uneven trail, sending both of them tumbling back to the bottom. He sat up, wiped his glasses with his shirt, and slid them into his chest pocket.

"We'll have to come up with an idea to get our friend up this trail, Buster," said Father Hughes as he sat and rested his arms and tried to devise a means to carry the alien up the trail to his car.

He began to feel the pressure of time as he considered ways to get the alien up the trail. So far, they had been lucky that no one else had stopped at the parking area, but Father Hughes knew that could happen at any moment.

"Ah, I think I have an idea for us, my friend," he said softly to the alien. He rose to his knees and removed the jacket he'd wrapped around the alien's shoulders. Then he pulled the jacket's cloth belt from its loops and set it aside. He then rolled up the jacket, leaving the sleeves stretching out from each end, and formed it into an improvised sling. He then ran the sleeves under the being's armpits and shaped the body of the jacket to create as wide a band as possible across the being's chest to spread the pressure of the sling over a larger area. Then he tied the sleeves behind the alien's back. He ran his hand under the sling to flatten a fold over the alien's chest that would have caused a pressure point and detected what he believed were breasts beneath the alien's jacket. "So, you're girl alien, it seems," he said in a low voice. "Forgive my clumsiness, child."

Next, Father Hughes tied the jacket's belt around the alien's torso and arms, just above the elbow, to prevent her arms and hands from dragging on the ground. Then he slid his walking stick under the knot tied behind the alien's back, turned the walking stick a quarter turn, leaned back, pulled, and dragged the alien a few feet up the trail.

"This idea will work, my child! This will work!" he said.

"Step back, lean back, and pull. Step back, lean back, and pull," Father Hughes whispered to himself as he tried to establish a rhythm to the work. After each pull, with sweat mingling with the drizzle on his face, he prayed for the strength he needed for the next pull. He tried not to think of the sharp twinges in his knees or the sting of the sweat-tinged rain dripping into his eyes, but instead, he kept speaking softly to the alien, "We're closer with each pull, my friend. Stay with us. If you can hear me, don't give up. Stay strong. I'll get you some help."

Step by step, pull by pull, they climbed the trail. Finally, with one last straining tug, they were beside the car.

Father Hughes, breathing heavily, his knees, his entire body rebelling with pain and fatigue, gently lowered the alien to the ground. He removed the belt and jacket, then gently lifted the alien's head to see if she responded to his touch. She was still shivering and did not react when Father Hughes patted her cheek and spoke to her. Buster, less cautious now, crept up to the alien, his nose nearly touching her face, and then he jerked backward and watched for a response.

"She's not well, Buster boy. She's in grave danger," said Father Hughes as he patted Buster's head. "We must try to save her, you and I."

Buster leaned again toward the alien, licked her cheek, and stepped back. The alien's eyes opened momentarily, then closed again.

Father Hughes opened the rear door to his small, old, four-door sedan, then as gently as he could, he lifted the alien and lay her in the seat, on her side with her knees bent, then covered her again with his jacket. As he and Buster were about to climb into the car, a helicopter passed overhead just above treetops and flew north along the highway. He stood and looked up at the helicopter as it passed overhead, thinking that the crew would find it suspicious for someone not to appear surprised and curious.

"Black and unmarked, Buster Boy," he said, "as if no one could guess they are Special Security Police. Let's not linger and give them a reason to become interested in us."

Father Hughes started the car and turned the heater and blower on high. Even though he dripped with sweat, he knew the alien was in danger of dying from hypothermia. As he turned onto the highway, he weighed the choice of either staying on the main roads to save time or taking the winding, less traveled minor roads to lessen the chance of running into Special Security Police checkpoints. The Special Security Police had been setting frequent, random traffic checkpoints to intimidate the public and to let everyone know that life in this country, and throughout the world, was different now. However, Father Hughes had lived in this area of Oregon for many years and was reasonably familiar with the local roads. Driving the local and secondary roads would cost them extra time, but he believed they would be the safer choice. Father Hughes called Mother Catherine again and informed her they would arrive later than he had initially expected. Then he phoned his friend, Doctor Paul Griffith.

"Hello, Paul. It's Gerald. I've got an important favor to ask of you today. Actually, it's a favor I require of you."

"Well, yes, I vaguely remember someone named Gerald. Gerald Hughes, I think his name was—a famously bad golfer, as I recall. Hello Gerald, I hate to refuse you a favor, but I'm afraid I'll have to turn you down on this one. I am booked solid until . . . ."

"No, Paul!" Father Hughes interjected. "This matter is more important than I can explain now, so please listen to me and do me this favor. It's important, my friend, crucial. Gather whatever medical gear you need for a house call, and meet me at—how should I say this—meet me at Mother's little cottage as soon as you can."

Doctor Griffith paused, then replied, "Mother's little cottage? Oh, I get it. What's with the code talk, Gerald? What's going on?"

"I can't explain further now, Paul. Be there as soon as you can—no, Paul, you must listen to me—listen! You know me well enough to know I wouldn't ask this of you without a good reason. No, Paul, I'm telling you, listen to me! Whatever you have on your calendar today must wait, or you must find someone else to cover for you. It's that important. You will understand, I promise you. You must do this, Paul! I'm pleading with you as a friend—insisting if that's what it takes. It's of vital importance."

The phone was silent, and then an irritated sigh."Alright, Gerald, but this had better be something as important as you say it is, or you and I will have a very lively conversation afterward! I'll be there, but it will be around an hour and a half!" Then, Griffith abruptly disconnected the call.

Father Hughes then placed his phone into a Faraday pouch. These pouches and wallets were illegal, as was the black market phone Father Hughes used for this phone call. These clandestinely manufactured phones made it nearly impossible for the authorities to identify or track the person using them, so, predictably, there was a flourishing black market for the phones and the Faraday pouches, which blocked radio frequencies. As an extra precaution, many citizens kept their phones in Faraday pouches when not using them. The black market phones were inexpensive because their only function was to make and receive phone calls, so if necessary, these phones could be thrown away without significant cost to avoid being caught possessing one. The Resistance often sabotaged the regime's communication monitoring system, but the citizens were never sure of monitoring system's status, so they always assumed it was operational. Like many other citizens, Father Hughes used his legal, trackable, traceable phone only for a few mundane calls each week to avoid his phone call record being "flagged" for low phone usage, which triggered suspicion of possessing a black market phone. But, for Father Hughes and an increasing number of citizens, their primary phone was their black market phone. It wasn't a foolproof practice, but it helped. Citizens had quickly learned that the less the regime knew about them, the safer they were.

The mist became heavy rain as Father Hughes drove through the low coastal mountains. There was only light traffic, and so far, no checkpoints or more helicopters flying overhead. Father Hughes wondered if, perhaps, the helicopter he'd seen at the parking area had been looking for a crashed alien craft or the alien being who was now lying helpless in the back seat of his car. He hoped that he was the only person in the world who knew of the existence of his passenger. But what did he know about this passenger of his? Nothing, except that some calamity had tossed her into the ocean and that she had survived long enough to wash up on a wet, chilly beach. Was she the only survivor? For that matter, would she survive? How could it be a reality that he, an old retired priest, was transporting a shivering, unconscious, perhaps dying being from another world, whisking her away to Mother Catherine's convent and, in doing so, possibly bringing unforeseen dangers to Mother Catherine, the sisters, his friend Doctor Griffith, and himself? Among all the other unknowns, he didn't know the intentions of this seemingly helpless creature lying in the seat behind him. Was she benign by nature, or was she malicious? She had shown no malicious indications, but in her weakened condition, that proved nothing. What was her purpose for being here? Why had his instincts moved him to hide this creature from the authorities, who were probably better able to care for her than Mother Catherine and Doctor Griffith? Could his instincts, in this instance, have been mistaken? Yes, the new regime was wicked and corrupt, but would not this be a matter that even they would handle prudently and appropriately? He bristled against that notion even as it passed through his mind.

He had committed himself and the others to the consequences, whatever they may be, of several decisions he had made this morning. There were so many questions riding on the backs of those decisions he had already made and the decisions yet to be made this day, with nothing but his instincts, his "little voice," to guide him. His instincts had usually proven reliable when circumstances forced him to make hasty decisions of importance. Still, he was always tense until the outcome proved him right. More burdensome decisions were already queueing up as he drove: how would his friends react when they realized he had enlisted them in the task of saving the life of a being from another world? What would they do next if they successfully saved this creature? They couldn't hide her forever. Her appearance, while beautiful, was unmistakably nonhuman. She could never show herself in public. How would they protect her and care for her if she survived? If she died, how and where could they bury her discretely?

A thousand what-ifs spun through his mind, and he picked through each one, hoping that something would suggest a plan to follow, but no ideas presented themselves. He would have to proceed one step at a time until he understood their situation well enough to form a plan. For the moment, it would be challenging enough to avoid cops and arrive safely at the convent.

Finally, he turned onto the long, narrow driveway leading into the convent. Burrowed deep into his thoughts, he had nearly driven past it. Father Hughes parked in front of the cottage beside Doctor Griffith's car. A young nun, whom he recognized as Sister Clare, stood inside the cottage doorway, watching for him. As Father Hughes climbed out of the vehicle, he discovered he was now so stiff and sore that he could barely stand. Buster bounded through the driver's door after him. Doctor Griffith, Mother Catherine, and Sister Clare hustled out of the cottage and hurried toward the car to see who Father Hughes had brought to them.

"Stop! Please! Wait, just a moment!" shouted Father Hughes, laying his right hand on the car hood to steady himself as he walked around the front of the car. "I must first tell you something of vital importance."

Everyone halted and looked at Father Hughes as they awaited an explanation.

"I don't know how to say this in a way that won't be shocking, but the person lying in the back seat is . . . ." He paused, barely able to speak the words that he was about to say, "The person lying in the back seat is not human."

"What do you mean, Gerald? What are you talking about?" demanded Doctor Griffith.

"I'll explain, Paul, but first, you must understand this poor person truly is from another world. I'm serious. But do not fear her. I say 'her' because I think it is a female, though I'm not sure. She is unconscious now. I believe she's dying from hypothermia. We must try to save her!"

Sister Clare impulsively rushed toward the car and opened the rear passenger door. Upon seeing the face of the alien lying unconscious on the seat, she cried out in a half-gasp half-scream and stepped back from the car, her eyes wide, her hands covering her mouth. Mother Catherine and Doctor Griffith stared at the alien lying helpless before them.

"Who? What? What is that? What does this mean, Father?" shouted Mother Catherine, her tone blending fear with anger. "What are you doing to us? What have you brought to us? Oh! This can't be real! This can't be happening!"

"What do you expect me to do here, Gerald?" growled Doctor Griffith. "I'm calling the sheriff! This is a matter for the authorities! I can't believe that you—Gerald, I—if it were just you and me standing here, I'd—I'm so damn mad I can't even say what I want to say to you right now!"

Griffith pulled his phone from his coat pocket.

"Stop, Paul! Stop!" shouted Father Hughes. He rushed to grab Griffith's hand before he could dial, but his stiff, weary knees responded too slowly, and he stumbled, falling hard onto the wet blacktop driveway. "Put the phone away, Paul! Put it away!" he shouted as he rolled onto his side. "I'll explain it as well as I can! We can't hand her over! We can't! Hear me, friends, hear me! I found her wet and struggling on a cold beach, trying to pull herself out of the water. She had no strength left in her at all—none. She could barely whisper a pitiable moan. I, too, was about to call the authorities—for the same reasons as you, I'm sure. But I knew, within my heart, I knew that it would be wrong. I didn't know why it would be wrong, and I still don't know, but I know it would be. As sure as I'm looking at all of you now, I was sure I shouldn't give her over to the authorities. So, instead, I carried that poor creature of God for a few hundred yards along the beach and dragged her another hundred yards up the path to the car, and not once did I sense evil or malice in her! Not even once, I tell you! Of course, I can't be sure, but I'm wagering there is no more evil in her than you'll find in you or me—perhaps a good deal less. But she'll soon be dead if we don't stop this bickering and get her inside that cottage, get her warm, and try to save her!"

He looked into the eyes of each of them as his Irish temper rose. His disappointment at his friends' reaction was turning to anger. His face reddened as he glared at them.

"So, what will it be?" he demanded. "Will you help this poor creature to live, or will you leave her to die? If you refuse to help her, I'll drive her to the sheriff's office myself, and no one will know that you'd ever laid eyes on her! No trouble will come to any of you! So, what's it going to be? Tell me now! What's it going to be?"

Father Hughes tried to stand but was about to fall again when Sister Clare rushed toward him, caught his arm, and helped him to his feet. Then they heard the alien sing two short, clear musical syllables as she lifted her head and tried to raise herself in the car seat. Through half-opened eyes, the alien looked at Father Hughes, reached for him, and then collapsed onto the car seat. Buster ran to her and began licking her face. She weakly lifted her head again and tried to speak but only managed a weak moan, then lost consciousness.

"Damn it! Just damn it all!" growled Doctor Griffith as he stomped toward the car. "Mother! Sister! Help me get this person inside before somebody sees us out here!"

UNTIL THE RESCUE SHIP ARRIVES

Father Hughes, too stiff and wobbly to help lift the alien, hobbled to the cottage door and held it open for the others as they carried her inside.

"Mother, rip down the shower curtain from around the tub and spread it across the bed to keep it dry while we get these wet clothes off her. Quickly!" Doctor Griffith commanded. "Now, Sister, throw some blankets into the clothes dryer and get them good and warm—not too hot, though. We don't know what a normal, comfortable temperature is for this creature."

As Mother Catherine laid the shower curtain onto the bed, Doctor Griffith, who held the alien in his arms, laid her onto the bed.

"Mother, help me get these wet clothes off her while Sister Clare gets at a stream of warm water flowing through the shower wand in the bathtub so we can rinse the sand and grit off her and begin warming her up. Be careful, though, Sister. Don't let the water get warmer than you would use to bathe a baby, and run the warm water over the bottom and sides of the tub before we set her in it. Oh, and you, Gerald, you look like hell. You'd better go home, clean yourself up, and rest those knees. We'll handle this part of it. Do you need anything for pain? Well, okay, then. I'll call you if there is a problem, but I won't be specific over the phone. I now understand the 'code talk,' as I called it, you used during our phone conversation."

"Thank you all for helping her," said Father Hughes. "I'll be back later. Do call me immediately if there's a problem. Again, I thank you, my friends. I'm sure this is the right thing to do, and I know you'll take good care of her. I think she knows we're trying to help her, but our argument frightened her, so please speak gently around her so she feels safe."

"Gerald, you may have forgotten that I've been a doctor for almost as long as you've been a priest. My bedside manner got as good as it's ever going to get decades ago. But I think even I can avoid deliberately terrifying a patient, regardless of where they're from—Earth, outer space, or even downtown Portland. One thing I already know is that you'd better do some praying about this patient. I don't know a thing about this creature's physiology, so I don't dare do more than try to get her warm and provide as much comfort as possible. Any medicine could be poison to her, him, it, or whatever gender it turns out to be. By the time you get back, though, I may have at least figured out whether or not this creature is a female—that is if their species has such a thing as male and female. Anyway, Gerald, go home and get some rest. We'll do what we can for her."

Chapter 2

It was nearly 6:00 p.m. when Father Hughes awakened from his nap. His knees were still stiff, as were the muscles throughout his body, but his mind felt refreshed. Even the extraordinary events earlier in the day hadn't prevented him from falling into a deep sleep after the stress and physical exertions of the morning. He fed Buster and then dressed in his "civilian clothes," as he called them since he did not expect to exercise any priestly functions during this brief visit to the convent.

As he and Buster were about to climb into his sedan, a black Special Security Police van drove up the street toward them. The van slowed as it drew near and then stopped. Two armed officers, one slender, the other soft and fleshy, wearing black uniforms and battle gear, climbed out and swaggered toward Father Hughes. Buster growled as they approached.

"Control your dog, citizen, or we'll shoot it!" demanded the fatter one.

" Control yourselves!" snapped Father Hughes, instantly angered by their demeanor. "I'll put him in the car, so you big brave men won't have to worry about him."

" Don't get smart with us, old man, and don't do anything stupid."

"I suggest the same for the two of you," replied Father Hughes as he pushed the reluctant Buster into the car. "Now, what's the meaning of all of this? You have no cause to approach me."

The fatter officer, who had been doing the talking, suddenly grabbed Father Hughes by the lapel of his jacket and slammed him against the car. "You're kind of mouthy, aren't you, old man? You should be a little more polite and respectful when you speak to us. We can stop and question anybody at any time, old man. We don't need a reason, and we don't need your permission. So, turn around, put your hands on the car so I can check you for weapons."

Buster, barking and growling, slammed himself against the car window in a vain effort to defend Father Hughes.

Father Hughes stood and glared defiantly at the officer who, unaccustomed to noncompliance and uncertain now about what to do next, loosened his grip on Father Hughes' jacket. "Okay, old man," he said. You look like you want a piece of me. What are you going to do? Are you thinking about getting tough with me? I see that look in your eyes. Go ahead, old man. Show me what you got."

"Let me tell you something—both of you—I'm long past being afraid of anything that any man can do to me, including the likes of you two!" said Father Hughes. "I'm a citizen going about my business, breaking no law, but now I have you two arrogant, uniformed bullies roaming about, abusing your authority, and blighting my day. If I've committed a crime, arrest me. Otherwise, be on your way! No, on second thought, I think Thomas Carnahan would insist on hearing about all the wicked criminal acts you two heroes caught me committing—you know, those wicked crimes, whichever ones you invented in your head to give you an excuse to drive up, shove me around, and threaten to kill my dog. So, I demand that you arrest and charge me. That way, you'll be on record for arresting a vicious evildoer, and your superiors will award you for your valiant crime-fighting efforts. So, get on with it! Arrest me right now, this very minute!"

"How do you know Major Carnahan?" asked the skinny one.

"That's not for you to know. Come on, get on with it!"

"Show me your identification?" asked the fatter one.

"Arrest me, and I'll give it to you when we get to the station."

"I could arrest you right now for refusing to comply with a direct order from an officer, old man. That's six months in solitary under the new laws—and that's just for starters. Yeah, I think that's where we'll start. Tuttle, get his plate number. We'll I.D. him through that.

"Then get on with it!" replied Father Hughes.

"Why are you so eager now to get arrested? Do you think you're special just because you know Major Carnahan? A lot of people know him. What makes you think he'll come down on us for arresting you for disrespecting an officer of the state and refusing to comply with a direct order? I've also decided to add suspicion of subversive activities to the charges. So, if you go crying to Major Carnahan, old man, you might find out how good he takes care of his officers and how hard he comes down on subversives."

"Very well, stop dallying and arrest me for—what did you say the charges were? Never mind, whatever they were, just go ahead and add spitting on the sidewalk and giving dirty looks to a couple of arrogant jackboots to all your other phony charges."

"You're really pushing it, old man. So, you think being old and being friends with the Major gives you the right to disrespect law enforcement officers?" replied the fat one.

Father Hughes detected weakness in the officer and decided to push it further. "I have always respected everyone in authority who behaves in a manner worthy of respect. The two of you, however, have disgraced and disrespected yourselves through your unprofessional behavior. You're not law enforcers. You're just bullying slobs in uniform. But enough of this! Arrest me and haul me in. I have nothing further to say to either of you."

The two officers stepped back, huddled, and conversed in whispers. Then, the fatter officer sauntered back toward Father Hughes. "Listen up, old man. You're really, really lucky that it's been a long, busy day for us with lots of things yet to do. We've decided to give you a break this time, but the next time we run into you, we'll expect your full cooperation, or we'll run you in regardless of who you claim to know." Then he turned toward the thinner officer, "Let's go, Tuttle," he said, and they climbed into their van and drove away.

Still angry and faintly tremoring from adrenalin, Father Hughes climbed into his car. Buster whined, licked Father Hughes's face, and attempted to climb into his lap.

"Easy now, Buster. Down boy, easy," said Father Hughes as he petted and reassured Buster. "You can't climb into my lap. You're not a little puppy anymore. Everything is alright. The bad men are gone now. I know, you would have bitten both of them, wouldn't you? I would have let you bite them, too. I may have bitten them a few times myself. They deserved it, didn't they, boy? Go on now. Move over onto your side of the seat. That's a good boy. Now let's go and see how our poor visitor from far away is doing."

Before driving away, Father Hughes slipped his black market phone into the Faraday pouch again, grateful that the cops hadn't patted him down and discovered it. He then drove a circuitous route to the convent. The rain became heavy and drummed steadily on the roof of the car. Like a tonic, the patter of the rain soon had Buster curled up in the seat asleep. In his mind, Father Hughes replayed the confrontation with the Special Security Police. He could barely believe his audacity during the encounter, just as he could scarcely believe that he had somehow instantly fabricated the suggestion of having a close association with Major Carnahan. He marveled even more at the unbelievable result that his bluff had worked, and the two officers decided that arresting him was a gamble they didn't want to make. If the two officers changed their minds and brought the encounter to Canahan's attention, Carnahan might look into it and create problems for him. But he thought it was more likely that the two bullies had already decided, for their benefit, to ignore the incident, not document the encounter, and never mention it.

In truth, he had been in Carnahan's presence twice: once over thirty years ago, when he had baptized him, and again three years ago, in the early months of the coup that ushered in the new regime when Carnahan, freshly appointed to command the Special Security Police, had called and asked him to visit his dying mother and give her the sacraments. Carnahan's mother had been a parishioner at Father Hughes's parish in the years before he retired. After Carnahan's baptism, she became a Christmas and Easter Catholic and eventually ceased attending mass entirely. Years later, however, near death, she asked her son to find him and ask him to visit her.

The Special Security Police Northwest Region, which Carnahan commanded, was part of the recently formed, poorly organized, and clumsily implemented enforcement arm of the regime, combining police and military personnel to serve as the muscle of the new police state. The citizens hated them and regarded them as little more than brigands because of their frequent criminal acts and the ever-descending character quality of the recruits and their superiors. Father Hughes wondered if even an ember of faith remained within Carnahan. He was sure Carnahan would have had to demonstrate to his superiors that he possessed the requisite contempt toward all religious expressions and moral principles before they promoted him to his current position.

The rain had eased to a mist when Father Hughes pulled up to the guest cottage and parked beside Doctor Griffith's car. "Stay, boy," Father Hughes told Buster as he stepped out of the vehicle, leaving the window open a slit for Buster's sake. Mother Catherine met him at the door.

"Come in, Father, I'm glad you're here. I am just overwhelmed by all of this. I'm both fearful and amazed. I hardly believe this is real. We've learned a few things, though. Perhaps Doctor Griffith can explain better than I."

Doctor Griffith stepped from the bedroom and into the cottage's tiny living room. "Gerald, I don't really know what to say either. And I still don't know whether I ought to sock you in the jaw for getting me involved in this or hug you for it—this is beyond historical. No other doctor on this Earth, drunk or sober, can truthfully claim to have made a house call on a patient from another planet," he said, smiling slightly for the first time since the incident began. Just like Mother Catherine said, I hardly believe this is real. But anyway, here's what I've learned so far about her. By all appearances, she is a young adult female of her species—just as you thought. She has no serious injuries, but I'm sure she would have died from hypothermia had we not warmed her up. She was halfway through death's door when you brought her here. I nearly fell over when I first took her temperature. It was only sixty-two degrees! We did what we could to raise her body temperature and clean her up. I had no idea what her temperature should be, so we just kept her warm and hoped her body would return to its normal temperature, which it seems to have done. Her temperature is now a steady nine-four degrees Fahrenheit. Something else I noticed when I examined her is that she breathes deeply and has remarkable lung capacity. I attempted to open her mouth to examine her throat when I thought she was unconscious, but she slightly opened her eyes and cooperated as if she understood what I was doing. The structure of her larynx and vocal cords is beyond my ability to describe. It appears to me that she probably can make many different sounds, and probably many sounds at once. And with her lung capacity, who knows how long she could go without taking a breath? I wouldn't be surprised if she could hold her breath for as long as a dolphin or a seal—no exaggeration.

"Surprisingly enough, she seemed to trust us right away after she woke up the first time," Doctor Griffith continued. "She speaks in some kind of sing-song style, but fortunately, she can speak English. It was Sister Clare who first spoke to her, but I let her tell you all about that. When I first spoke to her, it was a little hard for me to understand her until she got better at flattening out the sing-song aspect so we could understand her. At first, Mother and I could only make out some words here and there, but Sister Clare understood her right away. Through Sister Clare, we learned that she can eat some Earth foods. I guess I just invented a new term, didn't I? Earth foods," he said, smiling once again. "She can eat steamed or roasted potatoes and sweet potatoes, steamed or roasted fish, and poached eggs. She can drink water. I believe tap water is probably safe for her, but as an extra precaution, we run her drinking water through a water filter that Mother Catherine uses. At first, she was too weak to feed herself, so Sister Clare patiently fed her with a spoon, and she ate a dab of mashed sweet potato and a poached egg. I was encouraged to see that she ate every last bit of it, and after talking for a while with Sister Claire, she fell asleep again. After she had slept for maybe another hour, she woke up and seemed alert, so I had a good long chat with her. Maybe I questioned her too soon, for too long, but I was eager to learn a few things about her and her civilization while I had the opportunity—who knows how long she'll be here among us. She was a good sport about it, and I learned a lot from her. But I'll tell you about that later. Come on into the bedroom, Gerald. I'll let Sister Clare tell you what she has learned from our alien patient. She learned something surprising, but she'd probably hit me in the head if I didn't let her tell you about it herself."

In the cramped bedroom, Sister Clare sat on a wooden chair at the bedside of the alien being."Hello, Father, she's sleeping again," Sister Clared whispered. "I heard what Doctor Griffith was telling you, and yes, I can understand her just fine," Sister Clare said, smiling and widening her eyes as she patted her hands together in a silent clap with almost childlike excitement. "She seems to know English very well," Sister Clare continued, "but because of her pronunciations and, for lack of a better term, her musical accent, you may have to listen carefully at first to pick out what she is saying. With a little effort, though, you can understand her. In fact, she is improving quickly and becoming easier to understand with each sentence she utters. She told me she can speak several other Earth languages, too.

"For the first hour or so after we brought her into the cottage, she drifted in and out of consciousness. She didn't utter so much as a sigh while Mother and I helped Doctor Griffith get her out of her wet garments. We washed her with warm water, dried her skin as gently as possible, and then covered her with blankets we had warmed in the clothes drier to get her temperature up. After only about forty-five minutes of being covered with the blankets, she became restless and tried to pull them off. Doctor Griffith took her temperature; amazingly, it had risen to ninety-four degrees, so Doctor Griffith removed all the blankets except one light blanket. After he did that, she relaxed and slept for a while. Her temperature has stayed at ninety-four degrees, and Doctor Griffith believes that must be her normal temperature."

"So, what's the special something you learned from her?" asked Father Hughes.

"Ah, yes," replied Sister Clare, "I'm very excited about it—the first time I spoke to a person from another planet! Let me tell you the long version of it because, well, just because I want to relive the whole moment. I sat beside her while she slept, and I had dozed off a little myself when I heard her softly say three syllables. I looked, and she was lying on her side and looking up at me with those beautiful emerald-colored eyes she has. She raised her hand, pointed her finger at me, touched her ear as if telling me to listen, and then repeated the syllables more slowly. Then I realized she was asking me, 'Who are you?' I wanted to leap out of my chair! She could communicate with us! But I kept my composure. Speaking slowly and clearly, I told her who I was. I told her who you, Doctor Griffith, and Mother Catherine are and what this convent is. Then I asked her name, and she said I could never pronounce it. She told me to choose a name to call her that I could pronounce easily. My mind ran through dozens of names of famous people and various biblical names as I tried to think of a name for her. Then I thought of the name of my best friend from first grade. Her name was Laura. Maybe it's a silly name to pick for her, but I liked it and thought it would be easy for her to pronounce. So I asked her if I could call her Laura. I saw her lips moving as she silently tested the name, and then she repeated it in two half-sung notes, one note for each syllable. Then she nodded, and I saw her mouth widen into a straight line, which must be how she forms a smile. 'I will be called Laura,' she said. Then, we heard the other sisters singing in the chapel. 'Are they singing in your holy place?' she asked, and I said yes. Then she said, 'I will listen to them. Will you listen to them with me?' So we sat quietly and listened to the sisters singing, and I could see her moving her lips as if she were trying to learn the words to the songs.

"When the singing ended, I asked her if she was hungry, and she said she was. She told me the short list of 'Earth food,' to borrow Doctor Griffith's term, that her body could tolerate. Fortunately, the ongoing food shortages won't cause a problem for her because the foods on her list include fish, which we have in our freezer, eggs from our chickens, and potatoes and sweet potatoes, which we have on hand from our garden. So I prepared a poached egg and a portion of mashed sweet potato for her, which she quickly ate. I asked her how long it had been since she had eaten anything, but she said she wasn't sure. She thought she had been drifting in and out of consciousness for days, so I explained to her that she had only been with us for a few hours. 'Only a few of your hours?' she asked me, 'It was today that the good man brought me here?' I told her that was correct and reminded her that your name is Father Hughes. 'Yes,' she replied, 'Father Hughes. Father Hughes and his dog animal found me. I was cold, and Father Hughes brought me here. I remember. And there was a fight, not a dangerous fight,' she said, 'but angry talk, and the good man, Father Hughes, protected me, and the dog animal kissed my face and stood close to me.' Then she said, 'You were one of the people who did not want me here, yes?' I told her it was all true, just as she remembered it. I told her that, at first, we were afraid of her and what the authorities might do to us if they discovered that we were taking care of her. 'You say the truth,' she replied, 'It would be easy for you to lie to me, but you say the truth. You do not tell lies, do you?' she asked me. I said no, that would displease God if I lied to someone who deserved to know the truth. 'Yes,' she said to me, 'you are of those who worship the All-Holy One. You behave differently from most of the others of your race. I trust you because you care about the truth. I am happy that the good man, Father Hughes, and his dog animal brought me here. You are very kind,' she said. Then she paused and said, 'I am tired, Sister Clare. I, Laura, must sleep now. Thank you for the food, and thank you for being kind to me.'

"And that's when she told me something really exciting, Father!" continued Sister Clare. "She said, 'Before I sleep, I must tell you, I am not alone. There are two of us. After I have rested a little longer, I must find my—I forget your word for it—my . . . husband. Yes, that is the word you use,' she said. 'I must find my husband.' Then, she closed her eyes, and she's been sleeping since then. Can you believe that, Father? She is here with her husband! We must find him, Father! We simply must find him!"

Chapter 3

The cramped spacecraft shuddered, knocking both of them onto the deck. Propulsion system warning alerts blared and flashed on the control panels, indicating inequalities in the tunneling field that endangered the ship. The spacecraft automatically attempted to stabilize the tunneling field. Critical alerts in the navigation, control, and life-support systems followed. The two crew members pulled themselves up from the deck and activated the emergency shutdown of the tunneling system to transition the spacecraft to conventional linear velocities mode in a desperate attempt to avoid the spaceship destroying itself as it trembled on the verge of catastrophic failure. All the ship's systems communicated with the tunneling field, and these systems had to be running or at least functional to initiate an emergency shutdown and transition the spacecraft out of tunneling mode. Manually shutting down the tunneling system was impossible because the thousands of incremental, almost immeasurably brief buffering stages between the tunneling layers required precise, zeptosecond, and nanosecond timing as the system abruptly disengaged each of the individual layers of the spacecraft's tunneling field shroud, lurching the ship out of tunneling mode and back into three-dimensional space, propelling it then in conventional velocity mode at a velocity of Mach 115. The emergency tunneling shutdown procedure produced violent, jarring, hammering pulses and vibrations on the spaceship as it transitioned. The moment when the final tunneling layer shut down posed the worst danger because of the punishing stresses placed on the spacecraft as it dropped out of tunneling mode and slammed into the world of three dimensions. Once the spaceship achieved conventional velocity mode, the crew could continue under automated control of the craft, assume manual control, or eject if necessary and practical.

These emergency shutdown procedures, developed through controlled testing, had never before been implemented during an actual mission. This crew would be the first to do so. Failure in the tunneling system had occurred only once before in the history of that technology. In that failure, when the departing crew initiated tunneling mode after they were beyond the home planet's atmosphere, as was often the practice, instead of the spacecraft simply disappearing from view when it activated the tunneling system, the spaceship, along with its crew, instantly transformed into a glowing white ball of energy that lingered for days like a new star in their planet's night sky. Afterward, the engineers who investigated the incident attributed the failure to an almost immeasurably brief and unexplained voltage fluctuation in one of the tunneling field layers that enveloped the craft. After an extensive review of the tunneling system's design and retesting of all circuits and components in several other spacecraft, the technicians could not determine the cause of the voltage fluctuation and so did not recommend a total system redesign based on one unexplained failure out of several thousand successful voyages. They did, however, redesign the automatic tunneling field stabilizing system that temporarily maintained consistency in a malfunctioning tunneling field long enough for emergency shutdown. They also revised the sequencing of the stages of emergency shutdown for the tunneling system.

A spacecraft propelled by a tunneling system could travel between galaxies in days, weeks, or months if voyaging to a relatively nearby galaxy. While in tunneling mode, the crew did not experience distortion or dissimilarity in the passage of time relative to their points of departure and destination, and other systems in the spacecraft allowed the crew to avoid weightlessness and the effects of inertia during course adjustments. However, when the spaceship transitioned from tunneling mode to conventional velocity mode, the crew members again became affected by gravity, the lack thereof, and the laws of motion.

A new warning signal alerted the crew that the tunneling field had dropped to layer one, allowing the crew a final opportunity to secure their safety harnesses. Then, the last tunneling field layer shrouding the spacecraft dissolved. In that first few seconds of complete, unbuffered transition, only their harnesses prevented the crew from being violently hurled into the bulkhead or onto the deck as the ship shook, creaked, groaned, and banged as if being pummeled by a thousand hammers as the spacecraft emerged into three-dimensional space. Then, the violent battering of the ship ceased. The spacecraft now traveled at the conventional velocity of Mach 115. Because of the unavoidable, irreparable structural weakening of their spaceship caused during the unbuffered transition out of layer one, the crew could never exceed Mach 115 or activate tunneling mode again. Now, their only means of returning home was to launch a tunneling mode-capable rescue request orb to their home planet and wait for a rescue ship.

They were near enough to their destination, the alien planet called "Earth" by the race of beings who inhabited it, that reaching it under conventional velocities mode, assuming the ship's systems and structural integrity held, would require only two days as calculated on Earth. The two crew members worked in shifts, alternating between work and brief naps to stay alert, as they kept the fragile spaceship functioning and under automatic control until they neared Earth's outer atmosphere, where they assumed complete manual control.

As they guided the spacecraft downward through Earth's atmosphere, they steadily reduced their velocity as their altitude dropped to lessen the strain on their damaged ship until they leveled off at around 14,000 feet and flew at subsonic speed.

Despite their low velocity, the spaceship groaned and vibrated as it pushed through the resistance of Earth's atmosphere. As they flew eastward over the Pacific Ocean toward land, their power source, damaged by the ship's earlier convulsions, began to discharge at an increased rate. Then, one by one, each of the spacecraft's systems began to malfunction or fail entirely, either from the loss of power or vibration damage. The male alien retracted the outer shields over the craft's windshield when the view screen on the control console failed. The female crew member rerouted electricity from less essential systems to power the propulsion, navigation, and control systems so the male could maintain manual control and guide the dying spacecraft nearer to the shoreline where they intended to abandon the spaceship far enough out to sea to avoid being noticed by the humans, but near enough to shore they could paddle their way to land. If they were following the established procedure for abandoning their spaceship, they would have already launched or would soon launch the spacecraft's rescue request orb, but they had removed the ship-launched rescue request system's independent power cell when the damaged circuit from the ship's power source caused intermittent failures and used the power cell to power the position sensors for the manual control system, which required only minimal voltage. However, they still could launch a miniature rescue request orb from one of the wristwatch-sized bracelets packed into their emergency kits once they abandoned the spacecraft.

If they could maintain control of the spacecraft until they were within sight of the shoreline, they would activate the self-destruct systems, if still operable, and eject from the spacecraft. The ship's self-destruct system needed only a few volts from its independent power supply to trigger the self-sustaining process that would dissolve much of the spacecraft, reducing the likelihood of Earthlings finding evidence of their ship. Then, when they exited their individual escape pods, each equipped with an inflatable raft and other emergency items, they would activate the self-destruct system for the escape pods and paddle to the shore. Once ashore, they would launch a rescue request and evade detection until the rescue ship arrived.

After diverting the remaining power to the propulsion and navigation systems and the manual control system, which now responded more reliably to the controls, the male crew member held their course toward the shoreline. The female stepped up to the control console and, without speaking, gently squeezed the male alien's broad shoulders and then tenderly stroked his cheek in a gesture of her love and admiration for him. More so than he, she had kept the critical systems running while he fought to control the craft, but together, they had stabilized the struggling ship. She sang a short phrase, beginning slowly and softly in a single voice, then adding two of the additional vocal chambers in her larynx, entwining two more simultaneous harmonies in a short, soaring love song to him.

He touched her hand, turned in his seat, and looked into her eyes, those eyes that still captured his heart each time he gazed into them. She was his treasure, and she would always be his treasure. He had already decided that this would be their last voyage. They had discussed that idea several times since their previous journey. This near-fatal malfunction had settled the matter for him. It had brought them too close to destruction. When they returned from this voyage, they would never again leave their home. They would never again venture far from their broad, fertile valley separating two imposing mountain ranges. In that valley, they would live the simple life most of their race preferred. Together, he and she would work their land and produce enough for their needs and a surplus for sale and friendly barter as was the custom among their people who, despite their race's sophisticated technological capabilities, had learned, through the many millennia of their history, the importance of remaining close to the land, living simply, keeping fresh in their minds the wisdom and satisfaction gained from labors that left a little honest dirt and honorable calluses on their hands. They would raise their children according to the traditions that sustained their free and stable civilization. They would teach them the practical skills necessary for self-reliance and the social skills essential for a harmonious society. They would instruct their children in the collected wisdom that each generation handed on to the next, as they had done for many generations. Together, they would teach their children all the cherished ways of their people. Yes, this would be their last voyage away from their home planet. They had served well in the Distant Voyager Service, and now it was time to return home to their people and true lives.

As the male alien maintained their course and altitude, he attempted to respond to his beloved with his love song to her. He had to stop and restart twice because his emotions at that moment were so powerful that he could barely relax his throat enough to sing properly. His responding song required three voices, and she deserved only his best when he sang it to her. He inhaled deeply and began again. When he had finished, she leaned over, pressed her cheek against his, and whispered simple, unsung words of her commitment to him. Then she stepped away to retrieve an additional package of emergency ration wafers for each of them in preparation for abandoning the barely functioning spacecraft. As she slipped one of the rations into her jacket pocket, a jolting bang shook the spacecraft, throwing her to the deck, followed by the shriek of air forcing itself through a crack in the hull.

UNTIL THE RESCUE SHIP ARRIVES

The propulsion system failed, and the spacecraft arced downward. The male bellowed the command to eject, and they pulled themselves toward the tiny escape pods. The female latched her restraint harness, glanced at the male, and closed the hatch on her escape pod. The instant her escape pod hatch locked, the male slapped the auxiliary eject button on the control panel beside his escape pod. Her pod detached with a blast, followed by a roar of wind through the void where her escape pod had been. The male then slammed the hatch closed on his pod and hit the eject button without taking the extra second to lock his restraint harness. Nothing happened. As the arc of the falling spacecraft steepened, the male repeatedly struck the eject button, without result, until the ruined spacecraft smashed into the ocean. The impact slammed him against the hatch and momentarily stunned him, but it also dislodged the escape pod from the spacecraft, which had shattered upon impact. Cold seawater leaking around the damaged hatch seal of his pod brought him back to his senses, and he realized that the pod was sinking. He retrieved the pack containing the compressed and folded raft, the emergency kit, and the rescue request launcher from a compartment in the escape pod. He then attempted to throw the release lever for the pod's hatch. He gasped as a piercing pain ripped through his ribs on his left side as he strained to pull the lever, which refused to unlock. He simultaneously pressed the twin buttons next to the lever to trigger the small explosive charges that would blow open the pod hatch in such a circumstance. The charges failed to detonate. The pod continued to fill with seawater. He inhaled as fully as his cracked ribs would allow and tried to ignore the pain as he strained again to throw the lever to open the hatch. The escape pod was now a trap, nearly filled with seawater spraying around the hatch seal. He burned with anger at the fate that was enveloping him. Again, he pressed the button that should have blown the hatch open, and again, the charges did not respond. His anger then became pure animal rage. He could not escape from the pod to help his beloved get to shore, be rescued, and return home. He could not even sing her the short farewell song used at every parting whenever possible. He was about to become a casualty, not of a noble battle, but of an absurd, rare failure in the spacecraft's tunneling field circuitry and the first-ever failure of an escape pod hatch. As the air pocket inside the pod shrank, and despite the pain of his cracked ribs stabbing his side, he continued to pull on the lever to unlock the hatch. Failing at that, he made one last attempt to detonate the explosive charges, but the charges still did not blow. Then, he had one final, desperate idea. He raised his head and inhaled one last lungful of air, then he turned and pressed his back against the hatch. With his knees bent, his feet flat against the opposite wall of the pod, and in contempt for the pain in his ribs, he pressed against the hatch and pushed with his legs as if trying to lift a mountain. Straining, his leg muscles quivering, the escape pod now filled with seawater, he roared an ancient warrior song, five voices at once, into the water engulfing him. The air he forced from his powerful, capacious lungs generated a boil of bubbles in the cold water as he sang. In past eras, columns of warriors sang this song in unison, which reverberated around the enemy as the warriors assembled for battle. Its effect, if the singing warriors possessed clear consciences and bristled with fearlessness, was as dispiriting to the enemy as it was invigorating to the warriors who sang it. He felt his lungs emptying, and with the last burst of power remaining in his body, he slammed his back against the hatch and pressed against it so intensely that he nearly blacked out as he forced his muscles to burn all his remaining energy within the blackness of the escape pod. He spent it all: the remaining air in his lungs, all his strength, his will, his rage, his desire to save his beloved, his dreams for their future, all or nothing, success or death at the bottom of an ocean on an alien world. Then, as the last liter of air in his lungs roiled the water around him, he felt a dull thump. The lock had shattered. The hatch swung open. He was free.

Chapter 4

The small thrusters on the female's escape pod, designed only for landing, had barely enough time to slow her descent and allow the pod to splash gently into the water, where it held itself upright as it bobbed in the slow swells. She pulled the raft containing the emergency kit from its compartment and threw the lever to open the hatch. Next, she pulled the tab on the gas canister that instantly inflated the raft, and then she tied the raft to the pod to prevent it from drifting away while she assembled the paddle's handle sections and clipped the paddle's tether to the raft. She opened the emergency kit, pulled out the compass, knife, night vision goggles, and the rescue request launcher, set them aside in the raft, climbed back into the escape pod, and opened the valves to fill the pod with seawater and sink it during the self-destruction process. Then, she activated the pod's self-destruct system, which immediately began dissolving the pod in a process that would take several hours to complete.

The escape pod rapidly began to sink as it filled with seawater. Acrid steam caused by the disintegration process was already rising from the water. The female alien climbed out of the escape pod to untie the raft, but the point at which she had tethered it to the pod had already submerged, pulling the raft with it as it sank. She jumped into the raft, the stern of which was already rising out of the water as the sinking rescue pod pulled the bow under, grabbed the small knife from the emergency kit, and began cutting the tether. Within moments, the pod pulled her and the raft underwater as the effervescence from the dissolving pod gurgled around her. She gripped the tether and continued to saw through its tough fibers until, after a long descent, she cut through the last strand and, gripping its free end, rose with the raft as it lifted her to the surface.

She inhaled and pulled herself into the raft. As she did so, she inadvertently jammed the point of the knife into the raft's gunwale, causing her to lose her grip on the knife, which tumbled into the ocean. Immediately, she heard the hiss from the tiny puncture she had accidentally inflicted on the raft. She also realized all the other emergency items had fallen overboard while the raft was inverted underwater. Only the tethered paddle remained. She chided herself for the series of errors she had committed during the incident, errors she knew would only add to the challenges ahead of her. Oh, how her beloved would scold her if he knew, and rightfully so, she thought. She had let her focus slip badly. She would not do so again.

She grabbed the paddle and stared into the cloud-thickened darkness that surrounded her. Which way was the shore? How far away was it? She heard nothing but the rising and falling swells around her. She sang a four-note call to her mate, loud but in a single voice, and listened carefully for a reply, which did not come. Then she sang his name in all her voices simultaneously, but there was still no response. Fear for him flashed through her body, but she immediately rejected it. She did not sense the peculiar uneasiness that sometimes alerted members of their race if a loved one was in danger or had died, so she told herself that he was alive and fighting his way toward the shore, as was she. She knew his capabilities and chided herself for doubting his strength of will and resourcefulness. Her doubts and worries were useless, but she knew she would be battling these thoughts until they were reunited. She knew she must force herself to keep her mind in the moment and think only of reaching the shore.

UNTIL THE RESCUE SHIP ARRIVES

At the peak of each swell, she searched in vain, in all directions, for lights along the coastline that may have pierced the low clouds and mist to give her a bearing to follow, but she saw nothing. She decided to pick an arbitrary direction, hoping it was east toward the shore. She began paddling at a pace she could endure for hours as she raced against the leak in the raft and the unavoidable, debilitating effects of prolonged wet, cold, and fatigue that would be her unwelcome companions.

As she paddled, she, too, resolved that this would be their last voyage. She and her beloved had initially declined this voyage but allowed their superiors to persuade them to accept it because crewed missions were still preferred when live specimens were collected; even the best robots were far less efficient at collecting specimens than were flesh and blood, living Distant Voyager crews. But such considerations were now irrelevant. The specimens they would have collected would be dead or dying, scattered in the ocean inside their containers, along with shards and bits of the spacecraft. All that mattered now was for her beloved and herself to survive this final mission. Another chill of worry for her beloved crept over her in defiance of her resolve to resist such fears, bringing with it the unbearable thought of life without him. How could she possibly endure it if he did not survive, she thought? She caught herself and pushed the thought from her mind. Such temptations to emotional weakness were as much the enemies of their survival as were the cold, indifferent ocean and the yet unknown obstacles that the two of them would confront once they reached the shore. Yes, she would bear it and persevere even if he did not survive, she told herself. Whatever the burden or challenge, there was no other acceptable choice for members of their race than to endure and overcome. But without him, living would be an existence endured with an endless ache in her soul, just as it would be for him if she were lost. He was her husband. She was his wife. In spirit, they were now more one being than two individuals. They both must survive if either of them were to be whole. She knew his capabilities as thoroughly as he knew hers. He would expect her to do whatever was necessary to survive, reunite with him, and avoid the humans until the rescue ship arrived. She expected the same of him.

No race of beings they had thus far encountered, regardless of their technological development, were their equals in mental or physical toughness and determination in overcoming even the worst difficulties. Every child in their society learned to develop and exhibit these qualities along with all the other strengths and virtues their race of beings held sacred. Among their people, parents considered it an act of love to strengthen their children, in mind and body, and teach them to prevail over hardships, be resourceful, learn from challenges and trials, and gain wisdom from them. They infused in their children all the customs, traditions, and the collected wisdom of their people, which they, in turn, would hand to the next generation. Only by holding fast to the lessons gleaned from millennia of wars, struggles, upheavals, triumphs, and failures during their societal evolution could they maintain the stable, satisfying life and culture their race had finally developed, protected, and sustained for many generations. They had long ago identified the ideas and practices that produced ruinous results and forbade any attempts to revive such proven errors. Over time, they constructed a societal system that was not centralized and dictatorial but based on the principle of subsidiarity, handling issues at the lowest, most immediate jurisdiction possible. Thus, the citizens had immense control over their lives and communities, which they guarded jealously, and woe to anyone who attempted to tinker with that system. Theirs was not a perfect society, but it was a society of beings who treasured freedom, respected their duty to preserve it for succeeding generations, and understood the necessity of high standards of conduct for themselves and others to maintain that difficult balance between anarchy and tyranny. Occasionally, however, someone attempted to resurrect an old, failed idea they thought they could perfect and implement afresh. However, it was nearly always the citizens within their communities that crushed such efforts, violently if necessary, before the forbidden spore could become a widespread contagion as bad ideas always become when allowed to go unchecked. Vigilance was more than a word to their race because they understood the evils brought by lack of vigilance.

Onward, she paddled under the falling mist as the seawater penetrated her uniform, the fabric of which, even wet, provided at least a measure of insulation. She hoped she was paddling toward the shore and not just paddling in circles or, even worse, paddling farther out to sea. She tried to ignore her discomfort by whispering a marching song to time her paddle strokes, slowing the tempo when she felt her muscles tiring, then increasing the pace once her muscles felt rested. She sang to him twice more with a four-voice call but heard no response. She continued to combat the ever-returning fear that he may be dead. She countered this thought by telling herself that he was also fighting his way to the shore and that they would find one another soon after reaching land. If nothing else, this inner struggle with her thoughts kept her from focusing on her physical discomforts and helped motivate her to overcome her circumstances.

Soon, her raft deflated into an almost shapeless bladder. She stopped using the paddle, hugged the partially inflated raft like a pillow, and tried to cover the puncture with her body as she lay over it to perhaps slow the leak to some degree. Then, with steady, frog-like kicks, she swam in the direction she hoped was toward land.

Finally, the cold and the fatigue drained her, and she had to cease swimming and cling to the ever-shrinking remnant of the raft to allow her muscles to rest. For the first time since joining the Distant Explorer Service as a couple, she and her beloved now had to use the skills they had learned in childhood as Young Explorers, later hardened and enhanced in the Provincial Guards, and most intensely of all, during their Distant Explorer Service training. Distant Voyager volunteers were required to repeat the course until they either completed it successfully or proved to be physically incapable of doing so. Most volunteers toughened themselves enough to finish the course, even if they had to repeat portions of it. However, volunteers never incurred shame if the instructors declared them physically unable to complete the training. A volunteer's sincere but unsuccessful efforts were regarded as noble and virtuous, and they were discharged from Distant Voyager Service with honor and respect. However, to quit the training or feign injury or illness was a mark of shame that followed one for the rest of one's life. In the history of Distant Explorer Service, only two volunteers had quit or failed the course out of weakness of character. They were then shunned by their communities and compelled to live out the remainder of their lives in the Northern Provinces, where most of the residents were criminals or societal outcasts and where no one dared to question a stranger about their past without risking a fight. However, those who completed the Distant Explorer Service training developed an inner toughness and confidence that made them believe they could accomplish any challenge because they had already done the seemingly impossible numerous times during their training. They also gained the honor and respect of their fellow citizens, which benefitted them for the rest of their lives.

She resumed swimming and allowed her mind to wander at random, thinking of everything, anything, as long as it helped keep her mind off the cold, the grueling monotony of swimming and deflected the temptation to worry about him. When the raft finally deflated to uselessness, she slid under it, swam a few strokes beyond it, surfaced, and swam on, allowing the now useless raft to drift away. She lost all sense of how long she had been in the water and swam onward, her mind lost in a crowd of thoughts, defying fatigue, losing more and more body heat through her wet uniform until she finally had to rest again. She inhaled deeply to about two-thirds of her lung capacity and held her breath, which gave her enough buoyancy to relax and rest her muscles for several minutes. As she floated, she allowed herself to slip into a half-sleep. Then, feeling somewhat refreshed, she fully exhaled and inhaled to recharge the air in her lungs and continued swimming. She repeated this pattern of swimming and resting but was careful to avoid resting so long that her muscles stiffened.

For her active mind, the boredom of being a prisoner of the ocean was almost as punishing as the cold seawater that had long ago defeated her uniform's ability to insulate. She felt hypothermia settling into her. She offered a softly sung prayer for her beloved as she, in her mounting fatigue, again struggled against succumbing to fear and exhaustion, which threatened her resolve and fighting spirit. She could not permit herself to waste even a calorie's worth of energy or a tear's worth of emotion on defeatist thinking if she and her beloved were to prevail. To refocus her mind, she tried to think of a field-expedient way of fabricating a rescue request launcher from components available on Earth—an impossible idea, but it served as a distraction. The emergency rescue request launcher in her survival kit was now somewhere on the ocean floor—perhaps even in the stomach of some ocean creature, she thought. She surprised herself by laughing at the unlikely image of the rescue ship homing in on and inadvertently rescuing a wet, slimy, uncooperative sea creature that had swallowed the rescue request launcher. Perhaps hypothermia was beginning to make her giddy, she thought, so she again increased the rhythm of her swimming to generate more body heat.

The night became one endless, all-consuming moment. She longed to sleep but dared not take another brief nap to rest her muscles. Doing so now when she was so cold and fatigued could be fatal. She felt as though the cold, the wet, the exhaustion, and the concern for her beloved had settled into and saturated her soul and become a permanent part of her—and now thirst added itself to her miseries. Her race of beings could not drink seawater any more than could humans. Even so, there were several times when she nearly gave in to the temptation to swallow just a sip to wet her mouth. Again, her training and self-discipline prevailed, and she resisted.

She began to shiver, so she forced herself to swim incrementally faster to generate more body heat. As she swam, the waves grew as the wind increased. As she looked ahead, she thought she noticed a faint difference in the brightness of the sky. The horizon ahead of her appeared barely perceptibly lighter. Was morning near, or was she tricking herself? She halted and tread water as she studied the sky in all directions. Yes, the horizon in the direction she was swimming was faintly lighter than the sky behind her. She was sure it was true. And now she knew that she was swimming eastward toward the shore over which Earth's star would rise! How near now was the shore? Was it within the limits of her strength to reach it? Was the current moving her toward it or parallel to it? She shook her head to clear the fog of fatigue from her mind. "Concentrate on the swimming," she told herself aloud. "Nothing else is within my control. Swim. Just swim."

She again sang the marching song to help her maintain a regular cadence and keep her mind off her compounding miseries. But in the midst of it all, she still thought of him. What were his struggles now? Had he made it to shore? When she came within sight of the beach, would she see him rush out from a hiding spot near the shoreline and swim out to pull her to safety? She knew that was what he would do. Of course, such a scenario was improbable, she thought, but it was beautiful to imagine. But then again, why could it not be so? It was not a mathematical certainty that such a joyful reunion could not happen. Not at all. She allowed herself to entertain that possibility. Why not think it could happen that way? She created an entire drama of it in her mind. She saw him race down the beach and dive into the waves, swim to her with the speed and force of an indefatigable machine, and then pull her to shore and carry her into a little cave he had found where he had built a small fire with two fish roasting over the coals. Just a few paces away, there would be a cold, fresh, little rainwater stream trickling down, sweet and clear. He would carry her to it, and she would let the water run down her face as she drank it in greedy gulps. He would drape his uniform jacket over her and let her sleep near the fire until the fish were ready to eat. He would have his emergency kit and the rescue request launcher with it. And now that they had found each other again, he would send a rescue request, and in a few days, they would be going home—together.

Over and over, she reimagined the details of their reunion on the beach, changing bits of the story and hearing their conversations in minute detail. She imagined being warm and safe again aboard the rescue ship with her beloved at her side and, together, joyfully planning, as if they hadn't already done so a thousand times, the life that would be theirs once they were home, forever more at home.

Then she paused swimming and raised her head as the swell lifted her. She could see land! It was still a long swim away, merely a dark, hulking shadow rising from the ocean ahead of her in the faint pre-dawn, but she could see it! She was sure that it was true, not a hallucination! Yes, she could see it! If she could see it, she could—she would—make herself swim to it! Yes, she told herself, she still had enough strength to swim that far! Every muscle in her body ached with fatigue, and her shivering was constant, but she would make her body obey her will and continue swimming until she crawled onto that beach. She sang the marching song to herself again, but her body could no longer match the rhythm.

"I am almost there, my love," she sang after drawing a deep breath, momentarily interrupting her singing. "We both will survive. We will find each other, my beloved. We will return home, alive and together. We will, my love. We will."

And on, she swam.

Chapter 5

He thrashed his way to the surface and inhaled a full breath of air, blew it out, and inhaled again. He almost couldn't believe he had broken free from the pod and survived. He tilted his head back and bellowed a victory shout into the darkness, partly in defiance of the death he had narrowly avoided and partly in the hope of hearing a reply from his beloved. He then sang a brief song of gratitude to the All Holy One and added a petition for the protection of his beloved. He knew that while trapped inside the failed, falling spaceship, he had crashed far from where her escape pod had landed, but he would now spend all his strength and determination to find her and reclaim the remainder of their lives together, which fate had almost stolen from them. The cold water and the fresh air invigorated him, and for a moment, he ignored the pain in his ribs and once again sang out to her with a roaring five-voice chorus and then listened for her response. He sang out twice more but heard no reply.

As he trod water, something rose to the surface in front of him. The raft containing the emergency kit had jarred loose from the escape pod. He swam the few strokes to the still compacted raft, inflated it, crawled in, and pulled the emergency kit from its compartment in the raft. The items inside the kit included a simple, almost indestructible, magnetic compass specially designed for crews working on Earth and night vision goggles, similar in appearance to the eyeglasses that Earthlings wore but with a head strap to secure them. The goggles were also helpful in many daylight situations. The kit contained a packet of ration wafers, several doses of pain medicine, a roll of gauze-like bandages, an elastic bandage, a small knife, a non-absorbant blanket that also could be used as a small tent, a bladder to hold liquids, a small fire-starting wand, and the all-important emergency rescue request launcher on a wristband.

He fastened the rescue request launcher to his wrist, looped the compass lanyard around his neck, and stowed the rest of the kit back into its compartment. After connecting the paddle sections and tethering it to the raft, he opened the cover to the permanently luminous compass and maneuvered the raft until he was facing east. He tucked the compass inside his jacket and began paddling into the night, frequently checking his bearing.

From time to time, he sang out to her. He prayed that she had not encountered difficulties while escaping from the pod and tried to reassure himself by recalling he had seen her pod detach, so it was likely that her descent had been safe and controlled. Whatever challenges she may have met or would meet, if she was alive, and he believed she was, he knew she would fight with all her strength to overcome them. "Get to the shore, my beloved," he sang into the night, "I will find you, and together we will go home."

The constant paddling helped him combat the cold, but his cracked ribs rebelled at every paddle stroke. Nonetheless, he resisted taking one of the painkiller tablets in the emergency kit. She may need them if she was injured, he thought. He could bear the pain well enough for now; he would wrap his ribs with the elastic bandage when he reached the shore.

As he paddled into the night, at the peak of a swell, he twice saw the lights of what he believed to be container ships, but they were too distant for anyone to notice him in the dark. Nonetheless, he flattened himself in the raft to perhaps be mistaken for a piece of debris in the water if anyone on one of the ships had a night vision device and had seen him.

As he paddled, he planned for the work ahead of him when he reached the shore. First, he would find her. If he didn't find her at the shore when he arrived, he would seek a place to hide where he could watch the shoreline and wait for a few hours in case she was still paddling or swimming her way to shore. If she didn't arrive in whatever length of time seemed appropriate, he would assume that she had come ashore at a different location and then scout the shoreline for her, avoiding detection as much as possible. He knew this would be risky; it was almost inevitable that someone would see him. His uniform resembled clothing that humans wore, and he could be mistaken for a tall human from a distance. However, in a closer encounter, his broad, deep chest, thick neck, and distinctly nonhuman face would frighten any human who saw him. He had not practiced speaking any Earthling languages recently. If a human tried to talk to him, he could understand the human if they spoke clearly, but a human may not understand him until he had practiced speaking their language again, at least briefly. However, even if he could converse like a native, he knew he must avoid a face-to-face encounter with humans. But if that happened, he would have to escape quickly and hope that if someone reported him, the authorities would dismiss the report as nonsense. He had to balance boldness with caution to avoid anything that might interfere with finding his beloved. Finding her was the only task that mattered until they were reunited. Once he found her, they would do whatever was necessary to remain together and survive until they were aboard the rescue ship and on their way home.

Each hour dragged into the next as he paddled eastward toward the coast. To break the monotony, he repeated words and phrases in the English language until his tongue relearned how to form the simple, chattering noises that characterized all human languages. Occasionally, he called out to his beloved only to be answered by silence. He then grew bored with practicing speaking English and dug his paddle deeper into the water, paddling with a faster rhythm assisted by his subdued chanting of a warrior's marching song. Their spacecraft's system failures had prevented him from knowing precisely how far they were from the northwest coast of the United States of America when they had abandoned their spacecraft, but he thought he should be near to it now.

It was still dark and misting when he heard the waves rolling onto the shore. He quickened his rhythm, and when he was nearer to the beach, he retrieved the night vision goggles from his pocket and scanned the shoreline. He saw no humans, but neither did he see her. He paddled the remaining distance to the shore as the breakers helped wash him onto the beach. He rolled out of the raft and steadied himself with the paddle as he stood for the first time in hours. Then, he hoisted the raft onto his shoulders and looked for a hiding place. Through the night vision goggles, he saw that the beach had many boulders and piles of driftwood strewn along it. He saw no footprints belonging to her in the sand near the water's edge but he hoped to find the unusual tread pattern of her boot soles in the sand higher up from the water's reach. He walked toward a tangled heap of logs that would hide him as he watched the beach. As he walked, he continued to look for her footprints, but again he saw none. He settled in among the logs, which provided him a clear view of a long stretch of shoreline while allowing him to remain well hidden. He decided not to deflate the raft yet in case he needed it to rescue her from the water, and instead, just lay it under himself as a barrier to the cold sand as he watched and waited.

After over an hour, she still had not appeared, so he decided to scout farther down the beach before daylight. With morning approaching, he knew someone would see him if he paddled the raft parallel to the shore while searching for her, so he decided to abandon the raft and walk the shoreline wherever possible and swim when walking wasn't feasible. He put the wafers, pain medicine, and the knife from the emergency kit into one of his jacket pockets, deflated the raft, and buried it and the paddle and the other items in the emergency kit in the sand near the pile of driftwood.

He arbitrarily chose to travel south and jogged along the surf's edge. From time to time, he had to wipe the ocean spray from the lenses of the night vision goggles, but even when the goggles became spotted by mist and seawater, they were an indispensable tool. With them, he could see as far as he could if it were daylight, and if she were anywhere on the beach or swimming within two hundred yards from shore, he would see her.

He arrived at an area where a steep, narrow point of land jutted out into the ocean and blocked the beach. He climbed to the top of the point, crept to the opposite edge, and saw three people sitting near a glowing lantern on the beach below. The surrounding terrain was thickly wooded, and he considered hiking inland far enough to bypass the people on the beach but decided that created too great a likelihood of missing a chance to see her or discover her footprints or other signs. Reluctantly, he climbed back down the slope to the beach and, once again, waded out into the surf, swam out beyond the beach where the people sat near the lantern, and then swam south, parallel to the shore.

He continued swimming parallel to the beach but out far enough that no one could see him unless they, too, had some form of a night-vision device. He desperately wanted to sing out to his mate in case she was hiding somewhere ashore, but the risk of someone onshore hearing him and thinking that it was a distress call and responding to it or reporting it to the authorities was too high. So, in silence, he swam. He soon discovered other reasons why hiking overland would have been a bad idea. As he swam along the shoreline, he frequently saw lights from the windows of buildings glowing in the forest and along the oceanfront. Avoiding the humans and the animals that many of them kept as pets would have cost him too much time and effort had he chosen to go inland.

The sky lightened as morning pressed in, but he continued swimming, aching and fatigued, searching for a section of shore that appeared safe from chance encounters with humans. He was also hungry now, so he turned onto his side and reached for the wafers he'd shoved into his pocket. He discovered his jacket pocket was open, and the wafers, the knife, and the pain relief tablets were gone. So be it, he thought, those items would have been helpful, but they were not critical. He hoped his beloved was not also suffering from hunger or the cold and had found a safe, sheltered spot to hide near the beach where perhaps she would see him with her night vision goggles and call out to him. The thought of that possibility boosted his morale and helped him to force himself onward.

Long after daybreak, with the morning gray and heavy with clouds and mist, he found a narrow, empty stretch of beach below what appeared to be a highway cut along the side of a long, steep slope, where the trees grew thick down to within a few yards of the surf. Here, he thought, he might find a place among the trees near the beach to rest and watch for his beloved.

He lay in the water at the surf's edge and scanned the area before crawling higher onto the beach. In the sand in front of him, he saw footprints indicating someone had been there earlier. The prints were large and almost certainly a male human. Out of caution, he remained low on the sand until he convinced himself that no one was still in the area. He slowly rose to his feet and was surprised at how much effort was required for his weary body to stand and walk, almost losing his balance as he took his first few steps. He walked south along the beach, following the tracks of whoever had been there earlier. He noticed a thin, shallow furrow in the sand alongside the footprints, as if someone had been dragging something. He also saw dog tracks in the sand weaving in and around the human tracks.

He arrived at a trail leading up the slope toward the highway. Here, he noticed that the sand at the base of the trail was stirred and disturbed. The person whose tracks he was following had stopped and had done something there. Had he fallen or dropped something he'd been carrying, he wondered? Then he noticed a pair of wider, parallel furrows, indicating that the person had dragged something up the trail. He crouched and pondered the furrows that ran up the trail but were not among the tracks in the sand along the beach. What had the human dragged up the trail that he had not dragged along the beach? Then, within the stirred spot in the sand, he noticed an impression of the tread on her boot heel! Then he understood. Her boot heels had plowed the shallow furrows leading up the trail! The human had dragged her up the trail!

His mind raced through all the good and the bad tangled together in that discovery. That would likely mean his beloved was alive at that time. Otherwise, the human probably would have called the authorities to report finding her body. It must have been a civilian human who had taken her because if it were the authorities, they would have carried her away on a stretcher, leaving no traces in the sand. If she was alive, as he hoped and believed she was, she must have been unconscious. If she were conscious, she would have fought anyone who tried to carry her away, and she was more than capable of defeating any human in a fight. Who was the person who found her? Where would they have taken her? What were their intentions?

As he wrestled with the avalanche of thoughts that swept through his mind, he squatted, picked up a handful of sand, and let it trickle through his fingers. Then, just a few feet away, he noticed a tiny bit of foil poking up through the sand. He leaned over and pulled the object from the sand. It was an unopened ration wafer!

He grabbed the wafer and clutched it to his chest as he summoned the fullness of his self-control to contain his emotions. He could not answer all the questions for which he so desperately needed answers at that moment. He could only endure the torment the questions inflicted. Silently, he prayed for her protection. He strongly sensed that she was alive, but such intuitions, while often correct, were not infallible. Fear for her and doubts about her strength and endurance troubled him. He shook his head and slapped himself to clear them away. She deserved better from him.

"You are still alive, my beloved. I know it," he sang in a single-voice whisper. "I know your strength and your unshakeable will. Know that I am near, my beloved. We will find each other. You know I will not leave this planet without you."

He opened his large hand and gently stroked the wafer package as if it were her hand. "We shall leave this planet together, my love, or we shall die here together," he whispered as if she were mere inches away. His entire body ached from the emotions welling within him, but he held them at bay. He would not permit emotional weakness now. Now was a time for strength and clear-headed reasoning, not emotional self-indulgence.

He ran up the slope, slipping and falling, rising again, sore and exhausted but bounding onward. At that moment, he did not care if someone saw him. He would deal with that if it happened. When he reached the parking area beside the highway, he searched the ground in vain for further clues. He felt almost sick at having missed finding her by such a narrow margin. Two hours, an hour, a half-hour—if only he had known, he could have closed that time gap somehow. How could circumstances have so perfectly conspired to keep them separated by such a thin barrier of time? He felt his temporary burst of energy dissolving as the reality of his fatigue reasserted itself. He knew that the only sensible thing now was to rest so he would have the strength and mental clarity to give her his best efforts. At that moment, he had no idea how to find her, but at least he had cause to believe she was alive when someone carried her from this beach. Although he had no clue where she was or her condition, he knew that if she were still alive, his beloved would not just be waiting for a miracle. She would work toward the same end as he—reunion and rescue. But right now, he was bitterly and utterly useless to her. He could neither think of a way to find her nor assume she was in benevolent hands. It was entirely possible that someone, taking advantage of her weakness and exhaustion, had bound her and carried her someplace for purposes for which he would kill the Earthling when he found them. Now that she was in someone else's control, he knew he had little chance of discovering her location alone. He opted to launch a rescue request. Even if she no longer had her rescue request launcher, which emitted a signal to guide the rescue ship to her, when the rescue ship arrived it would launch its defender orbs to search for her. The defender orbs would swarm out in all directions, transmitting a signal to activate the homing beacon inside the tiny, almost invisible skin patch attached near her armpit. When an orb located her, it would signal her location to the rescue ship, and he would be aboard when it arrived at that location. He and the defender orbs would do what was necessary.

If the fully automated rescue ship launched from the home planet, it could take four or five days to arrive on Earth. But if the rescue request orb detected one of the many rescue ships that randomly patrolled in conventional velocity mode at the extreme edges of their homeworld's galaxy, and thus immensely closer than the home planet, the rescue request orb would detect its presence, intercept it, and instruct it to respond to the rescue request. Depending on where in the galaxy the tiny rescue request orb located a rescue ship, the ship could arrive as soon as a day or two.

D. E. MILLER

He decided that during the dead time of waiting for the rescue ship, he would watch the parking area in case someone pulled in who, for whatever reason, caused him to think they may be the human who had found his beloved and carried her away. It may have been someone who came there often. The odds were long, but for now, it was all he had.

Fatigued almost to his physical limit, he looked at the nutrition-dense wafer he gripped in his fist. It could give him the strength and energy to keep him going for at least three days. Yet, out of sentimentality, since his beloved had so recently held it in her loving hands, he was reluctant to tear it open, and for a moment, he just held it in his palm and ran his fingers across it. Then he abruptly tore open the wrapper, broke the wafer in half, rewrapped the remaining half, shoved it into his jacket pocket, and tossed the other half into his mouth. The strength-giving piece of wafer quickly dissolved in his mouth, and then, in a faint, sing-song whisper, he said, "I will rescue you soon, my beloved, but now, it is you who rescues me."

He opened the cap covering the rescue request launch button and pressed it. The launch indicator light pulsed blue, then red, and then changed to a steady, unflickering orange as a small port opened on the face of the rescue request launcher, and then a white light flashed as a tiny orb the size of a pinhead containing the rescue request code launched and began tunneling through space on its journey from Earth to the homeworld. It would arrive with no time distortion relative to the two worlds. The alien snapped shut the cover to the rescue request launcher, dashed across the highway, up the slope, and into the forest to search for a nearby place to rest.

Chapter 6

"Also, Major, in this set of photos, we can see the debris the Coast Guard collected several miles offshore. It's only a few pieces. They're small and look insignificant, but look at these close-up images. Notice the strange markings—symbols or whatever they are—on these two pieces. The Coast Guard originally thought they were debris from an airplane crash. However, on closer examination, they became convinced the debris was from an unknown device or machine because of the embedded, fine mesh of complex circuitry woven into the pieces shown in this next image. So far, no one who has looked at it has seen anything remotely similar. No one can even guess the function of the network of circuitry. We've sent them on for further study, but who knows how long it will take to learn anything more about it."

Colonel Hodge then handed another set of photographs to Major Carnahan. "If what you saw in those images doesn't make you wonder if the debris may have an extraterrestrial origin, that's understandable. But this next set of images shows what we believe to be alien fingerprints discovered by the local police on a paddle handle and a deflated raft hidden near a pile of driftwood on one of the beaches north of here. An obedient citizen found them and reported them early this morning because he noticed unusual symbols and markings on a few items in the raft. The citizen thought foreign smugglers might have hidden the raft and that we would want to know about it. And he was right about us wanting to know about it. The paddle, the raft, and the other items are very low-tech compared to circuitry embedded in the other material, but I think they are connected."

"I've seen thousands of fingerprints, Colonel, but these look like imprints from something else. What makes you believe they're fingerprints?" asked Carnahan.

"At first, we didn't think they were fingerprints either, But we found more prints of a similar on the other items in the raft, some presumably from different fingers, as you can see in this set of images. Some of the prints match the prints on the paddle. But more importantly, we also have two witnesses. Several miles south of where the citizen found the raft, a man and his wife, who are also obedient citizens, had set up their video equipment on a cliff and were looking out to sea and taking videos from the cliff's edge near the highway. Through their zoom lens, they saw the suspected alien swim ashore five or six hundred yards from the cliff where they stood. They took as much video of him as possible, then reported the sighting to us and gave us their video file. We enlarged and made hard copies of these individual images from the video, just like we did with the other images I showed you. And on one of them, where is it—here, this one—they got a pretty good picture of this character's face as he looked around before crawling up out of the water—here, watch this. I'll play a short clip of it from the video for you. It's only about a minute and a half long."

Major Carnahan watched the video and reexamined the photographs. "And you are positive these aren't faked somehow, Colonel?"

"Come on, Major. Give us a little credit, huh? This isn't our first day on the job around here. Look at this guy. Have you ever seen a mug like that? He's not going to blend in with the locals down at the café, is he? For now, we will assume that he's hiding out there somewhere. I don't know what options he may have. Can his people rescue him? Is he stuck here until he dies? Is he dangerous, or is he a pussycat? We just don't know. But we're going to find out. We're going to find and capture Mr. Martian, or Mr. Wherever-he's-from, and we're going to find out what he knows. If he has the technology to travel here from wherever his world is, we'll make him teach us his technology. When we learn his technological know-how, there will be no stopping us! We'll build an advanced, integrated global empire that will never collapse or be overthrown! We may even be able to establish diplomatic ties with his world—embassies, an alliance, trade, and commerce—that is if we don't have to get too rough with our uninvited newcomer to persuade him to tell us what he knows. That probably wouldn't lend itself to cozy diplomatic ties, would it?

"But first, Major, we have to catch him. That is now your job. Finding this alien is now your only purpose in life. From this moment on, you will focus all your attention and all your energy on finding and capturing this alien and delivering him directly into my custody. You will immediately put all your personnel on overtime—rotating shifts, twelve hours on, twelve hours off until we apprehend him—no holidays, no weekends, no sick leave for anyone unless they're verifiably hospitalized. Everybody works every day. If somebody fails to show up, find and arrest them for desertion. We're playing hardball with this. No traffic of any kind, be it by land, sea, or air, passes into or out of this region without being inspected—I know you can only stretch your personnel so far, but you will pressure your officers to come as close to that goal as possible. You will use all available personnel to set up random checkpoints. Every vehicle that approaches a checkpoint gets inspected. Nobody gets waved through anymore, no matter who they are or who they know—every vehicle gets checked. Invoke your authority to seize provisional command of the municipal police and county sheriffs in this matter—we'll need the extra personnel they can provide. This operation will take precedence over all other law enforcement activities. Set up highway checkpoints on major traffic arteries, secondary highways, side roads, hiking trails, rabbit trails—everywhere. Work a checkpoint for an hour or two and then move to another area. Keep the people guessing. Keep them nervous. Keep them scared and compliant. This way, we can further assert our control over the citizens while we hunt for this alien, getting two jobs done for the same money. Tell your officers that if they have to get a little rough to get the job done, that's fine with me. There will be no repercussions—but ensure they know how to write a good incident report. With a good incident report, their actions will be deemed justifiable no matter what they do. We'll accept their version of the action at face value. If we accept it, those above us will accept it. Your officers won't have to worry about being questioned about anything—as long as they write good reports!

"Also, order all railroad workers to report any unusual activities or encounters—do the same with ports and airports. Patrol every port, every railroad track, every boat dock. Spread your people out and keep them mobile to cover as much area as possible. In short, you and your officers must appear to be everywhere at once. But you must always be vague regarding who and what we are searching for—even with your own officers. Tell your officers that, for national security reasons, the object of their search must remain confidential. Just tell them they will know they have found what we are looking for when they find it. Tell them that when they find it, they will understand why you couldn't be more specific. Absolutely none of them can know that it is an alien being we are looking for because even if only one of them knows that we're hunting an extraterrestrial being, the word will get out. By tomorrow morning, everyone in the Pacific Northwest will report seeing every kind of space alien monster they can imagine. We've already made sure that the citizens who made the video won't be spreading any tales, either. You'll follow a lot of dead ends until you get good information that leads us to him, but Major, you will find him because, until you do, hunting him will be your sole purpose in life. If you get a hot lead, you will notify me immediately. But if I'm unavailable when you call, don't wait. Don't delay for any reason. Act on that lead the instant you learn of it."

"What about our people working undercover trying to crack the Resistance, Colonel?"

"You will temporarily pull them off the Resistance and get them out on patrol. We'll deal with the Resistance later. As I said, finding and capturing this alien is now your only purpose in life—and that goes for all personnel under your command, too. With local police and your security forces preoccupied with this task, the street criminals and the Resistance will have a free hand for a while, but that's just how it will have to be until we find this alien."

"Colonel, right now, I have over a dozen people working under deep cover in this region," replied Major Carnahan. "The Resistance people aren't stupid. If all our people suddenly disappear from their undercover lives, their covers will be blown. And if anybody in the Resistance recognizes our undercover agents while they're running around in their uniforms, they'll be marked for death, if not killed on the spot."

"That's the chance that we will have to take, Major. This is science fiction stuff come true. We're talking about an intelligent creature from another world hiding in the back alleys or somewhere in the woods. Catching him must trump all other concerns. Is that clear, Major?"

"Understood, Colonel. All of the assets of the Special Security Police will focus on this task immediately, Sir," replied Carnahan.

"We will remain in close contact throughout this operation, Major. You and I will exchange any useful information we obtain, and you will send me a report every day before seven p.m. I want to know where your people were working and what they turned up in their inspections. Even if they don't find the alien during a vehicle inspection, they may discover something that leads us to him."

"Yes, Colonel."

"I am confident you will get the job done, Major. That is all. You are dismissed."

Major Carnahan saluted and walked out of the colonel's office. He already felt the weight of this needle-in-a-haystack hunt that was now on his shoulders. The burden was now on himself and his officers, as would be the consequences if they failed to find the alien. Carnahan believed the Colonel was correct about an extraterrestrial running loose, but it still felt unreal—a manhunt for an alien being. He laughed and shook his head as he struggled to digest what he had just heard and seen and the absurdity of Hodge's orders. He and his police force were now ordered to further anger an already borderline rebellious citizenry by imposing a massive increase in the disruptions and impediments to their daily lives, lives that were already complicated by shortages of essential commodities and by the dictates and impositions placed on them since the United States and all other nations surrendered their sovereignty to the heavy-handed, deeply-hated, "Supreme Global Federation" three years earlier, commonly referred to simply as "the regime" by the citizens. Now, he and his officers in the Special Security Police, which, at best, was a jerry-rigged integration of law enforcement and military services, would intensify their harassment and bullying of citizens who were only trying to get through their day. Carnahan knew that increasing the imposition on the citizens would strengthen their support for the growing Resistance movement.

At first, the citizens were compliant and fearful of the new system. However, acts of rebellion were increasing, and the citizens exhibited a more hostile and combative spirit when confronted by the Special Security Police. Carnahan couldn't blame the citizens.

He, too, had seen the rapid deterioration in the quality of personnel as, one by one, the best among them deserted. Resigning from the Special Security Police or the military was now prosecutable as treason, so the disgruntled personnel quietly arranged matters so they and their families could suddenly disappear and "go dark," abandoning most electronic devices, bartering for what they needed, resorting to crime if necessary, surviving however they could on the fringes of society. This option, although possible, was desperate and difficult and becoming more so each day for those who attempted it. Those whom the police caught living outside the system were arrested and never heard from again. Even if others witnessed the arrest, the authorities always denied any knowledge of the matter. Carnahan knew that some police and military who succeeded in dropping out had joined the Resistance, which sometimes agreed to help their families remain hidden and anonymous in return for performing the various and always dangerous tasks.

Shortly after its establishment, the Special Security Police aggressively suppressed thuggish street crime. However, when shortages of essential goods spread, and rationing began, it wasn't long before the more clever and better-organized criminals found ways to prosper in the black market. Citizens quickly embraced buying, selling, swapping, and bartering for goods privately among themselves and with black marketers. They regarded such practices as patriotic acts of defiance against the imposed regime that had stolen their freedom.

Carnahan knew that black marketers would rejoice when they realized the police were preoccupied. Even the unsophisticated street criminals would promptly notice that the police were suddenly too busy with other things to bother with routine law enforcement, leaving the citizens as vulnerable as lambs surrounded by packs of wolves. He knew that this forced dereliction of duty would soon prompt citizens to take matters into their own hands against street crime as a matter of self-defense and further acclimate them to defying the regime's authority.

With the Colonel now permitting abuses of police authority as long as the officers justified and sanitized their actions in their incident reports, the police forces under Carnahan's command would become even more brazen in their already frequent piracy and abuse of citizens, further stoking public anger. Even his dwindling number of relatively conscientious officers would soon become indifferent or completely corrupt as they grew frustrated and weary of the unrelenting hunt for a mysterious someone or something about whom he could tell his officers nothing except that they would recognize the object of their searches when they found it. In his mind, Carnahan could already hear the question he knew his officers would ask him a hundred times each day: 'How can we know if we've found what we're looking for if we don't even know what it is?' He knew the officers would keep asking until they grew tired of the same vague answer. And even then, that question would be unspoken in the minds of all the other officers who knew it was useless to ask. The frustration among his officers would grow until this campaign came to whatever conclusion was in store for it. How long would it be before his police, third and fourth-rate quality that most of them were, would themselves be near the point of rebellion if forced to work twelve-hour rotating shifts indefinitely to carry out these orders?

Carnahan and his Special Security Police were already doing much of what the Colonel had ordered. They were already working extended hours to make the police seem omnipresent. Even now, discipline was a problem, and with these new pressures, it could become a dangerous problem. Citizens filed complaints every day, accusing police of stealing their groceries and other belongings or physically abusing them during spot checks. Investigations of these complaints were handled higher up the chain of command and were deliberately slow and unresponsive. Only the most egregious incidents were handled promptly, although they usually resulted in a meaningless reprimand.

More than once, Carnahan, too, caught himself toying with the idea of packing up his family and disappearing during the night, as had other citizens, but where could he take them? He was too well-known in the region to hope to disappear into the crowd without someone recognizing him. There was nowhere else in the world to escape to that wasn't as bad or worse. If he were a single man, he might somehow manage to exist on the fringes of society, but he had a family to protect and provide for, and for him, there was no joining the Resistance in return for their help. They would kill him on sight. He had considered taking his family to an old, remote, almost forgotten stone cottage his family owned on the Eastern side of the Cascades, but he knew their safety there would be only temporary. He was stuck, so he would continue his duties and do what was necessary. Perhaps if he and his team managed to catch this alien, Colonel Hodge would get the promotion he coveted, which could mean a promotion for himself to replace Hodge. He thought that could make all this somewhat more bearable, and maybe, if promoted, he could gradually reform the Special Security Police and transform it into a respectable organization. But first, he had to accomplish the improbable task of capturing an extraterrestrial who was probably more motivated to avoid capture than his officers were motivated to capture him.

"Finding and capturing this alien is now your only purpose in life," Carnahan muttered as he imitated Hodge's remark. He exhaled with a long sigh over the absurdity of it all.

Chapter 7

"So, we'll know what it is when we see it, he says. I guess that means we are looking for a package with a big label saying, 'This is what you're looking for.'"

"Well, sure. That way, if we open up the trunk of a car and find something boring and ordinary like weapons and explosives for the Resistance, we'll know that's not what we're looking for, and we'll just wave 'em on through."

"That's fine with me. I may not know what they want us to look for, but I know a few things that I'll be looking for today—oh, and speaking of things I'm looking for, look at what's sitting in the passenger seat of this one rolling up. You handle the driver on this one."

"No, man, there's a little girl in the back seat. Just check 'em and let 'em go."

"That's not the attitude you had yesterday with that little redhead."

"She didn't have a little kid with her. Just give these folks a look-over and let 'em go."

"Nope, today it's my turn to play. We practically own these civilians now, remember? So, get the guy squared away, and let's have some fun."

The sedan rolled to a stop, and the officer on the driver's side tapped on the door window.

"Open your window, sir," commanded the officer as the other officer approached the passenger window.

The driver lowered his window just enough to hand the officer his license, registration, and insurance paperwork.

"Lower your window all the way, sir!" the officer shouted to the driver.

" It's low enough for what we need to discuss, officer."

"That's not for you to decide, citizen! We're gonna search your vehicle. I order you to step out of the vehicle!"

The other officer smiled at the young woman in the passenger seat, tapped on the window with his knuckles, and gestured to her to lower the window.

"What are you doing, Rhonda? Leave it rolled up!" shouted the husband.

"Honey, let's not make a big scene over this," she said as she lowered her window. "We have nothing to hide, officer. Please don't be angry with us. I know you have a job to do."

"Rhonda! I told you . . . ."

"Your wife is being sensible, sir," interrupted the officer on the driver's side, taking a calmer tone now. "Step out and place your hands against the vehicle, please. Standard procedure, sir."

"Yeah, I've heard about some of your standard procedures lately. You're not cuffing me or my wife—and you're not even going to touch our child."

> "Daddy, I'm scared. Let's go home, Daddy," pleaded the little girl in the back seat.

"Martin, please, you're scaring her. Just do as they ask," said the woman.

"Okay, folks, relax. We'll compromise this time," said the officer beside the passenger door as he gave a subtle wink to his partner. "We are required to have you step out and stand away from the vehicle while we search it, but we'll allow your daughter to remain in the car if you prefer, or she can step out with you—whichever you want."

"No! I already told you . . . ."

"Martin! Just stop!" shouted the woman. "I'm getting out, officer. We'll cooperate—Martin, just get out, please! Okay, officer, what do you want me to do now?" asked the woman as she stepped out of the car and held her hands up.

"Daddy, I don't want to get out!"

"No, Sweetheart, you just stay in the car!"

"Yes, Mandy," said the woman as she stepped out of the car, "just stay in the car like Daddy told you. We'll be finished pretty soon, and then we'll go home."

The officer on the car's passenger side nodded slightly to his partner. "Okay, ma'am," he said to the woman. "Just turn around and place your hands behind your head. I just need to frisk you real quick to check for weapons."

"I need you to do the same thing, sir, just to check for weapons," said the other officer to the husband.

As the man reluctantly turned his back toward the officer and raised his arms, the officer struck him with a kidney punch. The man grunted and fell to his knees. The officer then hit him in the temple with the heel of his hand. Then, the other officer grabbed the woman from behind, locking his hands around her torso as he pulled her tightly to himself.

"Martin! Martin!" she screamed. She tried to butt the officer in the face with the back of her head, but he anticipated her move and tilted his head to miss the full force of her attempted head butt. He pulled the screaming woman to the passenger-side fender of the car and bent her over the car hood, leaning his weight on her.

"Save some of your energy, Peaches. You and I are going right over there to the van. If you're smart, you won't give me any trouble."

"You filthy pig! Get your filthy pig hands off me! Martin! Martin! Help me!"

"Mommy! Daddy!" The screaming little girl climbed out of the car, ran toward her mother, and kicked the officer in the leg. "Let go of my mommy! Let go of my mommy! Daddy! Help us, Daddy!"

The other officer attempted to put the man in a chokehold. The man, however, was still full of fight and grabbed the officer's arms, raised himself to crouch, and drove himself backward against the officer. The officer, barely maintaining his hold on the man's neck, stumbled backward under the force of the man's momentum. The man continued driving both of them backward until the officer tripped and fell with the man now face-up on top of him. The fall broke the officer's grip on the man's neck. Instantly, the man rolled on top of the officer and began punching him in the face, growling like an enraged beast as he battered the officer. The officer managed to pull his pistol from his holster, but the man, strengthened by adrenalin and rage, ripped it from his hand. The officer struck the man's wrist before he could point the pistol at him, sending it tumbling to the ground beside them.

The woman twisted her body and stomped the feet of the officer who was trying to subdue her. She clawed and scraped her fingernails into his hands and tried to grab and break one of his fingers to force him to release her.

"Run, Mandy, run! Run and hide, baby!" she yelled.

"No, Mommy! I'm helping! I'm helping! Let go of my Mommy, filthy pig man!" yelled the little girl, imitating what she had heard her mother yelling in her struggle. "Let go of my mommy, filthy pig man!" again screamed the little girl as she cried, kicked, and punched the officer with her tiny fists. "Help us, Daddy! Help us!"

UNTIL THE RESCUE SHIP ARRIVES

The officer struggling with the husband turned his head and reached for the pistol, but the husband hit the officer squarely on the jaw, then struck him again, and the officer lay unconscious. The man grabbed the weapon, turned, and aimed it at the officer who was struggling with the woman. When the officer saw the husband raise the pistol, he threw the woman down on top of the little girl and drew his pistol. The husband fired at the officer, but the shot was wide. He pulled the trigger again. Nothing happened. During the husband's struggle with the other officer, one of them had inadvertently pressed the pistol's magazine release button, partially disengaging the magazine, which prevented the slide from stripping a fresh cartridge from the magazine after ejecting the empty cartridge case from the first round.

The officer fired, striking the man low in the throat, just above the collarbone.

"Martin!" the woman screamed as she sprang from the ground and clawed at the officer's face. The officer pushed her away and shot her twice in the stomach.

"Run, Mandy! Run, baby!" screamed the dying woman as she slumped to the ground. "Don't you kill my baby, you pig! Oh, Martin!"

The screaming little girl dashed across the highway toward the forest. The officer chased her, holstering his pistol as he ran. The little girl turned and, seeing the officer almost within reach of her, cried out to her dead parents. The officer seized the terrified child by her hair, then locked her in a chokehold and carried her, dangling from the crook of his arm, back toward the car. He maintained the chokehold on the little girl and crouched near the trunk of the vehicle. The little girl stopped struggling and lay limp in his arms. He kept her in the chokehold a few moments longer, then checked her pulse, laid her on the ground, walked around to the driver's seat, pulled the keys from the ignition, pressed the button on the keyfob to unlock the car trunk, laid the little girl inside.

He walked over to where his partner was lying, knelt, and then slapped him several times in the face. "Hey! Hey! Can you hear me?"

The other officer opened his eyes, lifted his head, sat up, and collected his wits. He saw the husband's body lying near him. "What happened, man? What happened?"

"I'll tell you what happened. Listen and understand me clearly because you will swear what I'm about to tell you is what happened. What I'm going to tell you is what your report will say. Understand?"

"What the hell did you do, man? Where's the wife and kid?"

" Just listen! Here's what we did, what we, you and I did. So, just shut up, listen, and remember. We pulled them over, just like you remember. You ordered the husband to step out of the vehicle so you could check him for weapons, and I ordered the wife to do the same, just like you remember. Then, you told the husband to open the car trunk so we could check for contraband. That's when the husband went nuts and started punching you. Here is where your report stops because that's all you remember until I brought you around to consciousness again.

"So, where's the wife and kid?"

"Shut up and listen. My report will say that when the man knocked you to the ground and grabbed your pistol, I had to shoot him before he shot us both. That's when the woman attacked me and tried to grab my pistol from my hand, digging her claws into my hands and face as I tried to maintain control of it. That's when I had to shoot her. But again, that won't be in your report because you were unconscious and don't remember that part. Do you understand? And then, after all that happened, I inspected the car because I figured they reacted the way they did because they had something

UNTIL THE RESCUE SHIP ARRIVES

in the car they didn't want us to find. Then I opened the trunk, and that's when I found what they didn't want us to find. She was still warm to the touch."

"Aww, no, man! Hell, no! No, you didn't do that! You didn't do that! That little girl? What the hell are you, man? What the hell are you? No, no, no! The officer buried his face in his hands and then yelled, "I've done some rotten things, man! I've done some rotten things out here! I crossed the line a bunch of times, just like you—just like everybody else out here—but this! No, man, no, I quit, man! That little girl! You dirty bastard! You dirty, dirty bastard! I'm done! I'm done! I'm just done! This ain't real! I ain't doin' this! I ain't goin' along with this! I quit! I'm sick, just sick!"

"You're wrong! It's as real as it gets!" replied the other officer. "And get this straight—you damned sure will go along with it! And you're not going to quit! You've been in this too long. You've seen too much. You know too much—just like all the rest of us. They won't let you quit. They won't risk you running off, joining the Resistance, and taking everything you know with you. If you leave, it will be to take up residence in a fresh-dug grave. You know that. But, anyway, as I was about to say before you started getting weak and emotional, that's when I found the body of that little girl. I was devastated. We both were devastated. Do you understand me? We couldn't believe it. We couldn't understand how or why anybody would do such a thing. 'Why would they do that to that poor little girl?' we asked ourselves. It broke our hearts, remember? Say it! Say you remember! It broke our hearts, didn't it? Didn't it? Damn it, you'd better answer me, man, or this story is going to have one more fatality in it! Now say it! It broke our hearts, didn't it? Say it! Okay, that's better. So, now you know how to write your report. That's what happened."

"No! I ain't! I can't! I won't! None of that is gonna fly. You know it won't. That won't hold up. I'm sick. No, I'm not doin' this. This went too far. Nothing's ever gonna be right again. I don't know what

I am anymore. I just feel dead, dead inside. A little girl, her mom, and her dad . . . . They didn't do nothin.' Nothin.' Now they're dead because of you! They're dead, and you killed 'em! You killed 'em!" As he spoke, he reached down to draw his pistol.

"You don't have it, remember? It's still lying on the ground where the guy who was going to kill us with it dropped it after I shot him," said the other officer as he grabbed the other officer's arm. "So, you think if you kill me, that's going wash all this off your conscience? It won't. You're weak. It was all fun and games before, wasn't it? Confiscating people's groceries, taking their money or something they had that you thought you ought to have, or having a little fun with the pretty women. Yes, it was all fun and games for you—until today, when things went wrong. Now you're ready to kill me to clear your conscience for something you're mostly responsible for."

"What are you talkin' about? You killed 'em. I wasn't even conscious when you killed 'em. You're not puttin' this on me!"

"Oh, so you're just a bystander, huh? You struck the first blow to get things started. But you couldn't get the job done, and he punched you out cold. You weren't tough enough to take a punch. He had your gun and was ready to kill both of us with it, so while you were taking your little nap, I had no choice but to do exactly what I did. If you'd been man enough to hold up your end of the game, we would have had our fun, and they'd be on their way home. Oh, they'd hate our guts, that's for sure, but they all hate us anyway. They'd still be alive, though."

"Nice try! You don't even believe that crap! I'm not gonna stand in front of a firing squad because you couldn't keep your hands off that guy's wife. I'm not gonna do it!"

"Your thinking is getting dangerous. You'd better get it straight right now," replied the other officer, "because it's getting dangerous for you, not me. You're not going to pin this on me. If I go down because you can't keep yourself together, you die. I don't have to be the one who does it, either. You'll never see the man who kills you. So—partner—you'd better get your mind cleared up. You weren't listening to Carnahan earlier today. There will be no investigation. Neither of us will be charged with anything. Nobody's going to prison. Nobody's going to stand in front of a firing squad. That's not how it works anymore. We're untouchable now. Get that through your head. You'd better listen really, really good. You'd better start believing everything happened like I said it happened. And you'd better understand that I won't let you create a problem for me, especially after I fixed the problem that you created. Neither of us will have to explain anything to anybody if you write your report the way I told you to write it. And buddy, you will write that report exactly as I told you to write it. The way it works now, what we write in our report becomes fact as soon as we sign our names to it. You should have been paying better attention when Carnahan explained all that to us this morning. It doesn't matter if everybody believes it or if nobody believes it. As long as we write a good report, and our signatures are on it, whether it's true or not, what we said happened is chiseled in stone. It becomes a part of history as far as the hotshots in administration are concerned. All they care about is that the paperwork says it happened that way. If family members or witnesses challenge our report, they will soon learn that challenging an official report is a very unhealthy idea. So, get this through your head. It all happened the way I said it happened. It is definitely best for your health to remember that. Do you finally understand? Good. Now, I need to call HQ so they can send somebody up here to do their ever-so-thorough fifteen-minute investigation, notify the next of kin and other concerned parties, etcetera, et-cet-er-a."

Chapter 8

Father Hughes pulled up to the front door of the guest cottage and climbed out of his car as Buster jumped out behind him. Sister Clare was already opening the door for them.

"Good morning, Father," said Sister Clare with her usual cheer.

"Good morning to you, as well, Sister Clare. How are you and our friend Laura today?"

"Well, Father, she says she is feeling strong and rested, and she is very anxious to find her husband. Shortly after you left yesterday, Laura awoke, and we discussed what name we could give him. She agreed to call him Erik, a Viking name. That name seems appropriate because Laura says he is courageous and has a warrior's fighting spirit. Doctor Griffith liked the name, too. Laura pronounced his real name to give me an example of how it sounds. It is simply beyond the human voice's ability to replicate. Imagine three humans simultaneously singing three different words in harmony. That doesn't exactly describe it, but that's as close to it as I can get. It's amazing how many different sounds intertwine in their language. And I don't understand why, but if she sings even a little portion of what, for her people, is a simple melody or even a simple word, I have to swallow the lump in my throat and wipe a tear from my eye. Her vocalizations are just so beautiful, almost angelic. She says they also use a kind of unsung verbal short-hand when they need to express basic information quickly when details aren't needed. I don't know how they ever learn to master their language, but she says that even their little children learn to express themselves very well by the time they're able to walk."

"I'm glad she can speak our language. We'd be in a real mess otherwise, wouldn't we?" replied Father Hughes. "Let's put our heads together and see if the three of us can come up with some ideas to find this Erik of hers. Once we have him with us, safe and sound, we can plan for whatever comes next."

Father Hughes and Sister Clare stepped into the kitchen, where Laura sat at the small table and sipped a glass of water. "Hello, Father Hughes and Buster," said Laura with her broad, straight smile.

"Good morning to you, Laura—Buster! Down boy! I apologize, Laura. I didn't expect him to try to jump up on you," said Father Hughes.

"I am not disturbed by Buster. He is my friend," replied Laura as she patted Buster.

"I'm glad to see you are getting stronger," said Father Hughes, "and your ability to speak our language seems to improve with each passing hour. Sister Clare said that you want to try to find your husband today. Do you have some ideas?"

"Yes, Father Hughes. If you will help me, I have two ideas. I know that all of you are taking a risk by assisting us, and I do not want to make things more dangerous for you, but I will need your help to him. I am confident that he is alive. If I survived, I am sure he survived. I do not know whether he came ashore north or south of where you found me, but I believe he is somewhere near there. Sister Clare told me that the forest is thick in that area, so perhaps he is hiding among the trees somewhere near the ocean and watching. Since he does not know where I am, I believe he would have already launched a rescue request unless he lost his rescue request launcher, as I lost mine. If my beloved has his launcher, the rescue ship will search for him first, so Erik will remain hidden until it appears. The rescue ship will find him, take him aboard, and then they will search for me. I am, however, very concerned about his safety while he waits for the rescue ship.

"What would happen if he has lost his rescue request launcher? Would you be stuck on Earth forever?" asked Sister Clare.

"No, if we do not return home or send a message or a rescue request within a specific amount of time, which varies according to our destination and mission, our people will send a rescue ship to find us," said Laura.

"What if Eric can't find you? Would he return home and leave you here?" Father Hughes asked.

"Never!" Laura replied. "My beloved would not leave unless I was with him. He would die here first, as would I, rather than leave without him."

"Good. That's what I hoped you would say. I think I'm beginning to like this Erik fellow," replied Father Hughes.

"But how can Erik or the rescue ship possibly find you?" asked Sister Clare. "Do you have some kind of a chip or detection device implanted in you to help them find you?"

"No! No!" replied Laura. "In our world, even suggesting such a thing is a crime deserving severe punishment. We have a temporary location device that we use only during our voyages or other special situations. We are very protective of our freedom, and we know such technology too easily becomes an instrument for tyrants to control others. Our race fought for many generations to crush even the smallest seeds of tyranny wherever we found them because the seeds of evil always grow. So, instead of an implanted tracking device, we wear a removable locator patch on our skin during voyages. We apply the patch before departing from our home world, and when we return home, we remove and destroy it before exiting the spacecraft. The signal from the removable detection patch is not as powerful as the signal emitted by the rescue request launcher Erik is probably wearing on his wrist. However, it is powerful enough for our ship to find us.

"So, how do you think we can find Erik and get the two of you reunited and on your way home?" asked Father Hughes.

"If possible," Laura continued, "I would like you to take me to where you found me. We would stop there, and I would sing the short version of his name to him—I believe your people refer to it as a nickname. He would hear me if he were within what you would measure as two miles. If he hears me, he will sing a short reply. Oh, how joyful I will be at the sound of his voice!" Laura paused to contain her emotions and then continued. "If we hear no reply from him in one place, I would like to try again at several other places if possible. If he responds, I could then guide him to us with my voice. After we are reunited, you can leave us there, and we will hide until the rescue ship arrives—or, if you and Mother Catharine are willing, perhaps we could bring him here if he thinks the area where he is hiding is not very secure. May we try to find him today, Father Hughes?"

"I think it would be too dangerous for you to leave the convent, Laura," replied Father Hughes. "I'm sure Doctor Griffith has mentioned the increase in checkpoints and random searches that the police are conducting. It's almost certain that we will be stopped and checked, and there is no possibility of disguising you as a human, Laura. You are a lovely lady, my child, but they would never mistake you for a local girl," he said with a smile.

Sister Clare giggled, then Laura, momentarily puzzled, smiled and said to Father Hughes, "I think I understand. That was a joke, yes?"

"Yes, it was, my friend," he replied, "it was a very little joke. By the way, has Doctor Griffith been here to see you today?"

UNTIL THE RESCUE SHIP ARRIVES

"No, Father," interjected Sister Clare. "He hasn't called either. He told me yesterday that he would come by to check on Laura sometime early this morning, and it's already almost noon, so I'm surprised we haven't heard from him. When he arrives, he'll be surprised and pleased at how rapidly Laura has recovered. Doctor Griffith wants to learn as much as possible about Laura and her while she is with us. Yesterday, he was asking her questions, examining her, and taking notes like he was studying for a test," she said with a short giggle.

"Perhaps the checkpoints, the searches, and all that nonsense have delayed him," replied Father Hughes. Checkpoints and searches—I hear myself say the words, but I still can't believe that, within such a short time, we have succumbed to the kind of dictatorship we have fought against over and over in other places around the world. As you said, Laura, the seeds of evil always grow. But, enough of my ranting. I think your idea is good, Laura, but I don't want to risk your being captured by the police at a checkpoint, especially if Erik has a rescue ship on the way for you. Who knows how much more dangerous and complicated matters would become if the police captured you? You said that you had two ideas. What was the second idea?"

"My other idea is to teach one of you a simple, three-syllable word to sing that Erik would recognize and know I had taught it to you. No one on Earth knows even one word of our language, so he would know it is a signal from me, not a trick or a trap."

"I have heard Sister Clare sing," replied Father Hughes. "She has a fine, clear voice. It may be best to teach Sister to sing the word. If I sang it, Erik might think he was hearing the cry of a wounded animal."

Laura smiled at Father Hughes's attempt at humor, and then, taking hold of Sister Clare's hand, she said, "Yes, I think you could do this well, Sister Clare. Would you learn to sing the word to Erik?"

" I would be overjoyed to do it, Laura, if it is simple enough for me to sing," said Sister Clare.

"It is simple. You will use only one voice. It is one of our simplest words. It should be easy for you to learn. I will sing it slowly as if it were in a song so you can more easily hear the changes in pitch and the duration of each syllable. That is very important. Here is how you sing it. Are you ready?"

"Oh, yes!" said Sister Clare with her characteristic enthusiasm.

"Loh-doh-loh," Laura sang softly. Yet, her voice surrounded them with an almost palpable presence, as if Laura's voice were emanating from every corner of the room and flowing from her barely open mouth with a delicate vibrato of nearly heartbreaking purity. The simple melody of the word flowed around and through them with the subtlety of a breeze. "Now you try it, Sister Clare," said Laura.

In those brief seconds of Laura singing a single word in her language, Father Hughes and Sister Clare were on the verge of tears induced by the inhuman perfection of Laura's voice, and for a moment, they just stared at her as they wiped their eyes.

"How do you do that, Laura? How do you do it? I can't sing like that! No one on earth can sing like that!" said Sister Clare.

"I know you cannot copy my singing, but you can do it well enough, Sister Clare. I have heard your sisters in your choir singing, and if you sing as well as they do, you can sing this well enough for Erik to hear it and know that it is a message from me."

"No, I can't do it. You were doing something more than singing. I don't know what it is, but when you sing as you did, something happens inside me that I can't explain—it happened to Father, too. We both were on the verge of tears, and I don't even know why. It's as if you—I can't even find the words to explain it, Laura. I've never had an experience like that. It touches something that I didn't even know was within me."

UNTIL THE RESCUE SHIP ARRIVES

"Music, especially singing, is a language that speaks to both the mind and the soul," replied Laura. "Your race has only limited abilities to express and understand it. You can sense its power in the best of your own music and singing. It can affect you in ways that words alone cannot, and you can feel moved by it, but you cannot express or comprehend it as fully as we do. Please, do not be offended by what I am about to say, but to us, most of your music is unpleasant noise, and, to our ears, most human singing sounds as harsh as the barking of your dog animals must sound to you—except for your holy music and singing. We perceive that much differently because we understand its purpose. Its purpose makes it beautiful to us because we believe singing is the language of Heaven, and we reserve the best of our singing for our holy songs—much as you and your sisters do."

"But Laura, the way you described our singing, that's precisely why I don't think I can do this. I would feel exactly like a dog trying to sing an aria," said Sister Clare, her enthusiasm gone.

"Sister Clare, I am sure that, for your race, you have a lovely voice. Do not be concerned that you cannot duplicate what I do. It is not necessary. I will teach you to sing this word much like some of your people teach those bird animals, parrot animals, I think you call them, to sing one of your songs. Even though a parrot animal does not sound like a human when it sings and does not know what it is singing, you can still understand the words. I can teach you to sing this word just as you teach a parrot animal. I am sure you can sing much better than a parrot animal, yes?"

Both Sister Clare and Father Hughes began laughing.

"Did I say a joke?" asked Laura.

"Yes," replied Sister Clare, "a perfectly timed joke."

"What does that mean?" asked Laura.

"Well, joke timing is hard to explain, Laura," said Sister Clair, still giggling, "but yes, you've convinced me that I can probably sing better than a parrot. I will give it my best effort, at least. By the way, what does the word I'll be singing mean?"

"It is the name of a common little flower that grows in our world. It grows almost everywhere, even near the poles, where the growing season is very short. Everyone loves them because they are so rugged and determined to thrive, and their simple beauty and sweet scent delight us. I sang the flower's name to you as our little children sing it when they are beginning to learn our language well. I will sing the word for you again, Sister Clare, and I will try to do it more simply and with less expression than before, and then you will sing it."

"Okay," said Sister Clare. "Promise not to laugh at me when I try it."

Laura sang the song once again. And then, after two attempts, Sister Clare sang the three-syllable word as perfectly, in pitch and duration, as the limitations of her human voice permitted.

"Excellent, Sister Clare. Try it five more times," said Laura.

Sister Clare sang the word perfectly each time.

"Yes, you are ready, Sister Clare," said Laura.

"Why isn't anyone getting emotional and wiping away tears when I sing it?" joked Sister Clare.

"Even though you did not make us emotional," replied Laura, "when Erik hears you sing that word as beautifully as you did a moment ago, you will make him rejoice and shout with joy."

"Oh, that would be so wonderful to hear! Do you really think it would make him happy enough to shout?"

"Yes, I do, Sister Clare, just as I would shout if I were searching for Erik and heard someone sing that word. When Erik hears you, it will prove to him that I am alive. After Erik hears you, he may sing the word occasionally to let you know he is coming to you. If you repeat it to him, it will help him locate you."

UNTIL THE RESCUE SHIP ARRIVES

"Sister Clare, I think we should do this right now," said Father Hughes. "We should not waste any time. I'll walk up and get permission from Mother Catherine for you to come with me and ask if she would allow us to bring Erik here. Perhaps she will come down here to stay with Laura until we or Doctor Griffith return. As for Sister Clare and I, if we run into a checkpoint and they start questioning us like they always do, we'll just tell them we are on the way to find some fresh fish for the convent. I'm wearing my priestly garb, and you're wearing your habit, so they should have no reason to inquire further."

"But Father, that would be a lie!"

"Not if we intend to do it. I know a place near where we're going that may have some good, fresh-caught fish for sale—if they're not already sold out. You know how quickly food of any kind sells out as soon as people know it is available somewhere. I had planned to drive by there today, so we'll stop there on the way back if we don't find Erik on this attempt. But now, I'm going to tell Mother Catherine our plan and get her approval, then we'll go and do our best to find Erik."

As Father Hughes stepped out the cottage door, he saw Bobby, an intellectually impaired teenager from a nearby group home whom Mother Catherine hired part-time to wash windows and do other light tasks, hiding behind his sedan.

"Bobby, I see you. Come here, young man."

Slowly, Bobby rose, holding his pail full of window cleaning materials, and stood silently beside the car.

"Why are you hiding from me, Bobby?" Father Hughes said as he walked toward Bobby.

Bobby stood silently and looked at Father Hughes.

"What's the matter, Bobby? Did you do something that you're not supposed to do?" Bobby remained silent.

Father Hughes walked up to Bobby and put his hand on his shoulder. Bobby looked down at the ground. "Bobby, we've talked about quite a few things, you and I, haven't we?"

Bobby glanced up at Father Hughes but then lowered his head again.

"Bobby, tell me, what did you do that you think was bad?" Bobby looked up at Father Hughes. "That's my Bobby. You know you can talk to old Father Hughes, don't you?"

"You're not mad at me?" Bobby asked.

"No, Bobby, I'm not mad. I doubt you've done anything I should be mad at you for. We're both reasonable fellows, aren't we? Now tell me, why were you hiding from me?"

"I heard a angel."

"Where was the angel that you heard?"

"In there."

"What did you do when you heard the angel?"

Bobby lowered his head again and didn't say anything.

"Did you look through the window to try to see the angel? Father Hughes asked."

"I'm not s'posa look at people through the windows when I'm washin' 'em 'cause it's rude and makes people mad."

"That's true, Bobby. And you have always been good about not doing that, haven't you?"

"Uh-huh, I don't do that 'cause the sisters won't like me no more, and I want the sisters to like me 'cause the sisters are nice, and I like the sisters."

"Did you make a mistake this time and look through the window to see if there was an angel in there?"

Bobby turned his face toward the ground again.

"Tell me the truth now, my young friend. You did look through the window, didn't you?"

"Uh-huh."

"Thank you for telling old Father Hughes the truth. Now, Bobby, I'm going to tell you the truth about the person you saw because we know that lies are tools of the devil, don't we?"

Bobby looked up and nodded.

"That lady," Father Hughes continued, "whom you thought was an angel, is not an angel, but she is a very special person. She's not from Heaven like an angel would be, but she is from very far away. And there are some bad people who would come and take her away and treat her very badly if they knew she was here. We want to protect her until we can help her return home. Now, Bobby, will you help us get her safely back to her home by never telling anyone about the lady you thought was an angel —not even the other sisters? Will you promise me to keep that secret and help us protect her?"

"Uh- huh, I promise. But are the sisters the bad people who would do bad stuff to the lady? Is that why I can't tell the sisters?"

"No, the sisters are the very best kind of people, but they might accidentally say something to someone who isn't as good as you or them, and then that person may tell the bad people that the lady is here, and then the bad people will come to take her away. We don't want that to happen, do we?"

"Huh-uh. I'll be good. I'll help. I'll pr'tect the lady. Can I see the lady? She sang so pretty, I thought she was a angel."

"Yes, I think she would like to meet you. Then she will know that you are helping keep the bad people away from her until she can go home. Let me tell the lady and Sister Clare about our conversation before you come inside, okay Bobby?"

"Okay."

As Bobby waited outside, Father Hughes explained the matter to Laura and Sister Clare, and he described Bobby's condition to Laura so she would understand why he behaves differently. Sister Clare and

Laura were uneasy about this breach of secrecy, but they understood that it might be better to allow Bobby to meet Laura so he would feel like he had a part in keeping her presence a secret.

"Come on in, Bobby," said Father Hughes. "You know Sister Clare. And this beautiful lady is Laura. Don't be afraid of Laura. She looks different from us because where she comes from, all the people look different from us. She speaks differently, too, but listen to her very carefully, and you'll be able to understand her just fine, okay?"

Bobby didn't reply to Father Hughes but stared at Laura.

"Hello, Bobby," Laura said slowly and clearly.

"You look pretty!" said Bobby. "I heard you sing, and I thought you was a angel, and I looked through the window, 'cause I thought you was a angel. I didn't mean to look through the window, but I thought you was a angel singin'. I want to hear you sing. Can you sing some more 'cause even the sisters don't sing pretty like you? Father said you're not a angel, but I thought you . . . ."

"Bobby," Sister Clare interrupted, "please! Give Laura a chance to say something!"

"Okay, I'll shut up and let her say sumfin'."

"I am not an angel, Bobby," said Laura, "but I come from a faraway place. Where I come from, we often sing when we talk. I was showing Father Hughes and Sister Clare how we say the name of a little flower that grows where I live. That is what I was singing when you heard me."

"Sing it again, Laura! I won't ask no more, I promise. Sing it again. If I say please, will you sing it? One more time, if I say please?"

Sister Clare interrupted Bobby once again. "Bobby, do you truly promise that you won't ask Laura to sing again if she sings that word one more time?"

"Uh-huh, I truly promise. I truly promise."

UNTIL THE RESCUE SHIP ARRIVES

"And," Sister Clare continued, "do you promise you will never let anyone know that Laura is here? Do you absolutely, on your very honor, promise that you will keep this a secret and not tell anyone?"

"I promise, ab'sutely, and I very ab'sutely honor that I won't tell nobody. I won't tell nobody 'cause I don't want the bad people to come and take her away and do bad stuff. Father told me about the bad people. I won't never tell nobody. I won't never tell nobody. Sing it again, Laura, please, please."

"Thank you very much, Bobby," said Laura, reaching and gently taking his hand. "You are a very good young man, Bobby, and I believe I can trust you. I will be happy to sing that little word for you again, but we must first have Father or Sister Clare look outside to ensure no one nearby will hear me."

Father Hughes stepped outside to check for anyone nearby. "It's all clear, Laura, and I'd like to hear you sing it again, too, even if it is just one word."

Laura smiled. "This time, I'll sing it slowly and simply."

Laura slowly sang the three syllables again with clarity and such beauty one would think impossible to convey within the two-and-a-half seconds it took to sing the word. Father Hughes and Sister Clare smiled at one another and shook their heads in amazement as they wiped their eyes.

Bobby laughed and shook his fists as he hopped around the room with glee. "That's pretty! That's pretty! I love you, Laura! Pretty, pretty, pretty! I'm so happy! How come you guys are cryin'?" he asked Father Hughes and Sister Clare.

"I don't know, Bobby," replied Sister Clare. "Maybe Laura knows why it makes you so happy, but it makes us a little bit teary-eyed."

"Yes, I do know why. Our singing evokes the sense of lost virtue and innocence in your people—a sorrowing over the purity you lost but inwardly yearn to reclaim. However, Bobby's conscience is pure, so he can hear our singing without his soul experiencing the inner sadness that you experience.

"Are you and your race so virtuous that your singing doesn't affect you as it does us?" asked Sister Clare.

"I do not want to sound rude, but we are more virtuous than most of your race. But even more importantly, our race is not affected by our vocalizations as severely as your race is. For us, singing is simply how we communicate with one another. But we sometimes use our singing as a weapon, too. Particularly in past ages, when large groups of warriors met for battle, the group with the most warriors singing could intimidate their enemy and weaken their effectiveness in combat. If the number of warriors was similar on both sides, much depended on which side sang more forcefully and was the more spiritually prepared.

"When we use our singing for battle, the effect on our race can temporarily weaken the enemy's morale, but it is never as incapacitating for us as it is for you. As you have already experienced, expressing myself in your presence like Erik and I normally sing to one another would cause you great emotional discomfort. If you heard us sing one of our holy songs or one of our war songs, it could kill you if your soul was darkened by severe wickedness. With our language, details, emotions, and relevant subtleties are woven into each word through the manner in which we sing it. And even though your race could never understand what we are saying, your mind and soul would be stirred and troubled because you can sense deeper, veiled expressions conveyed by the melody and other elements of the song. You experience this even in something sung in a human language you don't speak or in a piece of instrumental music with no words at all. For you, this ability is limited, but it is strong enough to generate feelings and moods within you, but you cannot explain why it does so. In a weaker, though similar way, even the tone of speech can affect your emotions, such as when you hear an angry tone of voice or a soothing tone. Even if the same words are used in each instance, the emotional effect on you differs. That is not a perfect explanation, but perhaps it helps."

"I think that explains it pretty well, actually," Father Hughes replied, "It seems you have a secret weapon to use against us frail humans if trouble comes your way. Unfortunately, you may need to wield that weapon before all this is over."

Then, turning to Bobby, he said, "Okay, Bobby, Laura was nice enough to sing for you, so you had better get back to your work now because Sister Clare and I need to get on with our work. Don't worry about washing the windows here at the cottage this time, Bobby. I'll tell Mother Catherine I told you to wait until next week to do that. You won't get in trouble, I promise you. Come with me, Bobby. Walk with me up to Mother's office, and we'll see if she wants you to change your routine today—oh, Sister Clare, I'll leave Buster with you and Laura until I get back. I see he likes being in Laura's company. Her singing put him sound asleep."

Bobby waited outside as Father Hughes stepped into Mother Catherine's office. Father Hughes told her the events of the morning and explained their plan to find Erik and, with her permission, bring him to the convent. He also told Mother Catherine of Bobby's promise to keep Laura's presence a secret and suggested altering his work assignments.

"Yes, I will give Bobby tasks that will keep him away from others as much as possible. He enjoys tending to the chickens and sometimes loses track of time just watching them, and he likes puttering around with the garden tools, so I'll have him spend more time on those tasks. And, of course, Sister Clare has my permission to go with you to find Erik and bring him here," said Mother

Catherine. "I'll sit with Laura while the two of you are gone. I'll pray that you find him. And please, Father, do try to avoid giving the authorities any reason to focus their attention on us here at the convent. You know they are looking for excuses to cause problems for religious organizations of every kind. As with every accursed tyranny throughout history, they want to be God. People never learn, do they? They just never learn."

"It's true, Mother. It's always the same prideful foolishness, century after century. I shall do my best to avoid bringing trouble to all of you here, Mother. And, yes, pray that we find Laura's husband, bring him here, and keep them safe until their rescue ship takes them home. Laura is a remarkable person, and I'm sure her husband, Erik, will prove equally remarkable. Did you ever even imagine, Mother, that you would someday provide shelter and hospitality to real, live extraterrestrial beings here at this convent?"

Mother Catherine shook her head, "I wish I were only imagining it now, Father. I am overwhelmed by the reality of Laura's presence here, but I am deeply, deeply concerned about the possible consequences. I will pray for your success in finding Erik, but I will just as fervently pray that trouble doesn't follow you back here. Please, understand me, Father. Erik and Laura are welcome here. I wouldn't turn them away now. I must admit, I'm ashamed of my initial reluctance to help Laura when you first brought her here. I must trust that God has a purpose for bringing them to us. I don't know what that purpose is, but He has a purpose for everything. I admit, though, I will feel a million tons of worry lifted off my shoulders when they go home. But enough of all that. You and Sister Clare had better get going, Father. I'll walk back to the guest cottage with you."

UNTIL THE RESCUE SHIP ARRIVES

IT WAS RAINING AGAIN when Father Hughes and Sister Clare left the convent. As they wound through the curves on the narrow secondary highways, Sister Clare prayed a rosary for their success in contacting Erik and reuniting him with Laura. Buster lay sleeping, curled in the back seat.

Father Hughes's cell phone suddenly rang.

"Hello, is this Gerald Hughes?" asked the caller.

"It is. Who's calling?"

"I'll skip my name for now. I have a message from Paul."

"Paul Gr...?"

"Shut up and just listen to me," barked the caller. "Something's come up that he can't get out of, so he has to cancel on you today. He knows you'll understand. He also says that your neighbors know your niece is visiting you, and they'll probably stop by unannounced if she stays in town for another day or two."

Then, the caller hung up.

Father Hughes drove in silence as he tried to make sense of the phone call.

"Is something wrong, Father?" asked Sister Clare after a few moments.

"I don't know who that was, Sister Clare. I think someone was trying to tell me in vague language that Paul is in trouble. Maybe he's been arrested. I think the caller was also trying to tell me, as I say, in vague language, that the authorities know about Laura. If that is so, the only way they could have learned about her is if they had Paul in custody and had been interrogating him. If they have the medical notes you said Paul was compiling on Laura, that will make them all the more aggressive in forcing Paul to lead them to her. Paul's a sturdy old boy, but they have ways to get anyone to crack if they think there's more to squeeze out of them.

"Sister Clare gasped. "Oh! Poor Doctor Griffith! And poor Laura, if they come swooping down on her! Father, we must find Erik today so he and Laura can get away from here and return home. But what can we do for Doctor Griffith, Father? What can we do? This is terrible! Do you really think that's what has happened to Doctor Griffith?"

"I don't know, Sister. The person who called was trying very hard to tell me something without actually saying it and without giving his name—you always have to assume the big ears of the regime are listening, you know. He didn't give me much information to work with, but that's the only interpretation I can make from what he gave me. Keep praying, Sister Clare. We'll need as much divine help as we can get today."

Sister Clare continued to whisper prayers as they drove. The rain had stopped for the moment, and thus far, they had not encountered any police vehicles or roadblocks, which Father Hughes regarded as a miracle considering the heightened police activity buzzing around the area. Soon, they arrived at the parking area just above the beach where Father Hughes had found Laura. Fortunately, the parking area and the beach below were deserted.

"Here we are, Sister. Down below on the beach, a little north from the bottom of that trail, that's where I found her. The fact that I was able to get her up here and into the car is a wonder in itself. Are you ready to sing for Erik?"

"Oh, Father, I will sing as I have never sung before, even if it is just one word. If he is anywhere near, he will hear me—Oh, God, please let him hear me! Please, please let him hear me!"

Chapter 9

In the forest on the inland side of the highway, the male alien found a spot where two large trees had fallen, one atop the other. He sat and leaned against a stump sheltered under the crossed trees. He pulled the hood of his jacket over his head, folded his arms across his abdomen, tucked his hands under his armpits, and closed his eyes. He leaned to one side to ease the pain in his injured ribs and tried to empty his mind and allow sleep to overcome him, but his thoughts were still too engaged in the events of the day. In his mind, he saw her face as she closed her escape pod hatch. He had noticed the fear in her eyes in that brief instant before she slammed the hatch shut. Then she was gone. He would not allow himself to think it would be his last memory of her. No, she was not lost to him, he told himself. Wherever she was now, she was alive, and he would find her. If the orbs from the rescue ship somehow couldn't locate her, after searching the entire planet if necessary, he would send the rescue ship with its orbs back to their home world, and he would remain on Earth until he found her or until he died.

He couldn't rein in his thoughts, so he allowed his mind to run unchecked until his thoughts became half-conscious, abstract mind clutter, spinning like debris in a vortex as his weary brain sorted and cataloged all that had occurred that day. Finally, his physical exhaustion and mental fatigue united, and he drifted to sleep.

It was dark when he awakened. He did not move but instead sat silently and listened. He did not know if he awoke because of restlessness or if his senses had alerted him. He silently retrieved the night vision goggles from his pocket and scanned the area. Through his goggles, the night became day, but there was little open space around him, so he watched for movement in the gaps between the trees and foliage. As he watched, he saw the ferns several yards in front of him wobble as a raccoon emerged and calmly wandered past him, searching for anything edible it could find. He watched as it waddled along until it was just out of sight among the ferns, and then he heard it splashing in a small stream that he had not heard flowing even though it was only a few paces away. He had ignored his thirst until that moment, but now that he knew fresh, running water was at hand, he suddenly craved a mouthful of cool water. As he rose and crept toward the stream, he realized his ribs no longer ached. The nutrients in the wafer his beloved had dropped were doing their work. The nutrients they contained greatly enhanced the body's restorative properties, healing or curing minor illnesses and injuries in one or two days and helping even severe wounds heal rapidly.

The raccoon disappeared into the forest when it noticed him walking toward the stream. He knelt and tasted the water. It had no taste other than cool and wet, and he began scooping handfuls of it into his mouth until he satisfied his body's too-long-ignored thirst. He rose and followed the little stream downhill to see where it may lead. If it led to a larger stream or a pool, he would try to catch a fish to eat to lessen his twinges of hunger. If no fish were available, the nutrition from the wafer would keep him going, but having something to eat would give him a psychological boost and provide an extra bit of nourishment.

UNTIL THE RESCUE SHIP ARRIVES

Less than one hundred yards farther downhill, the stream widened into a shallow, slow-moving creek deep enough for small fish to escape most land predators and too shallow for larger fish to prey on them. With his night vision goggles, he could see well enough into the shallow water to determine if any fish were there. He crept along the bank until he came to a pool holding a few small fish. He pulled off his boots, which were now nearly dry, and set them on the bank along with his jacket. Then, as slowly as a sloth, he crept into the creek and crawled upstream so any mud or debris he stirred would not cloud the water in front of him. He saw a small trout, no more than six inches long, holding near a submerged rock. With the patience of a determined predator, he inched himself to within reach of the fish. Then, faster than any human could throw his best punch, he thrust his hand into the water, capturing the quivering trout. He bit the fish's head, crushing its skull, then waded back to the bank. He scaled the fish with the edge of a stone and then washed the fish in the stream to clean off the tiny scales. Next, he tore open the belly of the fish, gutted it, and washed it in the stream once again. He picked the flesh from the fish with his teeth and fingers until he had eaten all but the head and tail. Then, he tossed the remainder of the carcass back into the stream where the crayfish, with their nimble claws, would finish the job. He then scooped a handful of water into his mouth to wash out any scales or tiny bones and then drank several more handfuls of water.

During the hours of darkness, he scouted the area around him with the aid of the night vision goggles. The highway and the ocean bordered the west side, but the several-mile circumference east, north, and south was uninhabited forest. That gave him a fair chance of remaining hidden until the rescue ship arrived. The rescue ship would first track the signal from his wristband. When it located him, if it had not already found his beloved and brought her aboard, he would immediately launch the defender orbs to search for the signal from his beloved's skin patch. He would remain on the rescue ship, which could render itself invisible to the human eye, while the orbs located his beloved. Once the orbs found her, they would transmit details and images of her precise location and who and what was around her, then hover, invisible to the eye, and await further commands. Then, with the assistance of the powerful orbs, he would free her, and they would go home.

He hiked back to the fallen trees to wait for morning. He began to think about the life to which they would return after they arrived back in their home world and settled once again into their own house on their own land. So often during the past few voyages, they had spoken of all the children they hoped to raise—as many children as the All Holy One gave them. They would never again miss the seasonal family gatherings and village activities they had so often missed during their voyages. So powerful was their yearning for the beauty and peace of the valleys, hills, and mountains of their province that the ache was almost unbearable. They longed to be back in their home on their own soil, on that blessed little patch of sovereignty that was their private little province within the greater province. Then, he and she would never again be separated by more than a few paces from each other. Each day, they would awaken to the view of their valley rather than the sight of the functional, technological sterility inside their spacecraft—little more than a speck of dust amidst the immeasurable voids of the indifferent universe. He longed to get his hands dirty in the soil again as he raised his crops and to feel the tools in his hands as he worked on his machinery and made other repairs. He longed to hear the deep purring of the small herd of those enormous but gentle beasts they would raise, whose wool, when sheared and spun, produced the soft and almost indestructible fabric from which most of the clothing worn by the people of his world was woven—including the uniform he was now wearing. He missed the evening holy songs, sung by one and all, in every town and village at day's end, lifting to the Creator a tapestry of songs of thanksgiving and praise woven in the air by the chorus of his family and neighbors singing with the many voices each of them could sing simultaneously. The evening holy songs lasted only a few moments but filled everyone with peace and serenity by expressing the otherwise inexpressible through song. It was a joy the humans could never experience, and he was grateful that his people had such a rich, almost multidimensional language that combined song and unsung words, enabling them to communicate even the most complex thoughts with perfect clarity. The coarse, limited languages of the humans required many words to express a complex idea that, for his race, could be sung with a short, multi-voiced phrase. He almost pitied these humans, babbling away the best they could in their languages that were less sophisticated than the beginner language the children of his world used before they matured enough to control the fullness of the many voices they each possessed and would soon master. The simplest, rudimentary phrase of his people's beautiful song language tormented humans. The soaring, full, open-souled choruses, or the aggressive war chants of his race, caused the humans to collapse in spiritual and mental agony and could even torment humans to death. Other Voyagers had first seen that happen among primitive tribesmen who had stumbled upon them and attacked them during a specimen-gathering mission on one of the earliest voyages to Earth. They discovered that, when hearing the singing of his people, the humans sensed within their souls their inner spiritual darkness, deficits, and burdens that are inexpressible through words alone, which, for humans, can only be inadequately and unsatisfactorily relieved through weeping and tears.

 He had seen and experienced enough of these humans and their world. He had learned enough about their endless repetition of the errors and follies that shackled them to mediocrity. His race had documented this seemingly uncorrectable human fault throughout the generations they had studied them and their planet. The humans were not less intelligent than his people or less capable of obtaining wisdom. They were, however, utterly disinclined to benefit from wisdom. They often pretended to value wisdom, but when given a choice between a wise but difficult option or an easy but ultimately foolhardy option, humans always seemed to choose the latter. And while their technological knowledge continued to limp forward, the humans were always ingenious at finding perverse applications for each technological discovery. They inevitably applied each technological advancement in ways that complicated and cluttered their lives more than it simplified them. Some among them recognized these errors and failures and tried to persuade their kind to follow a different path but with little success. Human civilization always followed the same pattern: rising, plateauing, then collapsing. Then, they would slowly patch themselves together again without gaining lasting wisdom from their experiences. Thus, they would stumble onward toward the next ruination.

He felt fortunate to have been able to compare the civilization on Earth and those on several other planets where they had discovered intelligent beings. His observations during his voyages gave him an even greater appreciation for his race, culture, and civilization. He understood that while he and his people were susceptible to the same failings as the humans, unlike them, members of his race endeavored to overcome their personal weaknesses, which they recognized as the seeds of societal weakness. They made every effort to crush the first hint of them at their source in their personal lives and their communities. Their universally expected code of conduct required self-discipline, respect toward others, and dignified public behavior, virtues that were barely detectable in most human societies. Through the enculturation of personal virtue, his people eventually built a stable, orderly society that provided abundant freedom, peace, and prosperity from generation to generation.

His people imbued each new generation with an appreciation for their history, customs, and traditions, which enculturated the wisdom to reject errors that had destroyed their earlier societies. Thus, folly found little fertile ground to sprout, let alone take root.

Even though he was now eager for his beloved and himself to resign and return to their home, he was proud of their service to their civilization, first, before they became husband and wife, as troopers in the Provincial Guards dealing with occasional troubles and rebellions in the Northern Provinces, and afterward as Distant Voyagers. He valued the experiences they encountered during those times and the life lessons they provided. Their work, and that of others in the Distant Voyager Service, had benefitted their world in many ways. However, he knew that many other eager young volunteers were waiting for their opportunity to become Voyagers, so when he and his beloved returned home, they would resign with honor and make room for two new Voyagers. Home was calling to them. It filled their every idle thought. He knew how deeply his beloved's heart now yearned for their home, so much so that she could barely speak of it without closing her eyes and inhaling deeply to control her emotions. They would be home again very soon, he vowed to himself. Together, they would overcome this present challenge. Together, as always, they would prevail.

As the morning light penetrated gaps in the clouds and trees, he hiked toward the forest's edge near the highway where he could remain hidden and watch the parking area where he knew the person who had taken his beloved had parked. Only a few automobiles passed by that were not police or military. Occasionally, he heard the distant thumping of a helicopter, and he briefly saw one fly low over the water parallel to the beach. Soon afterward, a police van stopped at the parking area, and two officers stepped out and scanned the beach below through their binoculars. They talked as they stood and pointed to areas that interested them for whatever reason, then drove away. He could only guess their interest in the area but assumed it was somehow related to his beloved. Had whoever had taken his beloved reported the matter to the authorities or handed her over to them, he wondered? The thought momentarily crossed his mind to surrender himself on the chance that if she were in their custody, the authorities would reunite them in captivity, and then the rescue ship would later free them with little trouble. He immediately squelched this foolish idea and muttered an insult to himself for entertaining it for even a moment.

Traffic lessened, and he sat, restless and frustrated. He heard the hum of an automobile on the highway decelerating as it rolled to a stop in the parking area. As he watched through the foliage, an older man dressed in what he recognized as the apparel of a priest and a younger woman dressed as a nun stepped out of the automobile. The man opened the rear door, and a yellow dog ambled out. Then the man clipped a leash onto the dog's collar, reached into the rear seat, retrieved a walking stick, and then walked to the front of the automobile. The man spoke to the nun as he pointed toward the trail and the beach with the walking stick.

"Could this be him? Was he the one?" he asked himself. He didn't want to allow himself to believe it. It was too easy and too fast, he thought. Such coincidences do not happen. It could not be him. Or could it? He moved closer to better see and hear their conversation. Then, the nun raised her hands to the corners of her mouth to create a megaphone and sang, "Loh-doh-loh!"

His heart leaped, his skin tingled, and he clenched his fists and lifted his face toward the sky in joy and half disbelief. As crudely as the nun had sung the syllables, she sang the subtleties within the word well enough that he understood that it was a message from his beloved! She had sent them to find him! Only she could have taught the human woman those syllables and how to sing them well enough that he could recognize them as a word in their language. His beloved was alive! Thanks be to the All Holy One! She was alive! And now he would join her, wherever she was, whatever the conditions may be, he would be with her. He stood and was about to sing the same word in reply when the nun again sang, "Loh-doh-loh!"

Suddenly, a black Special Security Police van rounded the corner near the parking area, abruptly swerved, and skidded to a halt in front of Father Hughes's sedan. With the lights flashing on the van's light bar, two officers armed and wearing combat gear climbed out and strode toward Father Hughes and Sister Clare.

"Sister, here, take Buster's leash and get him back into the car, please," said Father Hughes as Buster began growling.

"What are the two of you doing out here?" barked the fatter of the two officers.

"What you see is what it is," replied Father Hughes, stepping toward the two officers.

"Oh, we know this one, don't we," said the thinner officer, "he's the one who claims to be best buddies with Major Carnahan."

"Well, so it is, so it is. And he's got his girlfriend and his attack dog with him, too. It looks like his girlfriend is having a little trouble handling the dog. Maybe we should calm the dog down permanently," said the fat one with a sneer, "What do you think about that idea, old man? By the way, grandpa, your girlfriend is a little young for you, isn't she?" Then, stepping toward Sister Clare, the fat officer reached for her. "Maybe we should tire her out a little for you. What do you say?"

Father Hughes bared his teeth and. and struck the fat officer squarely on the cheekbone with his walking stick, staggering him. "You filthy sons of Satan!" he yelled as he hit the officer again on the forehead, dropping him to the ground in a heap, blood trickling down his face.

Buster bolted from Sister Clare's grip, charged toward the fallen officer, and mauled the half-conscious man's arm. The thinner man drew his pistol but hesitated, unsure whether to shoot Father Hughes or Buster. At that moment, a deep, reverberating roar blew over them like a storm front. To Father Hughes, it sounded like a dozen thundering bass voices from a Russian Orthodox choir. The thinner officer, his mouth gaping in terror, could not precisely determine the sound's source and waved his pistol in one direction and then another. Then, the roaring stopped, and they heard limbs cracking as a racing blur charged toward them through the undergrowth. Suddenly, a blur of fury dressed in tan leaped from the forest onto the highway, sprinting, dropping and rolling, jumping to its feet again.

The thin officer fired several times in panic at the charging menace, missing with every shot, then he dropped his sidearm and turned to flee down the steep trail leading to the beach. But it was too late. The male alien slapped him on the side of the head with an open palm, knocking him face-first to the ground. With one hand, the alien lifted the skinny officer by his tactical vest and threw him down again beside the fat officer, who was lying on his back, pleading for his life. Then the alien kicked them, leaned down and slapped their faces, grabbed both of them by their tactical vests, one in each hand, and lifted them to his eye level.

"I saw you!" he growled, forcing himself to speak in slow, flat tones unnatural to his language so the men could understand him. "I know what you were going to do! I heard every word you spoke! You are cowards! You are criminals! I saw you! I heard you! You are not worthy of another breath of life! Now, I will kill both of you."

The two men screamed in fear and begged for their lives.

"You beg like the cowards you are now that it is your turn to die. You abused these people without cause, but they did not fear you. That angered you. Yes, that angered you. You want people to fear you because you enjoy feeling powerful." Then he shook them like rags. "Do you feel powerful now, cowards?" The two men blubbered and begged for their lives as he shook them. "Do you hear yourselves screaming and begging? You enjoy seeing fear in the faces of others, but you do not enjoy fear when it is on your face! No, it is not enjoyable now. You are not laughing. But I will laugh. You will die now, and I will laugh as you die!"

Then, the alien slammed the two dangling officers into each other as he held them above his head. "Scream louder, cowards! I want you to hear yourselves scream before you die!" shouted the male alien as he carried them toward the trail.

"No!" shouted Father Hughes. "Spare them! It is best not to kill them. I know who you are! Your wife sent us to find you. She told us you are honorable and brave. She said that is the way of your people! You are right to say these men are weak and cowardly. They have become drunk from their abuse of power and deserve the punishment you intend to give them, but you have shown them how weak and contemptible they are. You have rubbed their faces in their shame and shattered their arrogance. Perhaps you have taught them a lesson that will change them for the better if you let them live. Rather than killing them, allow them to live and learn from this experience. Perhaps they will become honorable men."

The two men, stripped of all pride and self-respect, begged for mercy and swore they would become changed men if allowed to live. The male alien threw them both to the ground and slapped their faces again, causing them to plead even more pathetically. He ripped their tactical vests off them, then with his foot on the chest of the thinner officer, he lifted the fat officer to his eye level.

"Out of respect for this good man who has every right to kill you but is now asking me to spare your lives, I will let chance decide if you live or die. I will throw both of you down this hill as far as I can throw such useless trash," said the male alien. "If you live, you will run away if you see me again. You should hope I do not see you first. I have your faces forever in my memory. I will not forget you. If I see either of you again, anywhere, you will not escape me!"

Then the alien roared as he threw the fat one, who squealed like a terrified child as he arced through the air, outward and down, landing on his chest with a heavy grunt and then rolling down the trail in a tumbling lump to the beach below.

"Please! No! Please! Please!" begged the skinny officer as the alien grabbed him. Then, like a hammer-throwing Olympian, the alien launched the skinny officer into the air, cartwheeling and screaming until he slammed to the ground and rolled to a stop beside the unconscious fat officer. The alien then walked over to the Special Security Police van, turned off the ignition, smashed the computer and the two-way radio, grabbed the shotgun from its mount, set it aside, and with a low grunt, he lifted one side of the van and sent it tumbling an crashing down the trail, barely missing the two officers at the bottom as they lay motionless in the sand.

The alien walked up to Father Hughes, still holding his walking stick. The alien tapped the walking stick with his knuckles, "You are an old warrior!" he said.

"I am an old priest," replied Father Hughes.

"Yes, and a warrior. I watched you. You deserve much respect. Take me to her now, and tell me, is she safe and well?"

"She is very well, my friend. She is in a safe place, but I warn you, taking you to her will be very dangerous, especially now after this incident. The police will almost certainly discover those men and their vehicle before we get back to the place where your wife is waiting, and they will call many more police and helicopters to this area. The Special Security Police will likely stop us somewhere along the way."

Ignoring Father Hughes's comment, the alien picked up the tactical vests, yanked the radios from the vests, and smashed them under his heel. Then, he retrieved the officers' pistols from the ground and carried them, the shotgun, and the vests to the sedan. Sister Clare was in the front seat, weeping and praying a rosary. Buster cowered on the passenger-side floorboard of the backseat, trembling in fear and offering a low growl as the alien knelt just outside the opposite rear door.

"What is your dog-animal's name?" he asked.

"It's Buster. He's very frightened. He may bite you."

"No, he will not bite me. He is a warrior, too. I saw him trying to help you. He and I will be friends," replied the alien. Then, in a whispered, almost falsetto voice, the alien sang a simple, one-voice lullaby. At various points, he paused and whispered, "Buster." After a few moments, Buster stopped shaking, whimpered weakly, and closed his eyes. The alien continued with the lullaby for a few more syllables, then when he again whispered, "Buster," Buster opened his eyes and looked at the alien, who then patted his hand on the car seat and said, "Come, Buster, come to me." Slowly, Buster stood and stepped over to the alien, sniffed his hand, and allowed the alien to gently pet the top of his head and stroke his ears. The alien whispered again to Buster in a falsetto voice, and Buster began wagging his tail. The alien stroked Buster's head again, then set the tactical vests and the shotgun onto the floorboard, slipped a pistol into his pocket, and said to Father Hughes, "You will take me to her now," and climbed into the back seat.

"You must understand," replied Father Hughes, "after what just happened, the police may kill us if they stop us. We should find a place to park and hide while we think of a better plan to get you back to your wife."

"No. You will take me to my beloved now," said the alien. "I will protect you. There will be no danger for the two of you or Buster. If we have trouble with the police, they will see that I have weapons, and I will make them believe that you are my captives. So now, you will take me to her. We will go now. What are your names?"

"I am Father Gerald Hughes, and this fine, young nun is Sister Clare. We are friends of your wife. Sister Clare has been staying with your wife at the guest cottage, where we have looked after her since I found your wife on the beach. We call your wife Laura, and we've named you Erik—if you don't mind us calling you that."

"Yes, you may call me that. I realize you could never pronounce our true names." Then he leaned close to Sister Clare, "You have been caring for my . . . Laura?" he asked.

Sister Clare moaned and buried her face in her hands as she clutched her rosary.

"Do not fear me, little one. I would not harm someone who has helped my beloved."

Sister Clare wept all the more. "I . . . ," she coughed and fought to stifle her sobbing. "I am so . . . so . . . terrified!" She then bent forward and wept uncontrollably. Buster stood with his paws on the back of the front seat and whimpered, then climbed into the front seat and began licking Sister Clare's face.

"We've waited here too long. We must go!" said Father Hughes. "Sister Clare, please try to pray for us—we'll certainly need divine help today. Erik, if the police stop us, do what you believe needs to be done, but we will not pretend to be your captives. That would be as cowardly as it would be false and futile. If we die, we die with integrity."

Erik looked at Father Hughes, and a broad, flat smile grew across his face. Then, he shook Father Hughes's shoulder with his large hand. "As I said, you are an old warrior."

"And as I said, I am just an old priest, but I am as angry and as frightened as an old priest can be right now—Erik, please help Sister Clare put Buster back with you in the rear seat."

The rain fell again as Father Hughes sped down the wet, winding highway.

"Tell me what happened to my beloved after she ejected from our spacecraft," said Erik, "Tell me everything she told you and everything that has happened since you found her."

"Give me a few minutes first, Erik, to put some distance between us and those two policemen while I think of the best route to avoid police checkpoints," replied Father Hughes.

Father Hughes turned off the highway onto a county road, and then, after a few miles, Sister Clare suddenly shouted, "Father! Get off this road now, right now! Look! Right there! There's a driveway or something. Turn there! Get off the highway! Turn! Turn! Now! Now! Now!"

There was no time to argue. Father Hughes swerved and turned up the narrow one-lane driveway.

"Keep going, Father, a little farther up! Hurry, please! Please!" urged Sister Clare. "Okay, I think we will be alright here."

"What's this about, Sister?"

"I don't know, Father, but please, let's just wait here for a few moments. I just had a sudden panic attack from being on that road."

"Sister, the longer we delay, the more likely those two . . . individuals . . . that we left back there will have their comrades combing this entire area of the state to find us. We need to keep going. Please stay strong, Sister Clare."

Just then, a Special Security Police van on the highway passed the driveway.

"Well, Sister, I owe you an apology. Be sure to let me know if you have another panic attack, okay?" said Father Hughes as he patted her hand.

"Sister Clare. You saved us. You have a talent to sense danger, yes?" replied Erik.

"I don't think so, but I am so frightened, and I have been praying so hard. Maybe God gave me a little bit of grace to warn us. I don't know, Erik. Please, Father, please, just get us back home. Please!"

"Have courage, little one," said Erik as he patted Sister Clare on the shoulder, "I think you are stronger than you believe you are."

Father Hughes cautiously pulled onto the highway again. "This is the first time you have ever ridden in an earth vehicle, isn't it, Erik?" Father Hughes asked, trying to make small talk to calm Sister Clare, whom he knew was barely controlling her fear.

"Yes, it is. We have similar vehicles, but no one from our world has ridden in one of your vehicles other than my beloved and me. And after riding with you in this one, I understand why Sister Clare is so afraid," he said, smiling his flat smile as he nudged Sister Clare's shoulder. "I am making a joke, little one. It is funny, yes?"

Sister Clare couldn't help but chuckle at Erik's clumsy attempt to humor her. "Thank you, Erik. I am sorry for being so afraid, but I am just not prepared for all this."

"This experience is new to us also," replied Erik. "We have never interacted with humans, even though our people have studied everything about you for generations. My beloved and I have voyaged here several times. But all our studying could never tell us as much about your people as we will have learned about you during this mission. Please tell me now everything my beloved has experienced. I want to know everything."

"Sister and I will tell you everything your wife told us about her experience after you abandoned your spacecraft, and we'll tell you everything about her experience since I found her on the beach," said Father Hughes. "And with a little divine help, you will soon be with your Laura, and she will tell it all to you herself. I cannot express how happy we are to have found you on our first attempt, but our joy will be nothing compared to Laura's when she sees you step out of this old car."

Chapter 10

The interrogation room door swung open just as the two police officers were handcuffing Doctor Griffith's wrists to the arms of the heavy steel chair bolted to the floor.

"Has he told the two of you anything?" asked the broad-shouldered, stone-faced Major Carnahan as he entered the room.

"No, Major. He says that he won't say a word without his attorney present," replied the senior police officer.

"So, why haven't you escalated your techniques?'

"We were about to do so, sir. We pulled him out of his cell for questioning only twenty minutes ago."

"I see. Step back, please. I want to have a few words with him."

"Yes, sir."

" So, you are Doctor Paul Griffith, is that correct?"

"You have all of my information. You know damned well what my name is."

"You do understand why we arrested you, don't you?"

"Tell me again. Maybe it will sound more interesting when you say it."

"Oh, I'll be glad to. You were arrested bright and early this morning and brought here because of your belligerent behavior toward these officers when they pulled you over at a checkpoint and ordered you to step out of your vehicle so they could perform a routine search—the same belligerent behavior you're showing me now. When a citizen behaves like that, we assume there is a reason. People with nothing to hide are well-mannered and cooperative. Your behavior makes us wonder if, perhaps, you're a smuggler, a black marketer, or maybe you work for the Resistance. Maybe you're an angry, unaffiliated subversive or saboteur. Such behavior makes us very suspicious. It's very unwise to behave that way, Doctor, very unwise. But since then, matters have become 'more interesting,' as you put it. As I reviewed the content of your attaché case, Doctor, I found some interesting notes about a patient you've been treating who, coincidentally, might be someone we are looking for or have information about the person we're looking for. You will tell us where to find this patient of yours so we can discuss a few things with her."

"I don't say anything about anything without my attorney standing here beside me. Now let me make a phone call."

"It seems you already managed to make that phone call while these officers were searching your vehicle—a slight mistake by the officers in forgetting to confiscate your phone before conducting their search. I'll discuss that unprofessional faux pas with them later."

Griffith tried to avoid showing any reaction.

"That was very clever, Doctor, speed dialing his number and keeping the phone in your shirt pocket so that the officers thought you were just grumbling and mumbling to yourself while they searched your car. You're not the first to try that, but it is clever. But, despite the Resistance's sabotage of our communications monitoring systems, we captured that call along with your attorney's name, location—everything we needed to bag him. After I glanced through your notes, I realized that your attorney also likely knew the information we were interested in, so I issued an arrest order for him. The Feds had a vehicle near your attorney's location and arrested him less than fifteen minutes after I sent out an arrest order. We're not totally incompetent, you know."

"Spare me the crap! Either get him down here to represent me, or I'm not answering any questions!"

"Ok, Doctor, here it is, straight. Your attorney won't be available for you. He has his own problems now. We charged him colluding with a subversive, which is just as serious an offense as being a subversive, Doctor Griffith. Unfortunately, he was not very cooperative during interrogation."

"Colluding with a subversive? What the hell are you talking about?"

"Oh, they must not have informed you yet. You are the subversive. I have charged you with subversion and colluding with a foreign agent, Doctor Griffith—someone who is as foreign as a foreign agent can be, wouldn't you say? And now, here you are, a captured subversive, all alone, with no lawyer to manufacture a dubious defense for you—just you, all alone. You forget, Doctor, this is not the old system. We can dispense with the niceties and use much more productive means of dealing with matters of importance now. And we now have more effective methods to persuade stubborn suspects to cooperate. It really is to your advantage to cooperate with us, you know. We can be very forgiving of mistakes a suspect makes while in our custody. But we are not so forgiving toward suspects who persist in making matters uselessly difficult. So, tell us where we can find your unusual patient so we can have a conversation with her. It will be better for you and easier for me if we have a simple conversation to arrive at the truth about a few concerns. If you stop your belligerence and cooperate, we may discover that you committed no serious crimes, and you can be on your way. But first, I need to know the facts. I'm somewhat inclined to think that this matter may be just a collection of misunderstandings and honest mistakes lumped on top of one another, with no criminal intentions behind them. But as I said, I need all the facts to sort it out. We may even have a good laugh together after this is all over. I've seen this occur many times once the air has cleared and the whole truth has been established, even in cases that initially appeared serious. So, let's start over. Let's you and I get to the truth so everybody—including your poor attorney who, I am sure, has a family that is just as worried about his well-being as your family and friends are worried about yours. So, what do you say, Doctor Griffith? Are you ready to cooperate and give everyone some relief?"

Griffith said nothing. He realized that he and his attorney were doomed. His attorney, whom he had told few details beyond the short, vague warning to Father Hughes, would have had no further information for them. They would assume his attorney was holding back on them, so they would torture him until they were sure he didn't know anything more. Griffith knew that few people who survived interrogation were allowed to walk away afterward. He had treated two people who had miraculously survived interrogation and were released. The severity of their injuries rivaled some of the combat injuries he had treated as an Army medic many years earlier. Soon, he and his attorney would have their taste of it. Only the most hopelessly naïve suspects could believe Carnahan's talk about forgiveness and having a good laugh together afterward. Police states aren't in the business of forgiving and forgetting. He had long ago lost his fear of death, but he did fear torture. He feared he would break and tell them everything he knew. He hoped his loyalty to his old friend Gerald and his high regard for Mother Catherine, Sister Clare, Laura, and all the others at the convent would give him the strength to hold out as long as he could bear it. He would endure the suffering as long as possible to buy them enough time to devise a plan to save Laura and themselves. Perhaps Laura's mate, whom she spoke of with such loving reverence, also could help them.

"Carnahan, here's how it is," said Griffith. "My wife died eight years ago, my son hasn't spoken to me for seventeen years, and I still don't know why, and I don't own a dog, so there's nobody who needs me or depends on me. My patients can find other doctors—they know I'm semi-retired anyway. And I don't give a damn about what happens to my estate or my unpaid bills after I'm dead. So do whatever you're going to do to me. Just get on with it because I don't have a damned thing to tell you about anything or anybody, I'm tired of listening to your crap, and I'm tired of looking at your stupid face!"

Carnahan struck Griffith on the cheek. "As you wish, Doctor Griffith."

Griffith spat blood onto the floor. "Uncuff me, and let's try that again—just you and me," he said.

"Oh, that was just an attention-getter, Doctor. We have other activities that we'll be engaging in today. Secure Doctor Griffith in van number seven," Carnahan told the officers. "I'm taking him for further interrogation."

"Will you want us to accompany you, sir?" one of the officers asked him.

"No, I want the two of you to get back out on patrol—Highway 22. And don't just drive around. Stop cars at random and do spot checks. Do some work. And before you put Griffith in the van, let him use the toilet and let him rinse his mouth in the sink so he won't be spitting blood on the floor."

Doctor Griffith said nothing as the two officers led him to the toilet, then to the police van, and shackled him to the bench seat behind the front passenger seat. As they shackled him, Griffith watched Carnahan walk over to an older mechanic, put his hand on his shoulder, and guide him to an area near where another mechanic was running a grinding wheel. He saw Carnahan put his hand to his mouth and lean in to say something in the mechanic's ear. Carnahan returned to the van, climbed into the driver's seat, and then they drove out of the compound and into the busiest section of the city.

Griffith noticed Carnahan reach under the dash as if to retrieve something, but there was nothing in his hand when he drew it back. Carnahan then turned onto a secondary road heading out of town.

"Listen to me, Griffith. I have some things to tell you."

"No! You listen to me," replied Griffith, "I know how this is going to play out, so just shut up and do it. I've said all that I'm going to say."

"Your lawyer is dead," continued Carnahan, ignoring Griffith's remark. "The person who verified himself as Gerald Hughes during your lawyer's phone call apparently uses a black market phone, making it next to impossible to track or trace it to a specific person even with our partially repaired monitoring systems. There are several men in this region named Gerald Hughes, and the feds wanted to save themselves some time and legwork by forcing your lawyer to tell them which Gerald Hughes he had called, along with other details they believed your lawyer knew but wasn't telling them. But your lawyer must have had a weak heart. As soon as they shackled him into a chair, like the one you were shackled in, he slumped over and died. They were coming to take custody of you and start working on you next. That's why I came and got you. Fortunately, it was us, the Special Security Police, not the Feds, who arrested you, so I have the original notes you had in your car. So far, the Feds only know a few details I gave them about your notes regarding your patient, Laura."

"Come on," Griffith interrupted, "that's just a variation of the old good cop bad cop routine. I told you I have nothing more to say to you. Just put me in a morgue drawer next to my attorney!"

"As I was saying, the Feds only know a couple of details I fed them," continued Carnahan. "They want me to hand your notes over to them, but I told them I was checking them for fingerprints before they got pawed by a hundred other hands. I told them I would get the notes to them later today. They didn't like it, but they went along with it, so now I need to make good use of that little slice of time I bought. I've been doing a little thinking about the matter, and I have a hunch that your friend in question is the Gerald Hughes who lives right here in this town—the priest, Father Gerald Hughes. Am I right?"

Doctor Griffith said nothing.

"That would be the same Father Hughes who recently called you and pleaded with you to make a special house call. We caught that entire call, too. The system flagged it. I noticed it. I have the only transcript of that call. And I deleted the only recording of it."

Griffith remained silent.

"You may be surprised to hear that I know that particular Gerald Hughes," Carnahan continued. "He probably doesn't remember me, but he administered the sacraments to my mother some years ago when she was dying. My mother told me that he was the priest who baptized me."

"Well, I'm sure he'd be busting open with pride over your spiritual progress since then," Griffith replied.

"Good, you can still speak. I thought maybe you'd gone catatonic on me. As I said, Father Hughes probably doesn't remember me, but I remember him, and I didn't want any trouble to come his way if I could prevent it. I figure I owe him a favor or two. Also, I believe I know where your special patient is. With the transcript of that phone call and some clues scattered among your notes, a little kid could figure out where your special patient, Laura, is hiding. We can find your patient hiding among the nuns at a convent not far from here, isn't that so, Doctor?"

Doctor Griffith said nothing. Carnahan already knew, so denying it would make no difference.

"That's alright, Griffith, no need to answer. We're going there now because if I can figure it out, my colonel and his federal crew, working together with military intelligence, will also figure it out soon enough. They'll get impatient and go to my office to demand I hand over the complete notes, but I won't be there to help them. They'll tear my office apart trying to find your notes, then go to my house and do the same thing, but there won't be anyone or anything there that's of any use to them. They'll send several teams to visit every Gerald Hughes in the Pacific Northwest and eventually narrow it down to the one your lawyer called. It won't take them long. I figure they'll be raiding the convent tomorrow or the day after. They'll swoop in on the place as if it were wartime. We have to get there first. I haven't yet figured out how best to protect your patient and Father Hughes, but I have a pretty good idea about what will happen to them if they're captured. They'll interrogate and then kill Father Hughes, and then they will lock up your patient at one of the obscure military facilities that almost no one knows exists. They'll treat her like a prized zoo animal while they try to extract as much technological and other information as possible from her. But if they can't charm the information out of her and she doesn't cooperate voluntarily, they'll realize they've painted themselves into a corner. They won't release her, and although they don't know how her people will react if they come to rescue her, the only other option they have is to continue to use ugly methods to pry technological secrets from her, and they won't stop until she cooperates or dies. Once she's in their custody, nothing good will happen to her ever again? And woe to unto us if her people discover what happened to her.

"Why are you telling me all of this? If you're so sure you know everything, why all the drama and games today? Why don't you just swoop down on the convent, or wherever you think she is, with all of your uniformed thugs, grab her, and kill anyone who gets in your way? That's how all you jackboots like to do things, isn't it? And don't expect me to swallow that crap story of your not wanting to cause trouble for the Gerald Hughes your mama knew. If you think you know where my patient is, just get on with it!"

"Griffith, it may please you to know both of us are outlaws now. While we were mixed up in the downtown traffic, I turned off the tracking system for this vehicle. This vehicle is the only one in the fleet altered for that option, and only the head mechanic and I know about it because I had him rig up the switch. I also conveniently left my phone in the interrogation room, which is shielded so that no phone signals can be received or transmitted from there, landline calls only, so not having a tracking signal from my phone will seem normal, at least for a while. We are now completely dark, as they say. Altering this van's tracking system would put me in prison, but adding to it the crime of unauthorized transport of a prisoner—that prisoner being you—makes me your accomplice in escaping from custody. So now both of us have a death sentence waiting for us. And if you're steaming up with hate because you think I've made matters worse for you, I'm not. They'd kill you anyway once they finished interrogating you, so I haven't put you in any greater jeopardy than you were in already. Are you beginning to believe me yet, Griffith?"

"You still didn't answer my question," replied Doctor Griffith. If you think you know everything, why bother busting me out of jail and taking me with you? Why didn't you just go wherever you think my patient is hiding and leave me out of this little adventure?"

"You're my peace offering, Griffith. You're my token of friendship to your co-conspirators. If I lay you at their feet, maybe they'll let me join your club, which could lead to additional options for me."

"And what if they tell you to go to hell?"

"Then I'll take the slowest, most indirect route there. But I'll let your friends keep you as my special gift to them—no extra charge. And hopefully, I can use my breaking you out of jail as currency to buy the trust of the Resistance."

To Doctor Griffith, Carnahan's story sounded plausible on the surface, but he knew it could just as easily be a ruse. He knew that people in Carnahan's line of work are skilled liars who say whatever they think will get them what they want.

"Carnahan, I don't buy your story, so why would you think anyone in the Resistance would buy it? Even if they did believe you, they'd figure you're just a traitor on the run trying to save his butt by switching sides until something better came along—that's how I'd see it if I were them. They'd never do it. They'd never trust you. Why should they? They'll just put a hole in you and dump you somewhere in front of lots of witnesses who will spread the news that Special Security Police Major Carnahan is deader than a canned sardine and it was the Resistance who killed him. And your story about being concerned for Gerald Hughes doesn't wash, so you'll have to try a different sales technique on me. I'm not buying what you're peddling. And I won't endanger anyone I know by letting you use me to gain their confidence. You're not going to scare, bully, or sweet-talk me into endangering my friends. As soon as I see them, I'll warn them that you're using me as bait to entrap them all. Furthermore, I hope the Resistance or your jackbooted buddies kill you."

Carnahan was silent. The only sound was the hiss of the van's tires on the wet pavement and the rhythm of the windshield wipers. Then, without taking his eyes off the road, he said, "Okay, Griffith, I'll tell you as clearly as I can even though I don't have it all put together in my mind yet. As this new order, regime, whatever you want to call it, grows and entrenches itself, the more evil and oppressive it becomes, and so do I. I have come to detest the regime and detest myself for being one of its instruments. Last night, after spending the better part of the day wrestling with my thoughts, I decided to desert the Special Security Police. I gave my wife some complicated, precise instructions that may allow her and our young daughter to disappear from the system, at least for a while, and hopefully, protect them from the retribution they would suffer because of my decision. As you may know, resigning is not an option for those of us who work for the regime. Resigning is regarded as desertion—a treasonous act in their book. And so, to kill the pathogen of treason, the regime would execute me and my wife and daughter, too. If they were in a generous mood, which they never are when dealing with traitors, they might allow my wife's elderly parents and mine to live as slave laborers separated in different labor camps. But in all likelihood, they would just execute all of us, one at a time, while the others watch and wait for their turn. That's how they've been doing it lately. But live or die, I've decided I can no longer be a part of this. I'm going underground, and I'll try to put my inside knowledge to work in the Resistance if they accept me. I know who the better-organized Resistance cells are. They don't know my plan yet, and, as you said, they may kill me when I contact them. But that's a chance worth taking.

"I wanted to make my last acts as Commander of the Special Security Police beneficial and honorable," Carnahan continued, "I know it doesn't make up for any of the things I've done, but it mattered to me. After studying your notes on the alien named Laura, I initially thought you were trying to write a piece of fiction. But I soon understood that what I was reading was not part of some poorly written science fiction story. No, you were writing about a living, breathing alien being who had traveled a long way to get here. And even though she was, for the moment, under the care of a handful of good people, I knew she was at risk of being captured by the regime. I also saw the possibility that this regime, out of sheer stupidity, could, if they mistreated your patient, bring down upon us the wrath of a race of beings technologically superior to us. And after I learned of your lawyer's death, a fate that I knew was in store for you after they wrung you dry of information, the same fate would fall on Father Hughes, all the nuns at the convent, and possibly all their family and friends. I decided to hobble the investigation at least long enough to give everyone a chance to escape before my colonel sends his federal men and the Special Security Police down on all of you. That's why I need to get to the convent, meet everybody involved, and figure out a plan to evacuate everyone somewhere safer than where they are now. Time is not on our side, Griffith. So, what do you say? Will you help me?"

Griffith didn't trust Carnahan's story. He knew this was precisely the sort of trick that could get everyone at the convent killed—including Laura. No one could have sounded more sincere, but Griffith knew that sincerity coming from the mouth of a man like Carnahan meant nothing. Griffith did not know if refusing to help Carnahan could save his friends, but he did know that any help he gave him would kill them if Carnahan were setting a trap.

"How about it, Griffith? Do you believe me yet?"

"It's a great performance, Carnahan, but no Oscar for you."

Carnahan swerved abruptly to the shoulder of the road, braking to a hard stop, climbed out of the van, walked around to the side door, opened it, unlocked Griffith's restraints, drew his pistol, and opened the slide just enough for Griffith to see a portion of the brass casing of the cartridge that was in the chamber.

"Okay, Griffith. Look, do you see the cartridge? This weapon is loaded. The keys are in the ignition, and the fuel tank is full." Then, he shoved the pistol into Griffith's hand and said, "So, here you go. I'm three feet away. Even you couldn't miss me. Shoot me and then drive like hell to warn your friends."

Griffith held the pistol and tightened his grip. He felt the urge, but he could not make himself pull the trigger.

"Come on, Griffith! You haven't got all day! Remember that smack on the side of the face I gave you a while ago? Here's your chance to get even! Now pull the damned trigger and get the hell down the road before you get caught!"

Griffith threw a left jab into Carnahan's jaw. Carnahan could have easily blocked or slipped the punch, but he just stood and let it land. His head rocked backward from the force of the blow.

Carnahan rubbed his jaw with a hint of a smile growing at the corners of his mouth. "That might have hurt if you hadn't been sitting down when you threw it, Griffith. So, what's your decision? Do you believe me yet, or will you pull the trigger?"

Griffith glared at Carnahan, then shook his head. "I'm done, Carnahan!" Griffith snarled. "Damn it! I don't trust you, but I'm not sure enough that you're lying to kill you—and don't think for a minute that I wouldn't kill you if I knew you were lying. I damned sure would. And if I find out you are lying, I will kill you. But, as I see it, I either play this out with you or sit here until some of your buddies show up. Either way, it stinks. But let's go. I'll keep your pistol in my hot little hands in case I change my mind along the way."

Carnahan grinned. "Climb into the front passenger seat, Griffith. We'll talk on the way.

Chapter 11

Special Security Police vehicles patrolled Highway 101 and the secondary highways north, south, and east of the parking area above the beach as helicopters crisscrossed the sky over the surrounding forests and backroads. At the parking area, as a tow truck prepared to winch the wrecked police van up from the beach, an unmarked black van rolled in and stopped at the parking area. A tall, trim officer with the silver oak leaves of a lieutenant colonel on the collar of his gray uniform stepped out of the van, slammed the door, and strode to the ambulance where a paramedic was treating the two officers who had been thrown to the bottom of the trail by the alien. He opened the rear ambulance doors. One of the paramedics was applying a bandage to the forehead of the fat officer who was sitting on the stretcher. The other paramedic, who had finished attending to the thin officer's injuries, stood beside the bench where the thin officer sat.

"What is the condition of these men?" said the officer.

The paramedic paused his bandaging of the fat officer and replied, "This man has several puncture wounds from a dog bite on his right arm, numerous contusions, and a superficial cut to his forehead—actually, they both have a variety of scrapes and contusions...."

"Nothing broken?" the colonel interrupted.

"No, sir, fortunately, by some miracle, all relatively minor injuries, but painful nonetheless. I should take them in for x-rays, and the dog bites may require...."

"None of that will be necessary," said the colonel, cutting him off again. "Would any of their injuries affect their eyesight or prevent them from moving their arms and legs?"

"Well, no, sir."

"So, they have no injuries that should prevent them from recognizing a superior officer and standing to salute him?"

Both men leaped to their feet and snapped a salute.

"Sorry, sir!" shouted the fat one.

"Me too, sir!" replied the thin one.

"Have the two of you finished treating them?" the colonel asked the paramedics.

"One moment, sir," said the paramedic as he finished applying the bandage to the fat officer's forehead. "There, sir, I'm finished."

"Thank you," replied the colonel. "Remember, anything you heard or saw regarding this incident is classified. Your report will say that you treated these two officers for minor injuries sustained in a minor accident—nothing more specific or detailed than that, regardless of who is asking. Here is my card if your supervisor or anyone else insists on more details. Tell them to contact me, and if your superiors continue to pressure you, contact me immediately. Beyond that, you were never here, and you know nothing about it. I've read your names on your badges. I will not forget them. If I hear so much as one isolated detail of this incident from anyone who wasn't here today, I will know that someone didn't keep their mouth shut. If that happens, you will see me again. Do you understand the seriousness of what I am saying?"

"Yes, sir. I certainly do," replied the paramedic.

"And you?" said the colonel to the other paramedic.

"Yes, sir, I understand."

UNTIL THE RESCUE SHIP ARRIVES

"Very good. You may go." The colonel then pointed at the two officers and shouted, "Now, you two get your butts out here!"

The two officers hustled out of the ambulance, trying to button, tuck, and straighten their dirty, scuffed uniforms as much as possible.

"Stand at attention! The colonel glared at them. "You are Anderson?"

"I am, sir!" replied the fat officer.

"You are Tuttle?" asked the colonel, looking now at the thin officer.

"Yes sir, Colonel," he replied.

"Clean the mud off your name tags!"

"Yes, sir!"

"Do either of you know who I am?"

The colonel stared at them, allowing a long, deliberately uncomfortable silence as the two officers stood rigidly and tried to recall the colonel's name. Then Tuttle replied, "Are you, Colonel Hotch . . . Colonel Hotchkiss, Sir?"

"Close, but no! The name is Hodge, Lieutenant Colonel Dwayne Hodge. Since both of you are completely ignorant regarding the chain of command, which doesn't surprise me, I will explain where I fit in. I am Major Carnahan's superior officer. The Major is currently unavailable; therefore, I have assumed operational command of the Special Security Police in his absence. That means you two incompetent embarrassments to mankind belong to me until I decide how best to deal with you. You are the sorriest pair of human beings I've seen wearing any uniform other than prison garb, but I have to work with the personnel I have. I have been briefed on your encounter here, and I think there are a lot of missing pieces to your story. I understand that you were engaged in a routine spot check involving an elderly priest and a young nun who were standing here next to their sedan. Is that correct?"

"Yes, sir!" the two officers said in unison.

"And the priest, without provocation, suddenly struck you with his cane and . . . ."

"It was a long, heavy hiking stick, sir," interrupted Anderson.

The colonel struck Anderson on his right cheek with the back of his hand. "Don't ever interrupt me again! Is that clear?"

Anderson paused long enough to be sure that the colonel had finished speaking. "Yes, sir. Sorry, sir."

The colonel continued. "And after the priest, without provocation, struck you and knocked you to the ground, a large alien being emitted a horrifying yell and bounded out of those trees over there on the other side of the road and attacked the two of you. And you, Tuttle, shot at the alien several times as he charged toward you, missing him with every shot. Then the alien beat up the two of you, threw you down the hill here, and then rolled the van down the hill after you. Then, after you came to your senses and collected yourselves, you crawled back up here, where a passing Special Security Police patrol van found you approximately a half hour after the incident began. Is that right?"

"Yes, sir!" the two replied.

"And meanwhile, the old priest, the nun, and the alien fled the scene?"

"Yes, sir!"

"And they took your shotgun, pistols, and tactical vests containing your extra magazines?"

The two officers were silent, afraid to answer.

The colonel continued, "Have I gone deaf, or have the two of you become mute?"

"You are right, sir. They took our weapons and ammunition," replied Tuttle.

" So now we must assume that they are well armed and capable of killing many of your fellow officers, is that correct?"

The two officers were now trembling. They knew they could be executed for allowing a suspect to disarm them.

"Is that a correct assumption, Anderson?" demanded Colonel Hodge.

"Yes, sir," he replied weakly.

"I didn't hear that, Anderson."

"Y'—Yes, sir."

"And you, Tuttle, do you also confirm that these three suspects are now well-armed and capable of causing many casualties among your fellow officers?"

"Yes, sir."

"Do you think that handing over your weapons was justifiable because saving your own cowardly lives, rather than aggressively defending yourselves and subduing the assailant, as you were trained to do, was a more sensible option?"

"Sir, uh, Colonel, I think it's bad that they have our weapons. He ambushed us, sir. It all happened so quick...."

"That's enough, Tuttle! Shut up!" Hodge shouted. "As I said a moment ago, your story does not convince me. Oh, I believe an alien attacked you. As you may have already figured out, finding that alien was my purpose behind expanding these spot checks. We suspected that he was out here somewhere. We are investigating the connection the priest and the nun have with the alien. We will sort that out soon. But what doesn't quite work in your story is your claim that an old priest attacked you with a stick for no apparent reason while you were conducting a routine vehicle search. I think that there is something more to that story. But, in compliance with my latest order regarding incident report documentation, if that is what you write in your incident reports, officially, that is what happened.

"Now, regarding your weapons, they will not remain lost because the two of you will recover them. That is how you may, possibly, escape being shot in disgrace in the presence of your fellow officers whom you have shamed and endangered. I'm confident they would unanimously insist on that sentence if they had their choice. You look like you want to say something, Tuttle."

"Yes, sir. Thank you, sir. How can we recover our weapons, sir?"

"Here's how that will happen. The two of you will ride with me as we search for these three individuals. We will patrol together, following every lead and hunch I get. We won't eat until I get hungry—and I don't eat often during an operation like this. We won't rest until I get tired—and I can go a long time without sleep when necessary. What I do, you will do. Where I go, you will go. And when we find these three, wherever they may be, the two of you will take the initiative to capture or kill them and recover your weapons and gear."

"Will we be issued replacement weapons until then, sir?" asked Tuttle.

"I see no need for that. The alien didn't have a weapon when he took your weapons from you. You will take them back the same way."

"But sir," said Anderson," that thing must have been over seven feet tall and stronger than any man in this world."

"And he swore that he would kill us if he saw our faces again, sir!" added Tuttle.

"I may kill both of you before he does, you gutless cowards! Each of you will grow a backbone and conduct yourselves like men for the duration of this operation. You will recapture your weapons and capture or kill the alien and his friends, or you will die—either in the line of duty, by firing squad if you fail, or by a bullet from my pistol if you show your cowardice again. Do you understand how thin a string your lives are hanging by?"

"Yes, sir!" they shouted in unison.

"Get in the van!"

Chapter 12

As Carnahan sped down the narrow secondary highway, he watched the monitor on his dashboard that displayed active checkpoints and police vehicles in the area, allowing him to bypass them by turning onto side roads and sometimes backtracking.

"So, Griffith, regarding this husband of Laura's, does anyone have a plan for contacting him?" asked Carnahan.

"Not the last I heard, but a lot can happen in a day. I'm sure they will have thought of something," replied Doctor Griffith.

"And Laura says that her mate is something of a warrior type?"

"From what she told me, all the young boys of their race undergo years of training in a kind of Samurai-like discipline of learning fighting skills and character building according to their values, as well as learning practical skills that the males of their race are expected to master—that's in addition to their family upbringing and basic education. She says the warrior skills training of the youth is broken up into seasonal sessions. In other words, they might train during the summer season of one year. The next year, they train during the winter season, and for the rest of a given year, they live regular lives, attend school much like our kids do, and work at incorporating all the skills and disciplines they're learning. They are serious-minded, principled creatures, it seems. Honor, courage, upright character—all the things we pay lip service to—they exhibit in their daily actions and expect the same from others. I'm sure they see us as contemptible slobs and savages by comparison. Laura said that if anyone in their civilization behaved as rudely and disrespectfully as we humans often do toward each other, that person would beaten on the spot by the offended party. In fact, the offended party would lose the respect of their family and community if they didn't knock the hell out of the offender. Serious crimes like murder, rape, kidnapping, and so on, while rare by our standards, do occur sometimes, and they always earn the offender the death penalty, which they carry out swiftly and publicly. As I say, they are very serious-minded, principled creatures."

"What about the females? Are they raised the same way?"

"The martial training training for the young females is somewhat less intensive than for the males, but judging from how she described it, the difference wouldn't fill a thimble. Their culture has an interesting way of separating the skills and duties of the two sexes to complement one another. Both sexes master skills unique to their societal role that they hone to perfection. However, both sexes cross-train so that in addition to their specialized skills, they become generalists in many of the opposite sex's skills. So, in a marriage—which is the norm for almost every young adult—one can take over the duties of the other if they're ill or injured. It sounds like a pretty interesting world to live in."

"How much do you trust this, Laura?" asked Carnahan. "Do you believe that she is as friendly as she seems, or could she be play-acting until she doesn't need you people anymore? How do you know if, once she and her mate are reunited, they won't become hostile if that's what it takes for them to get back home."

"Well, sure, Carnahan, that could be the case. But I don't think it's likely from what I have seen of her behavior. I've only known Laura for less than two days—and really only one day since you people decided to grab me and knock me around. That first day, I had a couple of hours or so to examine her and talk to her. Everything she told me could be a big fat bucket of lies, but I believe her—considerably more than I believe you, I might add. But I'm taking a gamble with her just as I am with you. I'll find out soon enough if either or both of you are lying—slow down! Slow down! That's Gerald's car up ahead! I'd recognize that faded old heap from a mile away!"

"You're sure?"

" I wouldn't have said so if I wasn't! They must be driving back to the convent. If they had run into a spot check, Gerald's name would set off bells and whistles when they ran his identification. How did they manage to get this far without getting caught?"

"Luck, just crazy luck," replied Carnahan. Look! There's somebody in the back seat! They looked at us through the rear window, then ducked down again. It looked like a big somebody, too. Could they have picked up Laura's mate already? Oh, damn it!"

"What?"

"The monitor shows another checkpoint a few miles ahead. They'll blunder right into it! I've got to stop them."

Carnahan stamped down on the accelerator pedal and lit up his flashing light bar but didn't turn on his siren.

"I see a side road ahead on my monitor—little more than a trail, really—but, with this vehicle, we can probably use it to detour around the checkpoint, but Hughes's little car wouldn't make it. They have to come with us. You've got to do some persuasive talking to convince them to ride with us, Griffith, or they're dead."

"They're slowing down," said Doctor Griffith, "Yes, that has to be Laura's husband in the back seat, and I think that's Sister Clare in the front with Gerald—oh, I forgot to tell you, Sister Clare and Laura decided to have us call her husband Erik because we couldn't begin to pronounce his real name. Okay, they've stopped. I'll get out. You stay in the van until I talk to them. Here, take your pistol back. I don't want to make anybody nervous by carrying it with me—especially if that's Erik in there."

Carnahan saw the hulking alien male in the back seat holding a weapon. Next to him, a dog watched through the rear window while two other figures crouched in the front seat. He pulled in behind them and rolled to stop but stayed back about ten feet.

"Just stay put, Carnahan. Don't get out, you hear?"

"Do it fast, man! We don't have any time to waste."

"I know. Shut up and let me handle this!"

Doctor Griffin climbed out of the van and ran to the car.

"It's Paul!" shouted Father Hughes. "Don't shoot him, Erik! He's a friend! Buster, down, boy, down!"

"You do not know if this man is still your friend! He is with the same police that attacked you!" exclaimed Erik.

"Don't harm him, Erik! I don't know what's happening, but Paul would not work against us!"

"If it is a trap, I will destroy them both. They will not use us to capture my beloved."

"Gerald! Gerald!" yelled Doctor Griffith as he ran to the driver's door. "Gerald, you have to come with us—all of you! Now! There's a checkpoint just ahead of us! They'll kill all of you if you keep going! And you," he said, looking at Erik, "you must be Laura's mate. Trust me, everybody, this is not a trick. We are going to the convent, too. There's a rough backroad ahead of us before we get to the checkpoint. We can follow it to get around the checkpoint, but it's too rough for your little car, Gerald. The van has four-wheel drive. It can make it. All of you have to come with us. We have to get going now! The roads are crawling with cops, and we may have only seconds to get out here before one comes along!"

"What happened, Paul? Why are you with a cop? They beat you, didn't they? Why are you with him?"

"Gerald, we don't have time for that now! That can wait until we're in the van. All of you, get out and come with us now! Now, Gerald! Now! You, too, big fella—bring your weapons and kill us all later if that's what you want to do, but get into the van now before we have more cops swarming around us than you have bullets for. Now, get your butts out of this car and into the van. Bring the dog, too! Now!"

"Who's the cop in the van?" asked Father Hughes.

"Major Tom Carnahan! The two of you can catch up on old times as we're driving! Now get moving, all of you!"

"Believe him, Erik! He's not a liar," said Father Hughes. "He's telling us the truth. Let's go! Come on, Sister Clare, quickly. Bring the weapons, Erik, in case we run into trouble."

Father Hughes pulled the keys from the ignition. "Don't bother to lock the doors. They'll just bust out the windows to get in and check it out. Come, Buster," he said as he trotted toward the van.

Carnahan opened the side door for them. Erik ran toward the van ahead of the others.

"Do you know who I am?" Erik asked Carnahan in flat, staccato syllables.

Carnahan felt an almost liquid cold churning in his stomach at the sight of Erik, who stood over seven feet tall with short-cropped hair and a broad but lean face.

"I know who you are. You are the mate of the one they've named Laura," Carnahan replied.

"You are correct. If you harm the priest or the sister, I will kill you."

Carnahan would not allow himself to be intimidated or permit this alien to regard him as fearful or submissive. Carnahan locked the alien's eyes in the coldest stare he could muster."

"Well, tough guy, if I do either of those things, you have my permission to kill me. But until then, remember this: You are in my world now. You are an intruder here. I am trying to help all of you, as you will see. So until I get all of you to the convent, you will listen to what I tell you, and you will do as I tell you because if you ignore my orders or directions and endanger these people, it will be I who will kill you! Do you understand me?"

Neither Erik nor Carnahan flinched in their stare-down while the others climbed into the van. Then, after a moment, Erik nodded and replied, "You speak with courage. I will trust you. If there is fighting, we will fight as one."

"Everyone buckle yourselves in. This may be a rough ride," yelled Carnahan. "Erik, take the rear seat and watch behind us. I'll have to concentrate on the road and everything ahead of us. Griffith, you can keep watch from the passenger side up here."

Father Hughes and Sister Clare buckled themselves into the middle bench seat.

"Father, pray for me," Sister Clare whispered. "Please pray I will have courage and not fall to pieces again. I want to be of some help. I don't want to be crying and whimpering. I don't want to be a burden on the rest of you. You all are so brave. I want to be brave, too."

"Oh, my dear Sister Clare, did you forget that you already saved us once from being captured when you ordered me to turn off the highway? I'm beginning to think that you and Erik want to steal all the glory today," Father Hughes said, smiling tenderly at Sister Clare. "Promise me that you'll let the rest of us get a chance to show a little gallantry, too," he said as he patted her hand in which she clutched her rosary.

"Okay, Father," replied Sister Clare. "I promise to let the rest of you have all the glory and gallantry you want—it's all yours. I'm quite content just to pray."

Carnahan turned onto a backroad that was little better than a jeep trail. The intermittent drizzle of the previous days made the road muddy and slick, but apart from the lurching and bouncing over ruts and stones, the van, with the four-wheel drive engaged, lumbered along steadily.

"Father Hughes, do you remember me?" Carnahan asked.

"Indeed, I do, Major Thomas Carnahan," Father Hughes answered. "And I remember your dear mother, as well."

"I wasn't sure you would remember us—my mother and me. I remember you, too."

"We priests tend to remember the souls that the Lord sends us to look after, even after some of them turn away to follow a perilous road."

Carnahan chuckled. "I don't think you're referring to the road we are on now, are you?"

"No, Thomas, you know quite well the road I'm speaking of."

"Well, as your friend Griffith, sitting next to me here, can testify, I've suddenly taken a turn down a different but equally perilous road. I'm now a deserter, a traitor to the regime. That's why both he and I are here together. We're all on the same road now."

"Then why does my friend's face indicate that he didn't escape your police station hospitality?"

"Oh, stop with all that crap, the both of you! The two of you will be yapping for the whole ride and still not get anything said," growled Doctor Griffith. "Gerald, I'll tell you what's been going on—the business with me, the cops, Carnahan—the whole enchilada's worth. Don't interrupt me. Just listen until I'm finished. Oh, and Erik, I want to tell you I'm glad to meet you finally. Your little lady has been telling us what a special fellow you are, and it seems she wasn't exaggerating about how big you are either. You are quite the fellow."

"I think what you said is called a compliment, yes?" responded Erik.

"Yes, Erik. That's very much a compliment," replied Griffith.

"Thank you. I understand your language, but sometimes not as well as my beloved understands it. She is much better at it. You have spent much time with her, yes?"

"Not as much as Sister Clare has spent with her, but yes, I helped her recover after Father Hughes brought her to us. She's a tough girl, that one."

Erik smiled, "You may yet see more examples of how tough my beloved is. Thank you for saving her life and helping us reunite."

"Just give us your mailing address on whatever planet you're from, and I'll send you a bill when all this is over."

"Doctor Griffith!" gasped Sister Clare.

"You said a joke. I understand your joke. When I see my beloved, I will tell her your joke," Erik replied with his race's unique straight smile.

"I'm sure your little lady will have more important things to talk about when she sees you climbing out of this van," said Doctor Griffith. "She's pretty worried about you. But as I was saying before I distracted myself, I'll tell you how Carnahan and I ended up on the same team."

As they lurched along the road, Carnahan and Doctor Griffith described the events and experiences that brought them to this point so that everyone understood the circumstances and dangers they now faced. Erik briefly recounted their narrow escape from the spacecraft and told them about the rescue ship that would soon be coming for Laura and him.

"So, you and Laura could be on your way home anytime after tomorrow?" asked Doctor Griffith.

"It is possible the rescue ship could arrive tomorrow. It is more likely to arrive a day or two later." Erik replied.

"Something just occurred to me. I never really thought this far into it until now, but you know what, folks? After Erik and Laura go home, we're all as good as dead!" said Griffith.

"What do you mean?" replied Father Hughes.

UNTIL THE RESCUE SHIP ARRIVES

"I'll tell you what he means," interjected Carnahan. "When Erik and Laura are gone, our problems with the regime will still be very much with us. They know about Erik, and they are already looking for him. Soon, they will piece together the connection between Erik, Father Hughes, and his unnamed 'niece,' who is, of course, Laura, whom Doctor Griffith mentioned in the intercepted phone call from Griffith's lawyer to Father Hughes. Since they will learn that Father Hughes is a priest, someone will get a hunch to check out the convent and discover that Erik and Laura were hiding there and that we all helped them. All of us in this van have broken a long list of laws—if you want to dignify their dictates as laws—and we'll pay with pain for each one. So, all said and done, we humans, here in this van and at the convent, are as good as dead when they catch us."

Everyone fell silent.

"Allow me to think for a moment," said Erik. "Please, say nothing while I think about this problem."

No one spoke. The only sounds were the van's engine and the creaking of the suspension system as the vehicle rocked and swayed over the uneven road. Minutes passed as Erik stared through the windows of the van's rear doors. Buster began to sense something amiss with the unnatural silence and whimpered as he placed his paw on Father Hughes's knee. "Shh, shh," said Father Hughes in a barely audible whisper as he patted Buster on the shoulder and stroked his ear.

After a few more minutes, Eric said, "I will tell you what my beloved and I will do. But first, I will explain something. No Distant Voyager has ever been in a situation like this in all of our visits to your world, so we have no, what is your word for it—precedent, I think, yes, precedent. We have no precedent to guide us, no specific instructions for a situation like this—no protocols. We always avoid interacting with the people of your world, and except for a few brief, unavoidable encounters, we have been successful. If we have a problem and need to be rescued, we are to launch a rescue request and remain undetected while we wait for the rescue ship. If necessary, we are to defend ourselves to avoid capture or harm; otherwise, we must not interact with humans. Of course, we could not avoid interacting with you in this incident.

"But there is now this important problem that my beloved and I cannot ignore," Erik continued. "All of you have put your lives in danger to help us. As a matter of honor and gratitude, she and I cannot escape to the safety of our home world and leave all of you to suffer or die at the hands of evil people. You cannot possibly know how much our race despises those who lust for power and control over others. For many ages, we have severely punished such people in our world. We rarely encounter them now. So, we will go beyond our established procedures and help you in your struggle against your regime. Our people will understand our actions. It would be a sin on our souls and a shame on our race if we left you to suffer after you risked your lives for us. We will not abandon you. However, we are not permitted to overthrow the regime on your behalf. We could do so easily with our technological capabilities, but defeating them is your task. In this circumstance, however, we will disrupt and destroy some of their advantages, allowing you to fight them successfully using the means available to your people. Also, we cannot protect any of you by taking you with us when we leave here. Even though you could live in our world for several of our years, just as we can live on Earth for several of your years, there are enough differences in the biologies of the plants, animals, and microbes of our two worlds that eventually you would begin to suffer many illnesses, and your lives would be shortened."

Erik reflexively pulled back the sleeve of his jacket and checked the rescue request launcher. The light blinked slowly like a silent metronome, counting the moments until the rescue ship's arrival was imminent.

"The rescue request is progressing, but it is not near," said Erik. "When we arrive where you are caring for my beloved, you must provide a place where she and I can speak to each other in our language without you hearing us. Your emotions may be disturbed if you hear us conversing in our language, but she and I must be free to express ourselves without hindrance if we are to help you. After my beloved and I have made our plans, all of us must work together to carry them out."

"Thomas," said Father Hughes, interrupting Erik, "I know what your policeman's mind may be thinking, but Erik and Laura will not be scheming to double-cross us if they meet in private, so drop any such thoughts if you have them. We humans do, indeed, become emotionally stirred when we hear Erik and Laura singing in their musical language. Doctor Griffith understands this, too. And Erik, I think I know where you and Laura can meet once we arrive at the convent. I will ask permission from Mother Catherine, who runs the convent, and I'm sure she will approve."

"Thank you, Father Hughes," said Erik. Our meeting will not take long."

Carnahan stopped the van at the crest of a rise, scanned the road where it dropped into a gully, ran uphill for another hundred yards, curved to the right, and disappeared into the forest.

"According to my monitor, about a quarter mile around that bend, we rejoin the highway, said Carnahan. "I don't see any markers on my screen indicating police vehicles near where this trail connects to the highway, but I'm going to scout the intersection before going further. Griffith, can you drive this thing?"

"I can drive it as far and fast as I need to, Carnahan. Go do what you have to do."

"I will go," said Erik. "I know how to do these things very well, and I can move much faster and quieter than you, Major Carnahan. I will take one of these weapons with me. You will know what to do if you hear trouble."

"No, I will go, but if you want to assist me, you may," replied Carnahan. "They might not have labeled me as a deserter yet, so if we stumble upon them, I may be able to put them off guard until we can take them out. If you don't like that idea, Erik, you will stay here, and I'll go alone."

"Your idea is good, Carnahan. I will go with you and do as you say."

Carnahan turned toward Doctor Griffith. "Griffith, if you hear trouble, you won't be safe sitting here, and turning around and going back is suicide. They'll catch you if you turn back. And if you abandon the van and try to hike to the convent through the forest, you'll probably get lost or captured before you get there. So, if you hear trouble, just get this thing rolling as fast as you can and try to smash through whatever is happening at the other end, and don't try to stop to help us if there is fighting going on. Just keep going. Erik and I will keep them busy."

"But Major!" exclaimed Sister Clare, "you just said that we would get lost or captured if we were on foot. You and Erik will be on foot—what will happen to the two of you?"

"Erik and I can handle that, Sister. You and Father Hughes just keep your heads down and let Griffith get you through. We don't need to get too dramatic about all of this. There's probably nothing waiting for us up ahead except more drizzle and mud, but we have to be sure so we don't blunder into a trap."

"Just a moment, Thomas," said Father Hughes. "If you stumble upon the police, do try to find an alternative to killing them. We do not want to be murderers."

"Father, at this point, our options are surrender and be tortured and killed, or fight and maybe live. There's nothing in between those two options," replied Carnahan. "You may be surprised that I know a little bit about the doctrine regarding self-defense and just wars—even a guy like me can pick up a few bits of knowledge here and there. I believe this is a clear matter of justifiable self-defense because we have unjust adversaries who intend to commit evil against us. Since I carried out the regime's directives for several years, I think I am somewhat of an authority on their methods. Believe me, Father, when I say there is no peaceful recourse."

"Maybe so, Thomas. I'll have to think about all that, but step out of the van with me for a quick moment before you go."

"We don't have time for a chit-chat, Father. We can talk when . . . ."

"Hold your tongue and do as I say this time, Thomas. Out with you!"

Father Hughes climbed out and walked over to a tree a few yards away. Major Carnahan followed him and protested what he considered wasting of valuable time.

"Be quiet and come over here, Thomas," Father Hughes commanded.

They stepped several more yards away and turned their backs to the van as they spoke in inaudible whispers. Sister Clare noticed Father Hughes make the sign of the cross over Major Carnahan, who then rushed back to the van.

"Ok, Erik, let's go see what's up there," said Carnahan.

Erik grabbed one of the pistols, checked to ensure the magazine was fully loaded, racked the slide to chamber a round, then shoved two more magazines into his jacket pocket.

"Where did you learn to handle a pistol?" asked Carnahan.

"We have been studying your world and your ways for many generations. We have learned many skills that could be useful if we found ourselves in unusual circumstances while on your planet—including how to use many of your weapons."

"But I thought you outer space people only used ray guns."

"Stop the jokes. We must now think like warriors. We can say jokes later," grumbled Erik.

"Okay, Griffith, you know what to do if you hear trouble. Otherwise, give us ten minutes and then drive up fast. Ten minutes, no more," said Carnahan.

"Gotcha, Carnahan," replied Doctor Griffith.

Carnahan and Erik did not follow the road but instead slipped through the forest's edge roughly parallel to the road. Carnahan marveled at the ease and silence with which Erik moved through the undergrowth. Despite his size, he never cracked a twig or rustled a branch. A cougar could not have moved with more stealth. He realized how unprepared anyone who attempted to capture Erik would be for the endeavor. Suddenly, Erik stopped, turned, glared at him, pointed to Carnahan's feet, grabbed his ear and wriggled it, and then made a couple of exaggeratedly careful steps to let Carnahan know he was making too much noise. Carnahan shook his head to indicate he understood but stifled a chuckle. He had thought he was moving almost as quietly as Erik, but clearly, Erik didn't think so.

Carnahan could not move silently and still keep pace with Erik, so Erik was soon about forty yards ahead of him and near where Carnahan estimated the trail and highway intersected. Then Erik stopped, turned toward Carnahan, crouched, touched a finger to his eye, flashed three fingers, and pointed toward where the intersection should be. Carnahan crept to Erik's position and crouched next to him. Through the undergrowth, he saw an unmarked Special Security Police van, like his own, parked at the end of the trail where it intersected the highway, sitting just far enough back from the intersection that a vehicle on the highway would not see the van until it passed in front of it. He heard indistinct chatter between two officers, one sitting in the rear seat with the side door open and another smoking a cigarette and leaning against the van beside the open passenger door. Neither of them were carrying weapons. The driver was in too much shadow to see any details. Carnahan nodded, and Erik and he crept closer. Carnahan could now see and recognize the faces of the men.

"I know those two men, Erik," whispered Carnahan. Anderson and Tuttle are their names, and I think that van belongs to Colonel—yes, he just showed his face as he leaned over and said something to Tuttle. That's Colonel Hodge, my superior, sitting behind the wheel. He must be able to block his vehicle from being tracked just as I can. Otherwise, I would have seen it on my monitor in the van. He broke a few rules by making that little modification, just like I did."

"I do not know him," replied Erik, "but I know the other two. They are the men that I punished earlier today. It is unfortunate for them that they are here."

"We'll have to act fast, Erik. I don't want to do what we are about to do, but we're committed now. I noticed Tuttle and Anderson are unarmed, but I doubt they'll let us capture them as prisoners, and there is no way to drive around them. If Hodge sees us, he'll probably just start shooting. If he happens to be in a friendly mood today, he may order us, just once, to surrender and then open fire on us if we don't comply within a split second."

"Was that another one of your jokes?" Erik asked sharply under his breath.

"No. Just believe the part about Hodge shooting as soon as he sees us. But even so, Erik, I hate this. I don't want to have to kill those men. I have another idea. Let's get closer and then charge them. I'll yell, 'hands up,' as we're charging. I'm sure Hodge will start shooting, so if he even looks like he's raising his weapon, shoot him. The other two men are weaklings, as I guess you already know, but they may be more afraid of the Colonel than they are of you and me, so they may grab a weapon and try to put up a fight. But let's give them a chance. If they surrender, we'll handcuff them to the steering wheel of their van or a bumper or whatever, and then we'll smash their radio to buy us a little more time. If they run, though, we can't let them get away. We'll have to catch or kill them. Let's do it and see how it goes."

"I do not like your idea, Carnahan. I do not think it will work. But if they surrender, I will spare their lives again."

"Are you good enough with a pistol to hit what you're shooting at while you're running?" asked Carnahan.

"Yes."

"Okay, Anderson and Tuttle are relaxed and not paying attention. Hodge is watching the road and probably not expecting anything to come up from behind them on such a poor road as this. We won't get a better opportunity. But if the plan falls apart, follow your instincts, Erik. Do whatever you are trained to do."

"They will not escape. I promised the ones you call Anderson and Tuttle that I would kill them if I saw them again. They are dishonorable cowards. It will not go well for any of them today if they choose to fight—listen, I hear your van coming up the road!"

Carnahan glanced at his watch. "Oh, no! Griffith is on time, but we lost track of a few minutes while sneaking up here. We have to make our move! Ready? Now!"

Carnahan and Erik burst from the foliage and charged toward the van.

"Hands up! Drop your weapons!" yelled Carnahan.

Tuttle had just stepped out of the van. For an instant, he froze, then screamed as if scalded. "It's him! It's him! And the Major, too!"

"Colonel! Colonel!" screamed Anderson.

UNTIL THE RESCUE SHIP ARRIVES

Hodge turned in the driver's seat, and fear washed through his body at the sight of Erik and Carnahan as they bounded toward them. Hodge drew his pistol and fired several rounds through the open side door at the two charging figures. Tuttle inadvertently stepped in front of Hodge's line of fire and was stuck in the back of the head. Almost simultaneously, Carnahan and Erik fired at Hodge as they charged the van, one of their rounds grazing his right ear. Anderson reached for the shotgun mounted in a rack beside the passenger seat. Erik fired twice, and Anderson slid from the van and fell face-first into the mud.

Carnahan fired again as he charged the van, grazing Hodge on the cheekbone. He and Erik were now only a few strides away from Hodge. Hodge fired and struck Carnahan in the chest. Carnahan fired at the same instant, ripping a gash across Hodge's chest, causing Hodge to drop his pistol. Carnahan tumbled to the ground. Erik leaped over him and dove into the van just as Hodge slammed the transmission into gear and floored the accelerator pedal. The van's tires spun, caught traction, and lurched onto the highway. In mortal fear of the enraged alien now upon him, Hodge madly steered the accelerating vehicle to and fro, rocking it to keep Erik off balance. But Erik dropped his pistol, grabbed the back of the driver's seat, and struck Hodge an off-balance blow on his temple with his fist. The blow momentarily dazed Hodge enough to cause him to swerve off the highway and plunge the van into a shallow creek, throwing Erik against the windshield as they crashed. Hodge, shaken and bleeding, reached for the radio microphone. Erik, bleeding from a cut on his forehead, tore the microphone cord from the radio.

"Don't kill me!" yelled Hodge. "We need to talk! I want to help you! I'm not your enemy! We want—we want diplomatic relations with you—with your planet. You can help us. We can become allies!"

Erik noticed Hodge inching his hand toward his ankle as he pleaded. Erik grabbed Hodge's arm and twisted it as he rolled himself off the dashboard. He yanked Hodge out of his seat and pulled a small pistol from Hodge's ankle holster.

"This was going to be a gift of friendship for me, yes?" growled Erik as he pressed the pistol under Hodge's chin.

"No! Please! I didn't know what was happening back there! I didn't know it was you! I thought you were criminals attacking us! This is all a misunderstanding! Really! Let's start over. Let's...."

Eric let the pistol fall from his hands as he gripped Hodge's throat. "You are a liar and a coward like the two dead cowards lying in the mud next to my courageous friend who wanted to spare your lives! But I will not spare you. You are a servant of worthless tyrants who bring misery to your people. Now, you will die for what you have done to my friend and the evil you bring to your people!"

"No, you don't understand! Please! Listen to me!" shouted Hodge.

Erik grabbed Hodge's head in his powerful hands, and with a quick pull and twist, Hodge was dead. Erik searched the van and found his pistol. Then he climbed out of the wrecked, steaming van and ran back toward the intersection.

Father Hughes, now at the wheel of Carnahan's van, saw Erik running up from the ditch and raced down the road toward him. "Get in! Get in! Get in!" he yelled as he threw open the passenger door and helped Erik pull himself inside. "Doctor Griffith and Sister Clare are with Carnahan," said Father Hughes. "I don't think he'll live, Erik. The poor, brave man. His poor family. The other two officers are dead. That looks like a pretty bad cut on your forehead."

"It is nothing," replied Erik. "We must go."

Father Hughes turned the van around and sped back toward the junction. They rolled to an abrupt stop beside Doctor Griffith and Sister Clare, who struggled to lift Carnahan without injuring him further.

"Erik, get out and help us get him in the van!" shouted Doctor Griffith. "He's trying to breathe, and he has a pulse, but I don't know for how much longer."

They lay Carnahan on the floor of the van.

"Set him down easy, Erik. That's it," said Doctor Griffith. "Sister, there might be a trauma kit in one of those compartments if these cops have brains enough to be prepared for such things. Yes, Sister, that's what we need. Open it up! What are you doing, Erik? Oh, his pistol. Go, Gerald! Fast, but not crazy. No bumps. Go! Go! The bullet passed through him, and he has a sucking chest wound. What else the bullet tore up on the way through, I can only guess. Sister, see if there are any chest seals in there. Oh, good! Good! Hand them to me. Good, a vented and an unvented. Sister, clean the area while I get the vented one ready. Now help me turn him, and we'll do the same for his back. Carnahan! Thomas! Do you hear me? Thomas, we're helping you the best we can, young man, but you have to stay with us! Faster Gerald! Stay with us, Thomas. You have a family who needs you, Thomas. Don't you leave them! Don't you give up! Don't you give up, Thomas!"

"He must live, Doctor. He reclaimed his honor today. He proved that he is no longer on the side of evil. He will be of great value to all of you if he recovers," said Erik.

"Don't bother me now, Erik, I don't have time! Sister Clare, hand me . . . ."

Erik crawled to the rear door to watch for trouble from behind them. Buster lay trembling in the corner, and Erik gently stroked his head to calm him.

No one spoke aloud, but Erik could hear Sister Clare's endless whispered prayers as she assisted Doctor Griffith. Then Erik remembered the unused half of the wafer in his pocket. Would this help a human, he wondered? He could not think of any ingredients in it that were toxic to humans, but no human had ever tried it before. Since no other option was available, it would be reasonable to try it. He pulled out the foil wrapper containing the remaining half of the wafer. Would one-fourth of the remaining wafer be too much or too little for a human? After a pause, he broke off one-eighth.

"Doctor, I have something that may be able to help Carnahan. For us, it has excellent healing and nutritional properties. I do not know how it will affect a human, but if you think you can do nothing to save him, I suggest you try it. There would be nothing to lose in doing so."

Doctor Griffith, his hands covered in blood after applying the chest seal, paused, looked at Carnahan, and then looked up at Erik. "What have you got, Erik?"

"This," Erik said, holding out to Griffith the broken-off piece of the wafer.

"What are we supposed to do with that, Erik?"

"Since he cannot chew and swallow, you should crush a small portion of it in your hand until it is a powder and place it under his tongue. He will absorb it. It will dissolve quickly, but only give him more after the previous amount has completely dissolved and if it benefits him."

Griffith nodded to Sister Clare, "Sister Clare, I think your hands may be marginally cleaner than Erik's or mine. Go ahead and do as Erik says. We have to try it. There's nothing more I can do under these conditions."

UNTIL THE RESCUE SHIP ARRIVES

Sister Clare crushed the small piece of the wafer in the palm of her hand with her thumb until it was fine as dust. Doctor Griffith opened Carnahan's mouth, and she sprinkled the powder under his tongue.

"Erik, how long will it be before we know if it is helping him?" asked Sister Clare.

"I do not know, Sister. A human has never eaten one of our wafers. Our people with serious injuries begin noticing slight improvement within an hour, as you would measure time. Healing is not instantaneous, but it is greatly accelerated."

"I pray it works for him as well as it does for your people," replied Sister Clare.

"We're just a few minutes away from the convent," said Father Hughes. "We'll go straight to the guest cottage. Mother Catherine is probably wondering where we are and getting nervous. Erik, Mother Catherine is sitting with Laura today while Sister Clare is with us. Mother Catherine will be very angry with us because we are bringing trouble to the convent. She may not understand that we had no other realistic choices. I don't think I will be welcome at the convent anymore after all this, and I don't know how Mother Catherine will react to you, Erik, at least initially, so please try to be patient with her if she is angry when she speaks to us. She is a good and loving woman who is under much pressure. My friends, I truly hate some of the things we had to do today, but I don't know what else we could have done under the circumstances. I am deeply troubled by it all. Sister Clare, are you holding up alright, my dear?"

"I'm okay, Father. I was horribly frightened for a while today—horribly frightened. I was afraid of those police officers who were abusing us, and I have to admit I was afraid of Erik when he came charging out of the bushes. Even though Laura told me so many good things about him, I didn't know what he might do to you and me after I saw what he did to those officers. Along with that, I had never experienced such wickedness from our police officials—our own government trying to hunt us down, willing to kill us to capture Erik, and of course, Laura, too, if they got their dirty hands on her. And all of the gunfire and death back there. In the past, we heard of such violent things happening in other places in the world and to other people, but now it's happening here just like it is to everyone else in the world. But Father, I'm not afraid anymore—not for myself, at least. I think my fear became so intense that it burnt itself out. I don't feel any fear at all. I placed everything into God's hands. I don't think I will fear anything ever again. I just want to do my best from here on. Whatever I can do to help, I will do it. No matter what the earthly consequences may be. Regardless of what lies ahead of us, Father, with Mother Catherine's permission and yours, I want to stay involved with helping Laura and Erik return to their home. I want them to be safe at home, away from all this. I want to help all the rest of us deal with the problems that will surely fall upon us. Also, I pray that you and Doctor Griffith will stay at the convent with us until all this is over. We are all a team now. Actually, I think we're more than a team. We are all one family now—including Major Carnahan. I want to help him survive and get strong so that he can take care of his family and use his skills and knowledge to fight the regime. And Father, I am sure Mother Catherine will be angry with us, just as you said. Even so, Mother Catherine understands that you were right in bringing Laura to us. I'm sure Mother Catherine knows God has placed Laura and Erik under our care. I'm reminded, Father, of that scripture which says, 'Greater love hath no man than this, that a man lay down his life for his friends.' Even though we have barely met Laura and Erik, I would gladly lay down my life for them if necessary. I'm sorry, I guess that was a long, rambling answer to a short question, Father, but that's how I feel about our predicament now."

UNTIL THE RESCUE SHIP ARRIVES

When Sister Clare had finished, she looked up and noticed Erik sitting with his eyes closed and his chin in his hands as if in deep concentration. "Erik, is something the matter?" she asked.

"Little one, you have humbled me. As I listen to what you said just now and see how all of you behave in this situation we are in together, I realize that I have underestimated the courage and virtue within you humans. I would not have understood this if I had not witnessed it. With each moment that passes, I realize that I do not know your race of beings as thoroughly as I thought I did."

"Carnahan's pulse is a little stronger," Doctor Griffith shouted, interrupting Erik, "and his bleeding has nearly stopped. His breathing is still shallow, but he is breathing. Maybe that wafer of yours is already beginning to do something, Erik. By some miracle, the bullet must have missed his heart, or he would be dead by now, but you probably couldn't measure the margin the bullet missed it by. He needs to be in a hospital, but they'd just kill him, and us, too, if we took him to one. Let's hope your wafer somehow pulls him through."

For the next few minutes, everyone was silent and in their thoughts. Father Hughes turned onto the long driveway leading to the convent, driving as fast as he dared without jarring Carnahan. The brakes on the van squeaked as he pulled up to the guest cottage.

"Erik, Laura is inside this cottage," said Father Hughes, "and Mother Catherine is with her. Please allow me to speak with Mother Catherine before you or the others leave the van."

"Yes, I will wait," Erik replied.

As Father Hughes stepped out of the van, Mother Catherine stood at the open doorway with Laura behind her.

"Father! Where have you been? I had no idea you'd be gone this long. And whose van is this? Who is in there? Did...."

Father Hughes interrupted her. "Mother, I must explain some things to you." Then, turning toward Laura, he said, "Laura, your Erik is with us, and he is well, but please allow me to speak with Mother for a moment before you go to him."

Father Hughes continued, "Mother Catherine, I will explain what has happened and what is happening, but first, I must tell you that we have a seriously wounded man we need to bring inside immediately to care for him as much as possible. Also, Laura and Erik need a place to be alone to converse in their own language about some crucial matters. You know how their language affects us, so would you permit them to go to the convent's emergency shelter where it is less likely someone will hear them?"

"Father! What do you mean? Who is this wounded man? What, what have you brought to us? Have you brought more troubles from the authorities upon us? I just received word that the authorities arrested our bishop this morning. Our beloved bishop. Does his arrest have any connection with what you have done? Father, this is a convent, not a hideout for criminals and subversives, but is that what we have become now in the eyes of the regime? Oh, I wish we had dealt with this some other way. Oh, yes, Father, indeed, we must talk! Oh, yes! Oh, yes! You and I will certainly talk!"

Mother Catherine paused, covered her face with her hands for a moment, then continued. "We will have Eric and Laura wait here at the cottage until we can bring them up without the sisters seeing them. They can discuss what they need to discuss in the emergency shelter while you and I discuss these other matters. And Father, you will give me a complete explanation of everything, and I mean everything! But first, park the van so that the side door faces away from the convent. I don't want the sisters to see you carrying that wounded man into the cottage. I don't know where else we can put him right now. Have Doctor Griffith stay with him. Who is this wounded man, by the way?"

UNTIL THE RESCUE SHIP ARRIVES

"It's Major Thomas Carnahan of the Special Security Police. He saved our lives today, Mother."

"He's with the Special Security Police? Oh! They will destroy us! They will just destroy all of us! Oh, my!" Mother Catherine paused again, then with a sigh, said, "Go on, go on and bring him in, bring him in before someone sees him! Father, I don't have the words to tell you how angry I am with you right now. I just don't have the words."

"Believe me, Mother Catherine, I do understand. I will explain how the situation has become what it is, but now let's bring Thomas inside so Doctor Griffith can care for him as best he can. And we should give Erik and Laura a few moments together."

"Yes, yes, let them see one another. I want to meet Erik, too. But that will be after you and I have had our discussion."

Father Hughes repositioned the van. Erik and Doctor Griffith carried Carnahan into the cottage. Laura held the cottage door open and, without saying a word, delicately touched the cut on Erik's forehead as he helped bring Carnahan inside. Erik's brow furrowed, and his mouth tightened as he fought to control his emotions at seeing her.

"Sister Clare, you're a mess," said Mother Catherine. "Come with Father and me when we walk up to the convent. Go straight to my quarters and clean yourself up. Make sure no one sees you. I'll bring you a fresh habit and a basket to put your soiled habit in."

Laura spread the shower curtain over the mattress on the bed and then laid a sheet over it. Doctor Griffith and Erik gently laid Carnahan onto the bed. He was still unconscious, but his bleeding had stopped.

"Your wafer crumbs are definitely doing something for him, Erik," said Doctor Griffith. "As long as he is unconscious, he isn't feeling pain, and that's good because I don't have anything to give him for that. I'll wait a little longer before I sprinkle more of it under his tongue—I don't want to use it up too fast. It's the closest thing to medicine I have for him right now, and he seems to be tolerating it. I don't need your help with Carnahan right now, Erik, so if you're ready to get reacquainted with your best girl and devise a good plan for us, this would be a good time to do it. I have full confidence in both of you. And by the way, you're a heck of a man, Erik. I'm glad you're on our side."

"You also are, as you say, a heck of a man," replied Erik, who then turned, pulled Laura close, whispered a quick, song-like phrase to her, and then they walked to the doorway.

"Eric and Laura, I want you to wait here until I signal you to run up to the convent," said Mother Catherine. "I'll order the sisters to go to the chapel to pray for the recovery of a badly injured man, but I won't tell them yet that he is here with us. As soon as they are all assembled in the chapel, I will wave to you from the doorway, so watch for my signal."

Sister Clare slipped into Mother Catherine's quarters without being noticed by the other sisters. Father Hughes stepped into her office and waited until Mother Catherine had gathered all the sisters into the chapel to pray. As the sisters prayed in the chapel, Mother Catherine signaled to Erik and Laura, who dashed to the convent. She then guided them to the emergency shelter in the convent's basement and taped a large X across the doorway with masking tape to dissuade anyone from entering. Finally, Mother Catherine returned to her office and taped a handwritten note on her office door stating, "Private meeting / Do not disturb!" and then closed and locked the door.

She sat behind her desk, paused for a deliberately long moment, and then said, "Father! Tell me what have you done! What troubles have you brought upon us? Do you even know? How did that man get wounded? What are the—I'm going to stop right here. I have too many questions, and I'm too angry to speak. Just tell me everything, absolutely everything, Father!"

Father Hughes told Mother Catherine the whole story, beginning when they had pulled into the parking area where Sister Clare sang the word Laura had taught her. He recounted the events of the day, with as much detail as needed, up to the end of the gunfight at the intersection.

Mother Catherine gasped loudly and slammed her hands onto her desk. "Three policemen killed, and Erik, along with this Carnahan fellow, who had been one of them until today, just murdered them on sight?"

"' Murdered them on sight,' you say!" Father Hughes forced himself to pause, took a long breath, and then continued, "I described the details of that gunfight to you just as Erik described them to me. If anything, I would label it as justifiable self-defense. I explained how Erik and Thomas gave them a chance to surrender, but they didn't do so. It is true that Erik and Thomas killed them, but do not forget, Mother, that the men they killed were lying in wait for us—not to enforce just and reasonable laws for the common good, but to do evil. I had a previous encounter with two of those men myself when they tried to bully me around and threatened to shoot Buster. I experienced the malicious arrogance that infected them and their inflated sense of power. And, as I also told you a moment ago, Paul's lawyer died of fright while the police prepared to extract information from him. Had they captured us, they would have tortured and killed us, too. I'm certain of it. After they squeezed all the information they could from us, those devils would have come here, and who knows what they would have done to you and the sisters? I told you how I had to strike one of those same thugs today with my walking stick to prevent him from manhandling poor little Sister Clare. If I still had my youthful strength, I would have struck him even harder. A knowledgeable Christian knows there are circumstances in which violence is necessary to avoid a greater evil. Those circumstances often force us to make such decisions in the heat of the moment and under pressure, and we make those decisions as well as we can. As I evaluate the decisions we made today, I say we did the best we could with the options we had. Remember, Mother, we Catholics are not a heretical pacifist sect. But believe me, Mother Catherine, justifiable or not, this incident will weigh on me for the rest of my days."

Mother Catherine closed her eyes and sighed as if on the verge of tears. "Oh, Father, three men dead, and that man Carnahan may die. Our beautiful, peaceful convent, a refuge of prayer and holiness, will soon be swarming with police and soldiers doing all their wicked deeds. She shook her head and said, "How could this happen to us, Father? How could this happen to us?"

"Mother, I am truly sorry. I could not have known that things would turn out this way. But I know we are right in helping these two poor castaways from another world, marooned here on what, to them, must be a frightful, menacing planet, as they try to survive until their rescue ship arrives. Mother, you know we Catholics have a history of protecting and sheltering people who would have otherwise become victims of evil men and their schemes. Are Laura and Erik any less beloved by God than were those of our own kind whom we, over the ages, have tried to help, often resulting in severe consequences to ourselves?"

"Yes, yes, Father, I know what you are saying, and with reservations, I do agree, despite the sorrow, anger, and fear I am feeling. I know we can't turn our backs on those in desperate need. That's why I permitted Laura to stay here at the start of all this. But I am so unprepared for the trouble we have invited upon ourselves. I am too overwhelmed to know what to do about it now, Father. And what of the sisters? What will those wicked people do to them?

UNTIL THE RESCUE SHIP ARRIVES

When the authorities come, we know they will not suddenly behave as conscientious professionals toward us just because we're a religious community. That godless regime hates us and hates anything that reminds them of the fact that they aren't God. Thuggery and brutality are what they have become known for during the short time they have been in power. What they tried to do to you and Sister Clare today is just more proof of that. I simply don't know how to protect my dear, precious sisters in the face of all this, Father. I feel so helpless and useless to the sisters now. They need wisdom and guidance from me. I have neither. I am an empty vessel. I know that, ultimately, it is all in God's hands, but I have a responsibility to take care of these brides of Christ to the best of my ability. It's a responsibility for which God will hold me accountable. If I fail them, God may forgive me, but how could I ever forgive myself if I lost even one of my precious daughters to those wicked devils? I would sooner they kill me than harm one of them. But now, what can I do to protect them? There is nothing, no manner of training or experience, that could have prepared me for this. God help me! God help us all!

"Another thing, Father," Mother Catherine continued, "you know they have been arresting bishops, one by one, across the country whom they suspect disapprove of the new order of things and perhaps are sympathetic to the Resistance? There's never a warning. They just burst in on them, usually mid-day, to strike fear into everyone present as they haul the bishop off. None of those bishops have been heard from again. When someone inquires about them, the authorities brazenly deny that he is in their custody and deny any knowledge of his arrest. No one knows if these bishops are alive or dead, and there is no way to find out. Today, they arrested our dear bishop—one of the best in the country. Now, it is just us alone, without the benefit of his wisdom, guidance, and such influence as he may have exercised to help us. I have also heard that several priests have disappeared, too. Now they are after you, too, Father. Somehow, we must form a plan. We know they will be coming. We can't escape to a safer place, either. Even if it were possible to do so without getting caught en route, there is nowhere to go that is safe and free anymore. We will certainly continue praying our rosaries. They are the only weapons we have. May we wield them as effectively as David wielded his sling. If you have any ideas, Father, I am all ears because, at this moment, I am utterly void. I have absolutely no ideas to offer."

"Mother, I don't have any answers either, but Erik believes that he and Laura can put together a trick or two to help us between now and when their rescue ship arrives. Erik told us that, with a bit of luck, it could appear as soon as tomorrow, although that's a long shot. He said some of the rescue ship's defenses can remain here for a while to protect us even after the ship takes them home. I'm sure he and Laura will also form some ideas for the interim. And regarding our bishop, It's improbable his abduction directly relates to Erik and Laura or today's events. I believe his arrest was planned some time ago, and it was just a coincidence that they abducted him today. He knew he was under scrutiny because they couldn't force him to praise the new regime, nor would he compel us priests to do so. We must pray for him, and perhaps Major Carnahan, if he recovers, will have some ideas for learning what has become of our bishop and finding ways to help him—if that is still possible.

"As for the well-being of the sisters," said Father Hughes, "I don't think I have to tell you that I love those dear sisters as if they were my own flesh and blood daughters. I have heard their confessions, offered masses for them, counseled them, listened to their beautiful singing, and enjoyed the sound of their equally beautiful laughter. They are as precious to me as they are to you. I want to shelter and protect them as much as any father wants to protect his own children. Believe me, Mother, I accept my responsibility in bringing all this trouble upon everyone here. So, if God grants me a say in the matter, if protecting you and the sisters costs the life of any of us here, may God let it be my own. With that in mind, Mother, when the worst of the troubles begin, I appeal to your protective instincts to force yourself to remain inside with the sisters and keep them together, keep them occupied to help control their fear, and keep them out of harm's way as much as possible. I wish I had the authority to compel you to do so under obedience, but I'm not the bishop. But please, do as I ask for the good of the sisters and yourself. They need your motherly care. So, Mother, from here on, focus your efforts on keeping the sisters together and safe. Eric, Laura, Doctor Griffith, and I will handle the other actions and undertakings the circumstances may require—with God's help, of course."

Mother Catherine shook her head in resignation. "You hard-headed Irishmen, how did St. Patrick ever manage to tame you?"

"Tame us, Mother? Not entirely. I think it's time for us to check on Erik and Laura. Let's see if they have some ideas to avoid the worst of the worst. Ah, another thing, Mother, you should have seen Erik out there when he rescued us from the two officers near the beach. He is everything that Laura said he was: noble, courageous, and a terror in battle, but as tender as you could ever imagine toward someone who needs a bit of kindness. Sister Clare knows about that. I believe a dozen like him could crush this regime worldwide in a matter of days."

Suddenly, there was a tapping at the door. "Mother, Father Hughes, it's me, Sister Clare. I'm sorry, I read your sign, but you must let me in."

Mother Catherine rose and let her inside, then locked the door again, leaving the sign still posted. "What is it, Sister?"

"I ignored the tape across the emergency shelter door to check on Laura and Erik to see if they needed anything. They are finished. They said that they had a plan. The problem is that some sisters saw me coming out of the emergency shelter and began asking me questions. I told them to just stay out of the emergency shelter on your orders. Mother, I hope you will forgive my presumptuousness and dishonesty in giving orders in your name, but it was the only thing I could think of to say at that moment. I don't know how much longer we can keep Erik and Laura's presence here a secret. The sisters sense that something unusual is going on."

"I know you meant well, but you shouldn't have ignored my not-so-subtle hint to stay out of the emergency shelter. But other than that, you handled it well, Sister Clare. You are right. We can't keep Erik and Laura's presence a secret any longer. Things will begin happening very soon around here, so we must prepare them. They will have a lot to digest—not only the troubles coming from the regime but also the shock of having two amazing extraterrestrial beings among us who, I'm sure, will frighten them at first. We must find the right words to prepare them so they will not be terrified of Erik and Lara. Sister Clare, I'll have you gather the sisters into the dining room, where Father and I will brief them and prepare them to meet Erik and Laura. Then, when we're ready, we will have you escort Erik and Laura into the room and introduce them to the sisters. Go now and get the sisters assembled, and tell them I order them to hurry. Father and I will go to the emergency shelter to hear Erik and Laura's plan and prepare them to meet the sisters because, despite their calm, collected demeanor, I'm sure they are just as fearful as the rest of us are—maybe more so. Oh, how I wish we had more time to prepare the sisters properly for all of this. I hope so much shocking news all at once won't overwhelm them. But how does one prepare for a convergence of events such as has fallen on our heads? It's never happened before in all of human history. But here we are. Well, Father, shall we go now to speak with Laura and Erik."

"Indeed, Mother. Let's get moving," replied Father Hughes, who was already rising from his chair.

Chapter 13

The jumbled conversations among the sisters in the dining room instantly ceased when Mother Catherine and Father Hughes entered. All the sisters stood and stared at Mother Catherine and Father Hughes in anticipation. Mother Catherine nodded to Father Hughes to proceed.

"Sit down, please," Father Hughes began, "I want you all to try to relax, at least a bit. You are understandably nervous because of the unusual, hush-hush, hurrying, and scurrying by Sister Clare, Mother Catherine, and me since we returned today. There is no gentle way of explaining everything we need to explain to you, my dear sisters, so I will simply lay it out as quickly and clearly as possible.

"Some terrible things have happened today, and as a result, we will almost certainly be put upon by forces from the regime. I expect this to happen soon—perhaps today, but more likely tomorrow. That is a frightening thing, to be sure, but we are not without resources in dealing with this, my dear ones.

"All of this expected trouble," Father Hughes continued, "is because, for a couple of days now, your convent has been protecting a foreigner who became stranded here, and we have been hiding her to prevent her being captured and mistreated by the regime. Today, we also found her husband and brought him here with us. We hope to hide them until their rescue ship arrives to take them home. Unfortunately, as we were bringing the husband to the convent today, we had a violent encounter with the Special Security Police.

in which three policemen were killed. Another man who was with us was grievously wounded. He is here at the convent, and Doctor Griffith, whom most of you know, is caring for him."

The sisters murmured among themselves at this news. Others gasped and covered their mouths as they began to understand the seriousness of the matter.

"But there is another aspect to this situation, my dear sisters," said Father Hughes, "something you must know and appreciate because it makes this matter a historic event for all of us and the entire world as well. Our two foreign visitors are beings from another world – a planet in another galaxy."

The sighs and gasps swept through the assembly of sisters like a storm gust. Some sank into their chairs, and others stood silent and stared at Father Hughes as he continued.

"My dear sisters, Sister Clare and I are about to introduce you to our guests. Please do not be fearful of them. It is true we have only known them for a short time, but in this short time, we have shared some frightfully intense moments, and during all this, we have quickly come to love and trust them like family. These two wonderful people became stranded here after their spacecraft crashed into the ocean during a specimen-collecting mission. They became separated when they ejected from their spacecraft, but they miraculously survived and are now happily reunited. Their actual names are unpronounceable to us earthlings, so we have named them Erik and Laura. They have some unique talents and abilities that will help us deal with our troubles, at least in the short term. We shall find ways to deal with the long-term matters as they come. And we know we are not without God's help—he has proven that to us time and again, has he not? He will not fail to help us in this matter either.

"Some of you," Father Huges continued, "may blame me for bringing danger to you because it was I who found Laura and brought her here to avoid her falling into the hands of the regime. I entirely understand and accept my responsibility. But you know that we cannot turn our backs on our neighbors in need if we have the means to help them. That is why I brought Laura, the beautiful lady from far away, to us here. When I found Laura, she was struggling to crawl ashore, half dead from hypothermia but still trying with the last of her strength to pull herself out of the surf and onto the beach. The authorities would have captured her, or she would have died from exposure had we not taken her in. We can only imagine what manner of treatment she would have received from them. But her recuperative abilities are remarkable, and she is now strong and fit. Her husband Erik has told us that it is a matter of honor and decency, according to their culture, that they do not leave us to suffer mistreatment by the regime as a consequence of our helping them. They have vowed to assist us as much as possible, whatever the risk to themselves. Erik and Laura will not overthrow the regime for us. However, they have additional ways to help us overcome this regime once their rescue vessel arrives. But now, time is ticking, and we must prepare ourselves for what is coming."

Father Hughes turned and nodded to Sister Clare to bring in Erik and Laura, then continued speaking to the sisters. "We shall let Erik and Laura, themselves, tell us their plan to prepare for an attack on us by the regime. Do not be the least bit fearful of Erik and Laura, dear ones. They are true friends." Father Hughes paused, took a step toward the doorway, and said, "Erik and Laura, please come in and meet our beloved sisters. Sisters, please greet our new friends, Laura and Erik!"

Another rush of gasps filled the dining room as Laura and Erik entered. Erik and Laura smiled and held each other's hand as they bowed at the waist in a gesture of respect for the sisters. Two of the sisters fainted and had to be steadied and helped into their chairs by others near them. Others, some with tears of awe in their eyes, began applauding Erik and Laura.

"Dear sisters," said Erik, keeping his voice as flat and unmusical as possible, "I hope you can understand me clearly. Our language is very different from yours, and it is difficult for us to speak in a way that is understandable to you. I want to repeat what Father Hughes said. Do not be afraid of us. I know we sound and look strange to you. You sound and look strange to us, too," he said, to which a few of the sisters responded with nervous giggles. "But we are indebted to all of you, especially Father Hughes, Mother Catherine, Sister Clare, Doctor Griffith, and a man named Thomas Carnahan. My beloved, the one you have chosen to name Laura," Erik paused and pulled Laura close to him, "would have perished had Father Hughes and the rest of you not risked your safety to help her. Your acts of courage, kindness, and hospitality we do not forget. Out of gratitude for your help and in honor of our people and our traditions, we will defend you against attacks by the regime. There will be two phases to this. One phase will be easy, and the other phase will be difficult. I will tell you the difficult part first.

"Until our rescue ship with its powerful defenses appears," he continued, "my beloved and I will use the weapons we captured today from the police to protect you if necessary. However, the most effective weapon she and I possess is the effect our singing and our other vocalizations have on human emotions. We can use our voices as a weapon against the regime because our vocalizations can reveal to humans the condition of your soul. The greater the evil within your soul, the greater your agony and the more emotionally and physically debilitating the effects. The extremely wicked among the regime's forces could even die from remorse, but even the least wicked will be tormented by their faults. For this reason, you must do your best to avoid hearing what is happening when the trouble begins. We will leave it to you to find the best means for that.

UNTIL THE RESCUE SHIP ARRIVES

"I will not mislead you. Even though my beloved and I will defend you with all our strength and natural abilities, the regime will have the advantage over us until our ship appears. So, you must understand that our success depends on our rescue ship arriving before the regime launches an organized attack. The likelihood of our rescue ship arriving in time to help us is good. Once it arrives, then the easy phase begins. The ship's defenses will protect you. You will be safe, and it will be the regime's turn to learn the meaning of fear. Even if the regime fired all its missiles and artillery at you at once, nothing would touch you here. Also, I will order some of the ship's defenses to remain here temporarily with you after we return home, but I will explain that later. We will end this meeting now because time is short, and you must prepare to live in your emergency shelter until the rescue ship arrives. You must begin stocking the shelter with the supplies and items you will need for at least several days because there may not be time to do so later. Please make these preparations as quickly as possible because we do not know if the regime's forces will arrive in minutes, hours, or days. When you have gathered all the necessary items, you must remain in or near the shelter until our rescue ship has sufficiently damaged the regime's forces to prevent it from harming you. Also—I must emphasize this again—when the troubles begin, you must do whatever you can to avoid hearing what is happening outside the shelter.

Later, after you complete your preparations and have settled into the shelter, my beloved and I hope we will have time for conversations with you. This experience is new to us, too, and we would like to become better acquainted with all of you. If a few of you would like to take turns helping us stand watch at the windows, that would also allow us to talk to one another. Thank you all."

Then, turning to Father Hughes, Erik said, "Father, I suggest we bring Doctor Griffith and Major Carnahan into the emergency shelter as soon as you have prepared a place for him. They are not safe in the guest cottage."

Chapter 14

The thumping of a circling helicopter filled the air as Special Security Police units blocked the highway, and investigators examined the scene as the ambulances carried away the bodies of Hodge, Tuttle, and Anderson.

"It was a slaughter, just as the civilians who found them described it," remarked Captain Phelps, now provisionally in command of the Special Security Police, as he spoke to the two officers with him near the spot where Anderson and Tuttle had lain. "I'm surprised that the civilians who reported this had the nerve to check for pulses on Anderson and Tuttle here and on Colonel Hodge down there. They probably trampled on some evidence when they did that, but I would have done the same thing if I were in their shoes. You can't just assume everyone is dead without checking them—they could still have had a spark of life left in them. Tuttle puzzles me a little bit, though. I think he may have been killed accidentally by a round from one of the other two. I don't believe the perpetrators executed him. I think the alien we've been hunting killed Hodge—it's alright to discuss the alien among ourselves now, so don't worry about it. After Anderson and Tuttle's incident at the beach, it's no longer a forbidden topic internally. Externally, it's still hush-hush, but it's probably already in the gossip stream. But as I was saying, I think the alien killed Hodge because he wouldn't have tried to run from just another man. But if the alien were part of this, that would explain why Hodge took off in the van, maybe with the alien aboard. Yeah,

I'd bet a week's wages that this is the work of the alien and his friends we've been looking for, not the work of some rag-tag Resistance operatives. But I'll leave it to forensics to figure all of that out.

"Now we have to find out where they're hiding," Phelps continued. "Hodge's engine was still warm to the touch, and none of the checkpoints reported anything unusual, so they may still be nearby. I'll redeploy some of our units in the area to block trails like this one. Whoever these people are, they either know the roads and backroads around here pretty well or have access to one of our satellite systems to help route them around the checkpoints. If they're using our satellites, the story becomes even more interesting because only our people can access the satellite systems.

"There isn't much around here that I know of except for forest in every direction." Phelps continued. "I doubt that the perpetrators are just sitting in the woods in their vehicle, hoping we don't find them. Henderson, Brooks, do either of you know this area well enough to know of any potential hideouts—abandoned buildings, barns, and such, they might try to use?"

"Nothing specific comes immediately to mind, sir," replied Brooks, "but Henderson and I patrol here fairly often, so we know that, like citizens everywhere lately, people around here are staying home unless they really need to go somewhere because they don't want to be stopped and searched two or three times, coming and going. So, if those people are home most of the time, there may be witnesses if the perpetrators are roaming around looking for a hideout. There are some houses scattered here and there. Some of them are out of sight from the highway, making them possible hideout locations. We could knock on a few doors and ask if anyone has seen anything suspicious. And there's a convent, or monastery, or something like that a few miles down the road from here. Tuttle and Anderson's report from earlier in the day stated that they had been questioning an old priest and a young nun when the alien jumped them. I don't know if they have any connection to that convent, but I'd be inclined to check there before checking individual homes or trying to search the forests, but that's your call, Captain."

"If you know where that convent is, let's take a look, just the three of us," said Captain Phelps. "If we find something that makes us suspicious, we'll get some backup before we take action. You drive, Brooks, and not too fast. We'll watch for any potential clues they may have dropped along the way."

They scanned the road and the shoulders for possible dropped evidence as they drove. Finally, Brooks slowed as they approached the long driveway to the convent.

"This is the entrance to the convent, Captain. How do you want to do this?"

"How far is it from here to the convent itself?"

"I'd guess three or four hundred yards. As I recall, about half of that distance is just a narrow driveway through the trees, then it opens up to a big open area with a couple of buildings and a garden plot."

"Could we drive in and park off to the edge of the driveway without being seen from the convent?"

"No, the driveway is pretty narrow, just barely enough room for two vehicles to pass and no shoulder to speak of, and somebody at the convent might get a glimpse of us through the trees if we just pulled in partway and parked on the driveway."

Phelps thought for a moment. "Okay, we'll just park the van out here. Brooks, you know the place's layout fairly well, it sounds like."

"Only what I just described to you, Captain. I was in there just once a few weeks ago. I was patrolling solo and wanted to see where the driveway led, and then I turned around in the convent's parking area and left. One glance at the place, and you'll know as much about it as I do."

"In that case, I'll have you wait here and block the entrance so no one can get in or out. Henderson and I will walk in through the woods and see what there is to see. He has a little more experience than you, which could make a difference if we run into trouble. After we've looked around the place, I'll call you and have you drive in, and we'll knock on the door and ask a few questions. Don't call me on the radio unless it's important. I don't want the radio squawking while we're prowling around. I'll call you if I need you."

The two men crept parallel to the driveway through the wet undergrowth and dripping trees until they were at the edge of the cleared grounds of the convent. Phelps leaned against a tree and scanned the property with the compact binoculars he carried in his coat pocket.

"I don't see any vehicles or people," he said, "but let's work our way around to that little cottage sitting over there by itself and have a look from there. I think it's close enough to the edge of the trees to get to it without being seen."

As they worked their way through the forest's edge toward the guest cottage, Officer Brooks radioed Captain Phelps.

"I'm sorry, Captain, but I thought you'd need to know I have a woman detained here. She says she is coming to pick up a special needs individual named Bobby, who, she says, works there as a handyman. And, of course, she wants to know what's going on, why we're here, why I won't let her in, why this, and why that. She's sitting in her vehicle while I run a check on her. She can't hear our conversation, so what do you want me to do with her?"

"Well, isn't that perfect timing?" grumbled Phelps, trying to keep his voice low. "Stall her. Tell her you can only say that we're engaged in official police business. Do a slow spot check of her vehicle. Find out what she knows about the place—who's here, how many, what they do here., Ask if she has seen or heard anything unusual. Try to get some information from her that we can use, but stall her as long as possible and buy us some time. We will be close to the buildings, so don't call me unless it's a life or death matter. I call you back after we check things out a little more."

"Will do, Captain."

"Come on, Henderson. We're going to have to move faster. Brooks has a civilian trying to come in, and he's stalling her as long as he can. Keep low, but let's pick up the pace. I have a feeling there's something here for us, but I want to be sure."

They stopped at the edge of the woods near the south side of the guest cottage, where no one in the main building could see them. They halted momentarily, watching and listening. Then, they dashed across the open space between the forest and the guest cottage and pressed themselves against the cottage wall. Phelps slipped up to a window and tried to look inside, but the interior was too dark. Easing his way over to the corner of the cottage, Phelps crouched, peeked around the corner, and then motioned for Henderson to come alongside him.

"Take a look at that, Henderson," Phelps whispered.

"That's one of our unmarked field commander vans," exclaimed Henderson under his breath.

"That's right. Now that Hodge is dead, only two officers in this sector drive one of those vans—Carnahan and me. Let's make sure there's no one in the cottage before we check out the van."

Phelps and Hodge hugged the side of the cottage as they sneaked around the corner. Phelps gently tried the cottage door. It was locked. He then leaned to look through the window next to the doorway.

"Hey! You ain't s'posa peek through windows at people!" a voice yelled."

Both Phelps and Henderson instinctively crouched and turned toward the sound of the voice as they reached for their sidearms.

Bobby, on his way to the convent house from the chicken coop, stared at the two officers and yelled, "I don't know you guys! You ain't s'posa be here! You get outta here! I'm tellin' that you was lookin' through windows! I'm tellin'!"

Bobby ran toward the convent, yelling as he ran. "Mother Caff'rn! Mother Caff'rn! Come quick! Father Hughes! Father Hughes!"

Phelps and Henderson ran after Bobby, grabbed him by his shirt, and tried to calm him, but Bobby struggled and continued screaming for help.

"Calm down, young man," Phelps said, trying to sound friendly as he grabbed Bobby's wrists. "I'm a policeman. Is your name Bobby? Are you the handyman here?"

"Let me go! Mother Caff'rn! Mother Caff'rn! Father Hughes! Father Hughes! It's the bad people! They're gettin' me! The bad people are gettin' me! Lisa! Lisa!"

"Come with us. Your ride is here to pick you up. We'll walk with you up to the main building so that your ride can take you home," said Phelps.

Bobby struggled, punched, and slapped the two men as he tried to break loose.

"Grab his feet, Henderson. We'll have to carry him."

"No! No! No! No!" Bobby screamed and then kicked Henderson in the face. "Help! Help! Father Hughes! The bad people! The bad people! Mother Caff'rn! Lisa! Lisa! Help me!"

"Oh, Lord God! Someone is kidnapping Bobby!" yelled Mother Catherine. She and Father Hughes dashed out the convent door. Sister Clare and the other sisters dropped the items they were gathering and ran out the door after them, passing them as they all ran to rescue Bobby.

UNTIL THE RESCUE SHIP ARRIVES

"Let him go, Henderson!" yelled Phelps when he saw everyone streaming out the door and charging toward them. "I'll call Brooks and get him in here to pick us up. We'll need to get some backup. We have all the justification we need."

Phelps keyed the radio and was about to order Brooks to rush in when a blue minivan roared down the driveway toward the convent.

"Brooks! How did that woman get through?" Phelps yelled into the radio.

"She just hit the gas pedal, sir, and somehow squeezed between the ditch and the van before I could do anything! I'm coming to you right now!

"Get in here fast and pick us up! We'll get some backup and—what the hell is . . . !"

Phelps stared in disbelief when he saw Erik and Laura race past the others and charge toward them, leaping, bounding, and tumbling to make themselves nearly impossible targets to hit if the police tried to shoot them.

"Run, Henderson! Run!" The two officers ran toward the police van as it lurched and rocked across the grounds toward them.

Erik grabbed Laura by the arm, and they both stopped and yelled to the others to get down and cover their ears. They all remembered what Erik told them in their meeting and understood what Erik and Laura were about to do. Sister Clare and two other sisters rushed toward Lisa, the woman who had come to bring Bobby back to his group home. Lisa threw open the door of her minivan and ran to find Bobby.

"Bobby!" Lisa screamed, sobbing and horrified at the sight of the two aliens and the presence of the Special Security Police as she ran toward the sisters.

"Bobby! Bobby!" she wailed. "Where's my Bobby? Where's my little Bobby?

Several sisters helped Sister Clare pull Lisa to the ground with them. Lisa tried to struggle with them.

"No! I have to find Bobby! Where's Bobby?"

"He's here, Lisa!" shouted Sister Clare. "He's safe!"

"Those things! Those two creatures! What are those?"

"They are friends, Lisa. I'll explain later. Cover your ears! Now! Now! Now! As tight as you can!"

Erik then nodded to Laura, and they began to sing. Suddenly, the air filled with a cacophony of roars, screams, and wailings, like the horrors of Hell echoing across the convent grounds. The sheer volume of Erik and Laura's many voices muted the screams of terror from the Special Security officers as they tripped, stumbled, and repeatedly fell onto the wet grass as they ran, eyes wide, mouths agape, toward the van and threw themselves inside. The terrified Brooks, barely maintaining his self-control, nearly overturned the vehicle as he spun it around and tore weaving, muddy tracks through the grass as the van rocked and bounced back onto the driveway and sped away.

Erik and Laura stopped their vocalizing. Although everyone at the convent had pressed their hands tightly against their ears, they all were overwhelmed by the effect of Erik and Laura's brief vocal storm and lay helpless and crying in the wet grass. Then Erik and Laura began singing a slow, delicate, complex harmony of a dozen voices, and an almost palpable wave of peace washed over their human friends. Suddenly, they stopped weeping and looked at one another in amazement as this new chorus inexplicably soothed and calmed their souls and minds. They rose to their feet and stood in silent wonder at the almost instantaneous dissipation of the dark, black dread that seconds earlier had engulfed them.

"Where's Bobby? Where's my boy?" yelled Lisa as soon as she had regained her self-control. "Where's my boy?"

Then, they heard loud, joyous laughter from the far end of the driveway.

"Look! It's Bobby! He's laughing!" shouted Sister Clare. "How did he get way over there?"

None of them had noticed Bobby chasing after the police van as it sped away while Erik and Laura were singing. Bobby, laughing, running, and jumping with pure glee, bounded back toward the group.

"Bobby!" shouted Lisa as she ran toward him, threw her arms around him, and kissed him, "Are you alright, sweetheart? Did they hurt you?"

"Lisa! Did you see 'em? Did you see 'em? Did you see'em run away? That was funny! Did you see? That was funny! They ran away, and ran away, and ran away!" Then, still laughing, Bobby hugged Lisa and began hugging everyone else.

"Weren't you afraid, Bobby?" asked Mother Catherine.

"Hi, Mother Caff'rn! Huh-uh, I wasn't scared. I was a little scared, but they ran away, and I wasn't scared no more. They was scared. I wasn't scared. They ran away, and I chased 'em. Laura and, and, him, the big guy that kinda looks like Laura, they started singin' scary stuff, and the bad guys ran away. I was brave, and I chased them bad guys away. I wasn't scared of them guys. I was brave. I wasn't scared. I chased 'em, and they ran, cuz they knew that me and Laura, and, and, that big guy, was gonna beat 'em up. I caught 'em lookin' through windows, and I was gonna beat 'em up cuz they ain't s'posa be lookin' through windows at people. And then Laura and the big guy sang that pretty stuff! Oh, pretty, pretty, they sang so pretty, and everybody got happy again. Who's that big guy?" asked Bobby, still excited and animated over the event. "Laura's big, but she's pretty. He's big, but he ain't pretty like Laura.

"Bobby, that's Laura's husband, Erik," said Father Hughes. "We brought him here a little earlier today. I guess we were a little slow in introducing him to you. Didn't it scare you when Erik and Laura sang the sounds that weren't pretty?"

"Huh-uh, I wasn't scared of them weird sounds. Them guys was scared. They ran away all scared. I laughed, and I chased 'em."

Laura and Erik stood next to Bobby. "Our singing does not trouble you at all, does it, Bobby? " asked Erik. "You must be brave and pure in all you think, do, and say."

"Yeah, I'm brave and good how I think and do stuff, 'cause Father Hughes tells me I gotta be good how I think and do stuff."

Erik patted him on the shoulder and held out his right hand. "I would like to shake your hand, Bobby. Laura told me about you," he said slowly to make his accent easier to understand. Bobby looked at him momentarily, then reached to shake Erik's powerful hand. "You have a good, strong handshake, Bobby, as a brave young man such as you should have. I understand why those men ran away from you."

"You guys are space-people, ain't ya? I wanna see where you live. Can I go see where you live?"

"Our home is too far away, Bobby," replied Erik, "and all the people here need you and depend on you to help them take care of things."

"Are you from Mars?" Bobby asked.

"Even farther away than that, Bobby," interjected Father Hughes. "But Laura and Erik have some important things that they must help us with before those bad men come back, and I think Lisa would feel much safer if you rode back home with her before they return. Will you ride home now with Lisa and make sure she gets home safe and sound?"

"I wanna stay here! I don't want nuthin' bad to happen to Lisa, or Laura, or Erik, or Mother Caff'rn—and you and the sisters, too. I'm gonna stay here and chase 'em off again. Laura and Erik can sing and scare 'em, and I'll chase 'em away again."

"Father," said Lisa, "if Mother Catherine would permit us, I think I would feel safer if Bobby and I stayed here tonight. I'm so afraid of all those cops and," she swallowed to stifle a sob, "and I'm afraid of them too—Laura and Erik—but I am more afraid of those cops. Mother, if you allow us to stay, I'll call the group home and tell them that Bobby and I will stay here tonight. I won't be specific, but I'll tell them we don't feel safe driving back to the group home. With all the crazy things happening on the highways, with cops everywhere stopping and bullying people, I think I can convince them that it's best if Bobby and I stay here tonight. May we, Mother?"

"Of course, Lisa, you are welcome to stay," said Mother Catherine, "but I must warn you more police and soldiers will be coming because they are looking for Erik and Laura, and now they know they are here. You may be in grave danger if you stay. Are you sure you want to risk staying here overnight?".

"Yes, Mother. I think so. I have become terrified of the police. They have been doing such terrible things to people—even some of my friends. I think we are safer here. If the police grab Bobby and me when we leave the convent, we will be helpless. We might disappear like so many others have recently."

"Then it is settled. You and Bobby will stay with us until you think it is safe to leave. So, my dear, let's all go inside, and we will explain everything so you understand what is happening. And let me assure you, Lisa, you have no reason to fear Laura and Erik. You will see. Oh, and for you, Laura and Erik, we will prepare some fish and sweet potatoes for you to eat. I want everyone to get at least one more good, hot meal before things get more difficult around here.

We have a little kitchen area down in the emergency shelter, and we'll prepare a meal, all things permitting. So, all of you come inside. The sisters will finish gathering what we need for the emergency shelter. Father, would you, Erik, and Laura now bring Doctor Griffith and Major Carnahan to the emergency shelter? We'll make Major Carnahan as comfortable as we can. And Bobby, while the sisters finish working in the emergency shelter, I would like you to be a brave soldier and stay inside, close to Lisa and Sister Clare. You can help them watch outside for anything or anybody who might cause trouble, okay?"

"Uh-huh, I'm a brave soldier. I'll watch out for 'em, Mother Caff'rn. I'll tell ya if I see the bad people sneakin' around. I'll see 'em. Can I have supper?"

"We'll make a good, tasty supper for you too, Bobby. We'll bring you your supper when it's ready," Mother Catherine replied.

While Mother Catherine and sister Clare prepared the meal, the other nuns gathered necessary items and organized the emergency shelter to make it as comfortable as possible. Father Hughes and Doctor Griffith assisted Erik and Laura as they gently carried Carnahan to the emergency shelter and laid him on the cot the sisters had prepared.

"Were the two of you alright during the happenings outside?" Father Hughes asked Doctor Griffith.

"Carnahan didn't even stir. He's been unconscious this entire time. I was in the middle of cleaning him up when I heard Bobby yelling, so I couldn't just drop everything and respond. Before I could run outside to see what was happening, I heard the noises Erik and Laura were making, and I heard them a little too well. It put me on the floor. I covered my ears, but I still got pretty worked up. But the next thing they sang was like a tonic. It's incredible what those two can do with their voices. But, anyway, I guess the cops know where we are now."

UNTIL THE RESCUE SHIP ARRIVES

"Yes, there were three of them," said Father Hughes. "They were snooping around the cottage when Bobby interrupted them, and they tried to grab him. The sight of Erik and Laura charging toward them to rescue Bobby sent them running. They'll be back, though."

"Well, Erik, I hope you and Laura still have a few serenades left in your songbook for when they come back," said Doctor Griffith.

Erik stared at him momentarily, then turned to Laura, who whispered a phrase in their language into Erik's ear.

Laura smiled and replied to Doctor Griffith, "Yes, Doctor, we still have a few serenades to sing. Erik did not understand what you meant."

"Does anyone else have difficulty understanding you, Doctor?" asked Erik.

"No, only people from other planets have trouble with it. Dogs and humans understand me pretty well."

Carnahan opened his eyes slightly. "I'm thirsty," he whispered, then closed his eyes again.

"I will get him some water," said Laura, "if you think he should have it."

"We'll try it," said Griffith. "Get me a spoon, too. I don't want him to try to drink from a glass yet. I'll give you one tiny sip at a time," he told Carnahan, "so you don't choke on it. Gerald, would you help Laura find a spoon, please?

"Where are we?" Carnahan whispered.

"We're at the convent, down in the emergency shelter, Thomas," replied Doctor Griffith. "You were wounded pretty badly. Erik gave us some kind of nutrient wafer of his that I've been giving you crumbs from, hoping it will do you some good. How are you feeling? How bad is your pain?"

"Not too bad if I don't try to take a deep breath. I remember getting shot. Hodge shot me in the chest.

"Erik took care of him for you. At least his bullet missed your heart," said Doctor Griffith. "And you can be thankful those wonder crumbs of Erik's seem to be helping you heal and helping with your pain—oh, thank you, Laura. Here, Thomas, just a little sip from the spoon, now—easy, easy, that's it. A little more? Ok, easy. Just a spoonful at a time. Swallow it slowly, buddy. In case you didn't notice, the sisters hung a curtain on some rope around your cot so you could have some privacy. They're laundering your clothes for you, too, and they'll stitch up the bullet holes before they bring them to you. When you feel strong enough, I'll help you get dressed. I'll be here to help you whenever you need it, and so will Father Hughes. Sister Clare will help in any way she can, too. She knows a thing or two about nursing. I still have some of Erik's wafer left, so I'll crush up a little more of it and give it to you after we've wet your whistle a little bit. Here, try to take a few more sips."

"Have you seen any cops yet?" asked Carnahan weakly.

"Yes, three of them. They were here just a little while ago, but Erik and Laura did some powerful kind of screaming and yelling that scared them off—and scared the hell rest of us, too. You've never heard anything like it, I promise you."

"They'll be back. We have to prepare a defense," said Carnahan. "Don't leave me out of all this. I can do something. Give me a weapon and set me by a door, a window, or something. I'm part of this. I'm still part of this."

"I think Erik and Laura have a plan worked out that they haven't explained to you and me yet," said Doctor Griffith, "so let's wait until we hear their ideas before we start making plans of our own. At least their singing put the cops on the run this time. I guess they just don't appreciate good singing when they hear it."

Carnahan smiled at Griffith's remark.

"But you're right, Thomas. They'll be back," Griffith continued, "However, as your doctor by default, I'm ordering you to stay in your cot. I know you want to be involved, but you aren't anywhere close to being healed, young man. It's a miracle how much you've improved so soon after being shot, but even Erik's miracle wafer can't heal a gunshot wound in a couple of hours. You'll have to rest and try to heal. Giving you Erik's wafer crumbs and our own brand of tender, loving care is all we can do for you. We don't dare try to take you to a hospital, and I know I don't have to explain why. Just let your body rest and heal. We'll need your help when you're back on your feet—hey, mister Major Thomas Carnahan, can you smell that? Does the smell of the sisters' cooking make you feel hungry?"

"No, not yet, Doc. I'd like a few more sips of water, though. By the way, I'm not a major anymore, remember? I'm just another one of those wild-eyed rebels like those I've been arresting for the past couple of years." Carnahan paused, then said, "I've got to shut up now. I'm really tired, but I want to try to stay awake for a while. Let me just lay here," Carnahan said, his voice trailing away in a whisper.

Lisa carried plates of food upstairs for Bobby and herself and relieved Sister Clare, who was sitting with Bobby near a window overlooking a section of the convent grounds and the forest edge. Laura and Erik, eager to enjoy a warm meal, positioned themselves at different windows, where they scanned the remainder of the perimeter while they ate.

Father Hughes spoke to everyone in the shelter as they finished their meal. "As all of you have discovered, Erik and Laura can use their voices as potent weapons. Erik warned us that even while we're down here with our ears plugged and our radios at full volume, we won't avoid hearing their voices when the authorities return because they will sing more intensely with more incapacitating effects. So, after all of you have eaten, I shall hear confessions over in the far corner so that you will have nothing on your souls to increase the torment you may experience. We don't know how much time we have before the police return, so I suggest all of you take advantage of this opportunity. That includes you, too, Doctor Griffith. I recommend that you take your place in line as well. I've been after you to get yourself squared away for years, and there will never be a better time than now. As for you, Thomas, I'll pull up a chair beside you and start with you if you want. The quick, general absolution I gave you earlier today was appropriate under the circumstances, but I think we have time now for a proper confession. We will turn the radios on to make background noise and ensure everyone's confidentiality. After I hear Major Carnahan's confession, I'll ask the next two of you in line to go upstairs after your confession and relieve Lisa and Bobby in case either of them want to come to confession."

"Father, what about yourself?" asked Mother Catherine. There is no priest to hear your confession. Will you be alright?"

"Well, Mother, I will just have trust in the mercy of God, won't I? I'll make an act of contrition, and I ask you and the sisters to say a prayer or two for me today, will you?"

"Of course, Father, we all will pray for you."

Chapter 15

"We've come to relieve you and Bobby," said one of the two sisters who had gone to confession. "Father wanted you to know that he is hearing confessions down in the shelter if either of you are interested."

"Thank you," said Lisa, "I'm sure Bobby needs a little break, too, don't you, Bobby?"

"I see sumfin'. I see sumfin' in the woods. Over there in the woods, I see sumfin'. Bad guys. Bad guys in the woods."

"Yes! I see them too!" said the sister. "Lisa, Bobby, quick—go down and tell everybody they've returned!"

Just then, Laura ran into the room. "They are preparing to attack the convent! All of you go down into the shelter!" she shouted, unable to fully control the musicality of her voice. "Tell everyone to remain there as we have planned. You must let Erik and me handle this. We will tell you when it is safe to come out."

As everyone rushed to the emergency shelter, Erik and Laura dashed from room to room to ensure that all lights were off, making it more difficult for the attackers to see movement inside the convent. They pulled the hoods of their jackets over their heads to take advantage of their jacket material's ability to reduce the effectiveness of thermal imaging devices that police may have had. Then they opened all the windows in the convent to allow their voices to carry all the better. They spoke to each other in brief, sing-song clips of conversation as they assessed the actions of the police assembling just inside the forest's edge. Erik crouched near a south-facing window overlooking the long driveway leading to the convent. Laura positioned herself next to a window facing the grounds on the west side of the convent.

Erik flipped open the cover to his rescue request launcher. The blue light was still blinking slowly, indicating that the rescue ship had not transitioned out of tunneling mode. The spacecraft would be less than two hours away when it transitioned out of tunneling mode. It would then receive the updated location signal from the rescue request launcher and send an acknowledgment signal. How welcome would be that signal, he thought.

"They are coming," Laura said in a voice just loud enough for Erik to hear.

Erik ran down into the emergency shelter. Everyone was already huddling."Cover your ears, now!" he shouted, then ran back to his position near the window. He watched the police as they dashed out of the forest and ran toward the convent. When they were halfway between the forest and the convent, Erik prepared to sing.

He inhaled, filling his immense lungs, and then unleashed a thundering bass note that reverberated like the horn on a warship as it rumbled throughout the convent. The police halted in their steps and fell to the ground, some pointing their weapons toward the convent house while others aimed them in other directions as they tried to understand what was happening. From where the men lay, the sound seemed to emanate from every direction. As Erik continued singing the thundering bass note, he added several more simultaneous, individual voices of torturous screams of agony and horror. Next, he increased the intensity by engaging all his voices, spanning his full vocal range, weaving in a cacophony of grating, dissonant chords.

Laura burst forth with a harsh, piercing chord that sounded as though the heavens had split open. Erik then transitioned to a long tangle of tortured, guttural groans as Laura tore the air again with a chorus of shrieking howls. Then, in unison, they unleashed a vocal storm of shrieks and screams that settled into the minds and souls of the police as they scanned all around them for the hellish horde they thought had encircled them.

The Special Security Police ceased aiming their weapons and cradled them loosely as though they had forgotten they were in their hands while their faces, twisted by the terror welling within them, searched in vain for the source of the voices of doom. No longer the intimidating force they were a moment before, they were now only trembling creatures, eyes wide, mouths agape, their minds and souls now gripped by doom. Some men dropped their weapons and covered their ears while others rose to their knees as if about to run, only to fall to the ground and cover their ears again. Others rolled on the wet ground and screamed unintelligibly. To each police officer, the membrane between their mind and soul became transparent. Each could now see every evil within themselves clearly in every respect. They saw the consequences of each thought, each word, and each deed of their lives and the extent to which they had failed to live according to the dignity for which their souls were created. As they experienced the truth of their inner self, their shame, self-loathing, and horror consumed them and hurled them into black, inconsolable despair and, finally, into madness.

Suddenly, as if on command, several men sprang to their feet and ran toward the forest. Then, the remainder of them broke and ran, some leaving their weapons lying on the ground while others still gripped them reflexively as they ran, stumbling and falling as they crashed into the forest. Four men remained prone and motionless, face down on the grass.

Erik and Laura stopped singing. The only sounds now were the fading screams of the police officers as they tried to flee the terror they carried within them. When they could no longer hear the cries of the officers, Erik and Laura began singing a different song, a slow, tender harmony at a much more subdued volume that floated in the air like a heavenly lullaby. They continued to sing as they walked down the stairs to the emergency shelter and opened the door. Everyone was weeping and praying. Father Hughes lay curled on the floor, groaning. Erik and Laura held each other's hands and kept singing. As with the earlier incident, even without understanding the language of the song, everyone immediately felt its healing effect on their souls and minds. Everyone removed the makeshift earplugs and head coverings they had used to lessen the volume of Erik and Laura's earlier singing. Then they sat or lay on the floor and bathed their emotions in the restorative tones that now washed over them. Father Hughes regained his composure and sat up with his eyes closed, breathing deeply.

Bobby sat on the floor with Lisa, hugging and trying to comfort her. "Don't cry no more, Lisa. Don't cry no more. Erik and Laura got 'em, Lisa. Don't cry. Erik and Laura chased 'em away. Listen how pretty they're singin' now, Lisa. Listen. Hear how pretty? Hey, Erik! Hey, Laura! You chased 'em away, didn't ya! Tell Lisa. Tell Lisa, so she ain't scared no more. Tell all of 'em, so they ain't scared no more."

Lisa, regaining control of her emotions, wiped the tears from her face and held Bobby's hand. "Bobby, my dear Bobby. What a marvel you are."

"How come I'm a marble?"

Lisa laughed and hugged him. "No, my dear, sweet boy, I said you are a marvel. That means you are something special. You truly are."

UNTIL THE RESCUE SHIP ARRIVES

As everyone recovered their composure, Erik and Laura stopped singing and explained all that had occurred outside. "I am sure more will come," said Erik, "but it will not be any of those men."

"I think that was just a hasty, half-baked operation that they threw together with the personnel they had nearby," said Carnahan from his cot, emotionally recovered, and his voice was noticeably stronger. "Whoever organized that operation, if he's not among the casualties, will probably be shot for incompetence even though the failure wasn't his fault. When they return, they will be at least somewhat better organized. They'll bring everything they can throw together—helicopters, armor, whatever they can get their hands on that still functions. If luck is with us, they may have trouble putting it all together because the Resistance saboteurs have been steadily chipping away at the regime's systems and resources. Communication systems, vehicles, aircraft, weapons, ammunition—wherever they've discovered a weak spot in security, they've exploited it. But if they somehow manage to round up a few armored vehicles or aircraft, can your rescue ship knock them out?"

"Yes, our ship's defenses can easily destroy any weapon in the human arsenal," replied Laura, "and it also has an onboard medical facility that will help you heal more quickly. It is small and somewhat limited but much better than any of your hospitals. And the robot that will treat you is far more capable than any human doctor."

"Oh, you think so, huh!" replied Doctor Griffith, causing Erik and Laura to chuckle.

"If you think it can help me," said Carnahan, "I'll gladly be your robot's guinea pig. If the regime doesn't wipe us out before your ship gets here, I want to heal up enough to be a part of the fight. I don't want to be just a bedridden spectator."

"Speaking of health and healing, Erik," said Doctor Griffith, "I gave Carnahan the last few crumbs of that wafer. If you have more of them on that spaceship, maybe you could give us some before you leave."

"We will do that," replied Erik. "There will be many of them onboard. We will give you all of them. I suggest you save one of the wafers to analyze so you can produce them yourselves. I do not know your words for the ingredients, but all of them can be obtained or produced here on Earth. But enough talk for now. Four police officers are dead and lying on the ground. We must bury them. To our race, it is a shame upon us if we leave the dead unburied without good reason—even if they are enemies. Mother Catherine, do you have tools we can use?"

"Yes, we do. And I agree, we should bury them. For now, you can bury them in the open ground near where the driveway curves into the forest on the way to the highway. It should be relatively soft digging there. If we survive all this, we will let the circumstances determine what to do for their permanent graves. Lisa, would you allow Bobby to show Erik and Laura where the tool shed is?"

"Uh-huh, I'll show 'em, Mother Caff'rn. But when I'm outside, don't let Lisa get scared no more, Mother Caff'rn. I don't like it when she cries. Don't let her feel scared no more. Can I show 'em, Lisa? I'll come right back—right back. I ain't scared to do that. I'm a marble."

"Yes, Bobby, you can show them where the tools are. I trust Erik and Laura to protect you while you're with them," replied Lisa. "And Bobby, I said you are a marvel."

"Uh-huh, I know. Can I help 'em dig, too? I'm a good digger."

"No, Bobby, just show them where the tool shed is and come right back," said Lisa. "You and I will keep watch at the windows again. You are very good at that. You were the one who saw them coming. You are a very good watchman."

"Yeah, I'm a good watchin' man. I'm good at that."

"Yes, you are," replied Mother Catherine. "So, hurry back as soon as Laura and Erik have their tools."

"I'll go with them," said Father Hughes. I'm not much good at digging anymore, but I may yet be of some help to the souls of those poor wretches lying out there,"

"Some of the sisters and I can help them dig, Mother," said Sister Clare.

Erik spoke before Mother Catherine could answer, "Thank you, Sister Clare, but no. We ask you all to remain inside the shelter. My beloved and I can do this quickly. We are strong. We will do this alone. We will return Bobby to you when we have the tools."

Bobby led them to the tool shed. "You have to clean 'em up when you're done 'cause they go rusty if you don't clean 'em, and they break if they go rusty," he said as Erik and Laura each grabbed a shovel and a mattock. "Mother Caff'rn will be mad if you get 'em rusty."

"We will make them as clean as they are now, Bobby. Thank you for helping. Now hurry back to help Lisa watch," said Laura.

As they walked toward the fallen police officers, they watched to ensure that Bobby ran directly back to the convent. When they arrived at the spot Mother Catherine had suggested, they dropped the shovels and began hacking into the ground with the mattocks. They tore into the soil with an almost machine-like speed and rhythm, breaking up the soil and roots and shoveling it all out.

As they dug, Doctor Griffith walked down to where the officers lay."Carnahan asked me to pick up the weapons and ammunition from these poor slobs. He said that we might need them. I agree with him. I'll grab them and be out of your way in a few minutes, but while I'm out here, I'll look around to see if they dropped anything else we can use."

"Yes, that is good," said Erik, "we were going to do that after we finished burying these men. They also have grenades in their vests. As you said, we may need them."

In less than an hour, Erik and Laura finished digging the four individual graves. They set the tools aside and began carrying the dead police officers to the graves.

Father Hughes, who had offered prayers for the souls of the dead officers and their families, spoke to Erik and Laura as they lay the last officer in his grave. "So much has happened in the past couple of days—so much useless suffering for the same stupid, prideful reasons. It's always about power and control, without a care for governing justly, benignly, and wisely. That has been the repeating story of the human race throughout our history—the powerful forcing the powerless to submit until the powerless finally rise against them. Then, the powerful retaliate with all the savagery that animates them as they try to crush the rebellion. Sometimes the rebellion succeeds, sometimes it fails, but either way, the pattern repeats itself." After a long pause, Father Hughes continued. "But something good is woven into these past days, too—the experience of meeting both of you. My friends and I have barely had the time to ponder and appreciate the miracle of you being here among us. But here you are, two beings not from this world, living with us under the same roof as we struggle against the odds to help you return to the freedom of your world as we hope to reclaim freedom in our world. Until now, the possibility of a visitation by beings from another planet was just a fanciful musing or the stuff of science fiction stories—usually about fearsome, otherworldly monsters coming to destroy us all. But the reality is that the monstrous creatures have always come from among our own, not from galaxies scattered across the cosmos.

"Yes, here the two of you are. With the intensity of our situation seeming to alter my perception of time and circumstances, I almost feel as though you are long-time friends visiting us from another city rather than stranded castaways from another planet. You are so different from us in many ways, yet in very significant ways, so similar—but in all ways, you have shown yourselves to be of higher character than us humans. Yes, much, much higher, I would say. I have only known you, Erik, less than a day and you, Laura, for two days, but I must admit, I shall miss both of you after you leave us. You are truly noble, courageous, admirable people. How I wish there were a pill that we humans could take that would ignite those virtues in us, as well."

Erik looked at Laura, then gently slapped Father Hughes's shoulder and replied, "You do not realize, Father Hughes, how surprised we are by the qualities we have seen in you and your friends. We underestimated your race because we did not often see evidence of the virtues your race has within you. You and your friends have experienced terrible things today because all of you risked everything to help us. You, Father Hughes, could have abandoned my beloved on the beach and saved yourselves the troubles of today and the troubles yet to come. But that is not the kind of person you are. You did it because you believed it was the right thing to do. We admire that. Because of the bravery and kindness of you and your friends, my beloved and I will survive this voyage, return to our beautiful home, and resume our joyful lives. We will have many new things to tell our people about you and your race of beings.

"We are now as deeply involved in your plight as you are with ours," Erik continued. "You have done all you can do for us. Now, it is our turn to do all we can for you. The orbs from our rescue ship, by themselves, could destroy all the weapons, equipment, facilities, and identifiable personnel of the regime in your country in only a few days. The orbs from five rescue ships could destroy the regime's assets worldwide in the same amount of time. I am tempted to ask our people to launch such a mission. But that would be the wrong decision, as I have explained before. It would be improper for us to fight your fight for you. We are not meddlers, empire builders, or alliance makers, nor will we put ourselves in a position to be worshipped as saviors or false gods as many of the weaker-minded among your race surely would do if we intervened to liberate you from your oppressors. It is better that we disrupt the regime sufficiently to enable you and your people to destroy it yourselves. Then, your victory will come from your own efforts and sacrifices, and you will proudly and rightfully celebrate your victory forever.

Laura then spoke. "Father Hughes, I want to tell you that I will never forget your fatherly care as you carried me from the beach. I was sometimes conscious enough to understand what was happening. I did not have the energy to speak, but I heard you when you spoke to me. I know you were exerting yourself almost beyond your strength to save me. While I was struggling to crawl ashore, I was afraid that if I did not die on the beach, the authorities would capture me in my weakness and imprison me, perhaps even kill me. We know of them and their ways. But it was my good fortune that you found me.

"As you know," Laura continued, "I was conscious as you were pleading with Doctor Griffith and Mother Catherine to allow me to stay here at the convent to recover. You truly have the soul of a father. You are very dear to me, Father Hughes, and so are Doctor Griffith, Major Carnahan, Sister Clare, Mother Catherine, the sisters, and that dear young man, Bobby. If I may modify your comment from a moment ago, I wish there were a pill that all of your race could take that would make them exhibit the same character as all of you here at this convent."

Father Hughes smiled and replied, "Unfortunately, my dear friends, there is no such magic pill. We are a spiritually and intellectually lazy race that will, more often than not, choose the easy way even when we know it's the wrong way. Your race has the edge on us in that regard. But enough of all that. Here comes Sister Clare with some sheets to wrap these poor fellows in. We'll help you bury them, and then we all can get back to the house."

UNTIL THE RESCUE SHIP ARRIVES

"Thank you, Father, but my beloved and I can finish this quickly," replied Erik. There is no need for you and Sister Clare to remain out here in the open."

"Erik is right, Sister Clare," said Father Hughes, "let's go back inside and see what help we can be there."

Chapter 16

Laura and Erik returned from burying the fallen officers, washed their hands, and checked on the others down in the emergency shelter.

Carnahan called Erik from his cot as they stepped into the shelter, "Erik, I had Doc Griffith put all the firearms and gear under my cot. In addition to the four extra pistols and magazines, we now have fourteen rifles! While Doc was outside, he found ten additional rifles that those guys dropped as they ran away. We also have four extra pistols with full magazines, extra fully loaded magazines for them, and four tactical vests with grenades. I'll let you have all the rifles except one. I'll keep one rifle and my pistol with me—thanks for tossing it in with me when you loaded me into the van. If the goons make it into the house, I'll make them pay when they try to come down those stairs. All the extra weaponry is under my cot, so take it upstairs with you. You can pre-position the extra firearms near the doorways and windows so you'll always have a loaded weapon and extra ammunition nearby in case you need to move around to keep the attackers at bay."

"Yes, I will take them, Carnahan, and pre-position them as you say. I continue to hope our rescue ship arrives before the authorities do. If it does, we will not need the rifles and pistols, but your people have a phrase you sometimes say, 'Better to have and not need than to need and not have.' That is how you say it, yes?"

"That's how we say it, alright!" said Carnahan. "We have another saying, too: 'Don't get caught with your pants down.' And I don't intend to be caught with my proverbial pants down. If this becomes our Alamo, I'll be Jim Bowie on my sick bed, and I'll take down a few of them when they bust through the door."

"I do not understand what that means," replied Erik, "but I know you will do whatever you can, Carnahan. I am pleased that you are feeling stronger."

"I am feeling better. It still hurts if I forget and take a deep breath, but I'm alive and I'm healing because of your wafers. By the way, Doctor Griffith says he will have those wafers you said you'd give him analyzed and start manufacturing them as soon as this mess is over. He said he knows people who do such things and have the equipment and facilities to do it. So, don't forget to give those wafers to him when your spaceship gets here—and give me a few more of them, too."

"I will do so, and as I said, when our rescue ship gets here, we have medical equipment onboard that will help heal your wounds before we depart."

"You must have quite a world where you come from, Erik," said Carnahan. "I haven't had a chance to ask you about it. Tell me a few things about your world and your people, if you don't mind. For us Earth people, speaking face to face with alien beings from another planet isn't exactly something we get to do every day, you know. I'd like to learn at least a thing or two about your people before you leave us."

"Yes, Erik," said one of the sisters sitting nearby, "we know nothing about you and your world. We'd love to hear about it while we have a few quiet moments."

Agreeing voices rose from the other sisters gathered in the emergency shelter, asking Erik and Laura to tell them more about life in their world.

UNTIL THE RESCUE SHIP ARRIVES

"Lisa and Bobby are still on watch, yes?" asked Erik.

"Yes, Lisa and Bobby are still watching. Bobby is adamant about staying at his post and keeping watch for you," replied Mother Catherine.

"Good. I will tell you some facts about our world and our people. It is only fair that we tell you something about ourselves since we know so much about you, and you have been so kind to us even though you know nothing about us. But there are some things that we cannot discuss with you. We cannot reveal detailed information about our technology and science. We must not speak of our spiritual understandings because our experiences and relationship with the All Holy One differ somewhat from yours, so we do not want to create confusion. We cannot tell you which galaxy contains our home world. I can tell you that it is visible to you without a telescope on a clear, very dark night. Also, we cannot discuss details about our knowledge of the universe. However, there are many other things about our world I can tell you. I will speak of these things in the order they enter my mind, and I will try to brief, but when speaking of our home world, I may, as you sometimes say, 'get carried away.'

"Our society is ordered and governed through a simple hierarchy of authority that is entirely the inverse of that in your world. In our world, the family and its well-being are most important. We structure our families like small sovereign states, and we lovingly but firmly maintain order and set high standards for the conduct of our family members to ensure the family remains vibrant and respected by our communities. Each family is sovereign over its home and property. Property is not taxed or regulated, and no one has the right or power to tell someone else what they can do with their property unless someone is engaging in an activity that creates problems for others. If that occurs and the concerned parties cannot agree on a solution, which is very rare, they will ask the community to join the discussion to help arrive at an acceptable solution. Community involvement nearly always solves the problem because we understand the importance of maintaining harmony and goodwill with our neighbors.

"The next level down is the community. Communities are sovereign in managing their affairs unless the community does something that affects another community. This is also rare and usually quickly resolved, like disputes between neighbors.

"The next level of authority is the Provincial Councils. We have many provinces, and each community in each province appoints a representative to attend to their interests at the yearly Provincial Council gathering. These gatherings never continue for longer than sixty days and usually far fewer days than that. We have learned that short gatherings ensure that the council discusses only the most essential matters, reducing the temptation to expand the role of the Provincial Council.

The last level is the Provincial Forum, where representatives from all the provinces meet yearly to discuss important matters and resolve problems between or among the provinces. Provincial Forums are also limited to sixty days. We have no full-time, professional politicians. Our history is full of these contemptible schemers who, in the end, only serve themselves and bring ruin to society. We detest them and will never have them again.

"We have a court system comprising community courts that differ somewhat from yours. Our community courts handle nearly all crime and other legal matters. Our laws are few and simple. No one is ignorant of them. Justice is swift and firm.

"Our manner of living is simple. Even though we have highly advanced technologies, we use them only for essential tasks where their use is justifiable. In many ways, our homes employ less technology than do yours. With few exceptions, we do not clutter our lives with unneeded devices and novelties. To us, simplicity is a virtue. We shun unnecessary complexity and take satisfaction in limiting our possessions to things we need and use, most of which do not require complex technology. Our limited use of sophisticated technology and our preference for simple, durable tools, machinery, and appliances also preserve our freedom and self-sufficiency. We regard technology much like we regard medicine. We use only the necessary amount because too much is dangerous. I think your people are beginning to understand that, too. Technology always becomes a tool for those who desire to control others.

"We have what you call cities, but they are fewer and not as large as most of yours. Most of our people live on small homesteads within or near small communities. These small communities contribute much to maintaining our peaceful, happy, productive lives. We have frequent community celebrations and social events. No one is isolated or shunned unless they have committed a serious offense. Our families are large. We often have three, and sometimes four, generations living in the same house. Grown children have a friendly but vigorous competition for who will have the honor of having their parents and grandparents live with them when they are old. This honor does not always go to the eldest son and his family, as in some cultures in your world. Many factors determine who prevails. There is no shame in not being chosen, but it is always a disappointment.

"Our world was once filled with conflicts, much like yours. But now, serious conflicts are rare and brief because most people in our world are happy with their lives in their communities and provinces. They would not tolerate rebelliousness, crime, or other wickedness erupting in their communities. Over many generations, we have identified and stripped away the behaviors, ideas, and philosophies that have repeatedly led to strife and suffering, and we have no tolerance for them. We do not forget what our history teaches us, so we do not believe in giving lies and foolishness equal standing with truth and wisdom. We teach our children the ways that bring peace and contentment and also the ways that bring strife and misery so they, too, will recognize and reject them. We occasionally have people who commit crimes or create serious problems. When that happens, the citizens of our volunteer community militias deal swiftly and severely with the troublemakers without requiring further legal procedures. Your people call this vigilantism, which has a bad reputation in your world. However, in our world, our people are raised to know the difference between administering justice and taking revenge. Victims of wrongdoing are never permitted to judge the offender or carry out punishment. Other community members and members of the community militias take on those responsibilities for them. Sometimes, the militias hand over a troublemaker to their official community court if the militia believes the matter is beyond their ability or competence to judge or punish. But usually, the militias can judge a crime and decide if the sentence should be restitution, physical punishment, execution, or banishment to the Northern Provinces, which I will tell you about in a moment.

"The Provincial Guard serves and protects its home province and, when necessary, coordinates with the Provincial Guard in the other provinces, much as did your state and national guard organizations here in your country before the tyrants began using them against you. Our citizens are entitled to volunteer to serve in our militias and the Provincial Guards for as long as they wish, with a minimum of two years as measured in our world. Even though planet-wide wars are far behind us, we still have problems that erupt. That is why we have maintained our warrior training and spirit, traditional moral code, and personal self-discipline because they strengthen the core of our civilization and keep us unified. Also, maintaining our warrior skills and traditions helps us to overcome challenges in our daily lives.

UNTIL THE RESCUE SHIP ARRIVES

"We help our family members and citizens with disabilities develop skills to perform work according to their abilities if they wish to do so—and yes, despite our superior medical technology, we do have people with physical and mental disabilities. We treat them with kindness and respect and help them participate in society as much as possible. Those who are capable of working are much happier when they perform useful work each day—work they are eager to perform, regardless of how simple the task may be. It gives us joy to find ways for them to contribute their talents and participate in society.

"As I mentioned a moment ago, there is a region in our world known as The Northern Provinces. These are five provinces surrounded by an ocean. They function as what your race would call penal colonies. These lands are for outcasts expelled by their communities for various offenses. If someone exiled there commits further severe crimes, we execute them. Others go there voluntarily, for reasons of their own, to carve out a living however they can. Those forcibly exiled to the Northern Provinces are never permitted to leave. Only the children born there, the military personnel serving there, and the few who chose to move to the Northern Provinces can leave and reenter as they wish. If those exiled there reform themselves and behave honorably, they can live a decent life. But for our race, such a life can never be truly joyful and satisfying when separated from one's family and community. The substitute friendships and communities one forms in the Northern Provinces can never replace the families and communities of one's birth.

"The Northern Provinces are guarded and governed by a zealous, highly-trained branch of Provincial Guards recruited from all the provinces. They strictly enforce the rules of society, relying as little as possible on technology to deal with the offenders. We find it more effective and honorable to ensure that trouble-makers learn to fear us rather than fear our technology. My beloved and I served in this force before we joined the Distant Voyager Service. That is where we met each other.

"Since then, my beloved and I have served together in the Distant Voyager Service for three years as we measure them, adding to the knowledge gathered by several generations of Distant Voyagers. We have made twenty-one voyages together. Eleven of those voyages were to this planet. As you can imagine, we have spent very little time at home between voyages. Before this voyage, we had discussed resigning from the Distant Voyager Service, and the events of this voyage have settled the question for us. We will resign when we return home, and then we will do as over half of the people on our planet do—grow crops and raise livestock on our small farm. It is work, yes, but satisfying work. My beloved and I become excited when we discuss it. If only we could be there now. We have done our duty as Distant Voyagers. Now, we are eager to rejoin our family and community. But most of all, we want to begin our own family. We desire to have many children. There is no greater joy than having a large, happy, harmonious family.

"Talking about all of this fills my heart," Erik said. "Laura and I can barely wait to return home. We have a fine home in a long, wide valley with fertile soil, mild summers, and moderate winters. Along with growing crops, we will raise a small herd of remarkable beasts common in our world. They are slightly larger than the animal you call a . . . let me think of the animal's name . . . a rhin . . . a rhinoceros animal. These animals have long hair that we shear when the weather becomes warm, and from this, we weave the cloth from which we make most of our clothing and many other cloth items. These animals are the most docile, friendly creatures you could imagine—they are even friendlier than your dog animals. They will follow you while you are working, gently nudging you to let you know they want to be scratched and petted. They will follow you into your house if you are not careful. And despite their size, they are so nimble and gentle that they will even play with the children—chasing them, then having the children chase them—even allowing them to ride them. But when they have young calves, if an animal that they perceive to be a threat comes near their offspring, they will destroy the predator if it does not run as far and as fast as it can. They will gore the other animal with the cone-shaped horn on their forehead and trample it until nothing recognizable remains of it. They are just as protective of children. There are many stories of them saving children from attacks by other animals and saving children from drowning or other dangers."

"And as Erik said, he and I are eager to have children," interjected Laura, "as many children as the Great All Holy One grants us. There is nothing so sweet as the music of children when they sing and mutter their little sounds as they learn our language or their coos and squeals of joy as they play together.

"Erik will build an extra room onto our house so that they will have plenty of room to tussle around on rainy days and during the winter," said Laura. "I will make all of their clothing myself. I will sew the character representing each child's name on the chest pocket of their little jackets. Erik will make their little shoes and their little boots. Together, he and I will make their toys, their swings, and their, what is your word for them . . . teeter . . . teeter-totters, I think you call them. And yes, our children play very much like your children! They will follow us and learn by watching as we tend the crops and work with the animals—it will be so joyful.

"I can barely wait to step into our home again," Laura continued. "I can almost smell the sweet, subtle aroma of the wood from which it is built, the scent of which never dissipates regardless of how old the house is. And I can see in my mind the little stream that tumbles down the side of our nearby mountain and forms the pool from which our animals drink before it flows onward to join the river that we call, roughly translated into your language, the River of Triumph, where our ancestors, whose names we remember from generation to generation, defeated one of our ancient enemies. And in the evenings, after all the children are sleeping, Erik and I will stand outside and gaze into the lights of the heavens, and we shall search until we find the point of light that is your galaxy, and we shall say, 'There is the home of our dear friends who saved our lives and helped us return here to our home. Home, as simple as your word for it is, the sound of it is so beautiful to contemplate—Home. Home."

She turned her head and wiped her eyes as Erik pulled her to his side. "Laura and I will now take our posts and watch for the authorities," said Erik. "We will send Lisa and Bobby back down here to you."

Erik and Laura collected the firearms and vests from Carnahan. They were about to go upstairs when Carnahan called to Erik, pointed to the extra rifle, and said, "Here, take this one, too. I did some thinking while I was lying here, and I have to be honest with myself—I'm in no condition to use it. Maybe tomorrow or the day after, but not today. I'll keep my pistol, though, in case I have to pretend to be Jim Bowie at the Alamo today."

"Thank you, Carnahan," Erik replied. "You will soon heal, and then you will fight them."

"And we will fight them now, in our way," said Mother Catherine. "Sisters, your rosaries. Father, will you lead us, please?"

"Of course, Mother," replied Father Hughes as he pulled his rosary from his pocket and made the sign of the cross. "In nomine Patris, et Filii, et Spiritus Sancti...."

Chapter 17

Heavy clouds hastened the darkness of evening. Mother Catherine shut off all circuit breakers except for the emergency shelter, which was below ground, to avoid someone turning on a light out of habit. Erik handed Laura his night-vision goggles. While Laura kept watch, Erik opened the cover to his rescue request launcher and whispered a lengthy, detailed message using a non-musical shorthand version of their language, which the launcher understood and recorded. The non-musical code provided a more covert, subdued means to record a message to be transmitted later. In this circumstance, it avoided causing discomfort to the humans if they overheard it. Erik's message contained all the details of their experiences up to that point. He added specific instructions to the rescue ship so that, if he and Laura were injured or killed, the rescue ship would have not only a detailed record of their experiences but would also know the tasks that Erik wanted it to perform upon its arrival. Erik's rescue request launcher would automatically transmit the message as soon as the rescue ship transitioned out of tunneling mode and signaled it could receive messages.

When Erik finished, he closed the launcher's cover and gently lifted the night-vision goggles from Laura's face. "It is my turn to watch and your turn to rest, my beloved," he whispered in their language. Laura smiled and shifted her position so Erik could sit cross-legged near the window. She then lay on her side with her head on Erik's thigh and clutched his hand to her bosom as she drifted to sleep. As he scanned through the darkness, he stroked Laura's soft, short-cropped hair and remembered the tormenting thoughts that had surrounded him like a legion of demons when he sat, wet and cold in the forest, and wondered what had happened to her and prayed he would be able to find her again. But now those haunting demons were expelled. He and she were together. Whatever happened from this moment on, they would share it. Be it survival or death, they would remain together. He would not lose her again. There could be no true life for him without her. She was, without doubt, his gift from the All Holy One, a gift that filled a void within him that he did not know existed until the day he met her, but soon after meeting her, he understood that only after living an entire life with her could he feel that he had truly lived. Now, she was here with him again, asleep on his lap, as serene as if they were sharing a quiet hour in their home, and the wretched human enemies were galaxies away from them.

But the wretched ones were not galaxies away, and they would return, perhaps with more formidable weaponry. Erik knew that if the authorities attacked with armored vehicles, it would be difficult for their voices, which, at this point, was their best weapon, to have an effect. If the humans attacked with aircraft, the enemy would easily destroy them. But if circumstances prevented them from using their voices, they would use their captured human weapons and fight to their last cartridge, and then they would fight with any implement that fell into their hands. They would never surrender to the humans, and suicide was unthinkable and unforgivable. They would fight to their final heartbeat. They would fight not only for themselves but also for their vulnerable friends in the emergency shelter. As long as either of them could wield a weapon or throw a punch, he and his beloved would not permit the wretched ones to harm those defenseless humans who had risked everything to help them. Somehow, he and she had to disrupt the enemy and keep them disorganized until the rescue ship arrived.

An hour passed, and Laura awoke, sat up, and reached for the rifle Erik was holding. "It's your turn to sleep now, my fearless warrior husband," she whispered with a smile, "and rest well, for your fearless warrior wife will protect you."

Erik laughed and handed her the rifle. "Here then, my fearless warrior wife, I have kept this warm for you. Please avoid accidentally shooting me with it."

Just then, Doctor Griffith crept into the room. "I'm going to help keep watch. Give me a rifle, and I'll watch from the widows on the north wall."

"Doctor, I do not think you should do this," Erik replied.

"I know how to handle a rifle, Erik. You're not the only one around here who knows something about war. Right now, you need help, so give me a rifle."

After a pause, Erik replied, "Two rifles are leaning against the north wall, and loaded magazines are on the floor beside them. Take no unnecessary risks, Doctor, and do not shoot anything unless either my beloved or I give the command."

As they spoke, they heard the thumping of an approaching helicopter. "Stay away from the windows, Doctor, and get down!" shouted Erik.

The thunder of the helicopter grew louder, and they could tell that it was directly over them, circling the convent property. With his night vision goggles, Erik could see the helicopter, which showed no lights as it slowly circled the grounds. Then, it hovered directly over the convent house, sounding as if it were barely above the rooftop, the pounding of its blades thundering through the house. Thinking that soldiers or police may deploy from the helicopter, Erik lay prone and trained his rifle on the main entrance door. Suddenly, the helicopter engine roared as it abruptly rose and veered out over the open grounds away from the convent house.

"Listen!" yelled Laura from the east window. "I think they are losing control!"

As Erik watched through his goggles, the helicopter began spinning as it rose, as if the tail rotor wasn't functioning properly. Then, the pilot seemed to regain control and, for a moment, flew straight toward the trees, barely clearing the tallest of them. Then it abruptly headed toward the convent again, losing altitude, gaining it again, diving wildly as if about to crash into the guest cottage, then pulling up and away barely in time to avoid crashing into it. Then the helicopter stabilized, hovered momentarily, turned, and slowly flew northwest, the beating of its rotors gradually fading into the distance.

Carnahan tottered into the room, steadying himself against the wall as he walked. "I know I told you I'd stay downstairs and leave it all to you, but I heard the helicopter. I thought you might need some extra help. Where are the pistols? Give me an extra pistol."

"Carnahan!" Doctor Griffith shouted. "What are you doing up here? I knew I shouldn't have helped you get dressed. In case you forgot, you still have a bullet hole through your chest that's trying to heal. If it weren't for Erik's wafer, you'd be dead already!"

"We cannot do this! I have changed my mind!" barked Erik. "We cannot have all of you coming up here to help. You will only put yourselves in danger. Doctor, I want you and Major Carnahan to return to the emergency shelter!"

Doctor Griffith glared at Erik and stomped toward him. He thrust his face up as close to Erik's face as his shorter height could reach.

UNTIL THE RESCUE SHIP ARRIVES

"Who the hell do you think you are, yelling orders to us, telling us what to do, where to go?" growled Doctor Griffith. "You may be big and strong, rough and tough, but you don't give orders to us, mister! You don't run a damned thing around here. We don't jump when you bark, big boy. You need to remember that we, all of us humans here, are trying to save your alien butts! If you don't want our help, just pack up, get out of here, and do whatever you want. But don't you think for a minute that we're under your command, mister! Not for a minute! You aren't...."

"Ease up, Doc, ease up!" Carnahan interrupted. "We have to keep our heads clear here. Whether you like it or not, we're all in this together, and we don't stand a chance of getting out of this in one piece if we don't work together. Erik's probably right, Doc. Let's let them do what they're trained to do. We'll know if and when they need us to step up."

"Maybe so, Carnahan, but I mean what I say—and I'm looking right at you, Erik. You're not the boss around here. We don't take orders from you. If you try to boss me around again, I'll bust you right in the face, and I won't give a damn what happens after that. You got that big boy? Huh? You got that?"

"Doctor Griffith, please, allow me to speak to you," said Laura as she pressed herself between Griffith and Erik and gently held Griffith's arm. Turning to Erik, she said, "Beloved, take my place while I speak to Doctor Griffith."

Erik said nothing as he left the room to stand watch at the west windows.

"Doctor Griffith," Laura began, "I owe my life to you and Father Hughes. If it were not for the two of you, I would be dead. I am grateful to you, and I respect you very much. I cannot express how much it troubles my soul to know you are angry with...."

"I'm not mad at you, Laura," Griffith interjected, "but I am plenty damned mad at him."

"My beloved meant no disrespect to you, Doctor Griffith. None at all. We have a direct manner of speaking and behaving during moments like this. That is why Erik spoke as he did. He did not intend to anger you. He understands that it is our responsibility to protect all of you as well as we can. And we will do so to the limits of our strength. We assumed all of you had given us the authority to make decisions and take actions necessary to defend you. Perhaps we assumed too much. Please accept my apology if we angered you. I know Erik respects you very much, Doctor Griffith. He has told me how impressed he is at your efforts to save my life, disadvantaged as you were by not knowing anything about our physiology. Can you overlook Erik unintentionally offending you? Can we all work together? Will you allow us to do what we think is best for all of us, and will all of you cooperate with us as we try to do this? If not, as you suggested, we will leave the convent to avoid more disagreements, but we will remain in the forest, guarding all of you and attacking anyone who tries to harm you. Our honor requires this of us regardless of the circumstances. We will do this with or without your approval. We will protect all of you and defend you until we succeed or until we die. Tell us how you want us to proceed, Doctor Griffith."

Laura studied Doctor Griffith's face as she awaited his response. Griffith could not remain angry.

"I can only speak for myself, Laura. I don't speak for the rest of them. I can't order the two of you to do anything. I'm not the boss of anything around here, either. Besides, even if I could give orders to you, I wouldn't order you and Erik to go and hide in the woods. I just lost my temper, Laura, that's all. As far as I know, I'm the only one around here with a gripe. The rest of the people here would probably throw me out if I tried to throw you and Erik out over my little temper tantrum. You and Erik stay right here with us. Do whatever you need to do. I think that's what everyone else expects you to do. Carnahan is right. We all need to stick together and cooperate to get through this. I'll go make peace with Erik."

"That is unnecessary, Doctor Griffith," said Erik as he stepped back into the room. "I heard your conversation. Let us cooperate to defeat these people."

"That's what we'll do," replied Griffith. "I'll take Carnahan back downstairs whether he likes it or not. He knows he shouldn't be up here."

"Take the rifle with you if you choose," said Erik. "If we need you, we will call for you."

"If you and Laura do need help," said Carnahan. "I can post myself at a window while the two of you do whatever else you need to do."

"Thank you, Major, but my beloved and I work with each other and fight enemies together very effectively. We have done so numerous times," said Erik. "I suggest you listen to Doctor Griffith and let your wounds heal."

"Yeah, yeah, Erik, alright," replied Carnahan, "but there's something very unusual about what the helicopter just did. They weren't just flying around to scare us. I'm sure a team was on board that was going to deploy. But for some reason, that didn't happen. If they had deployed, we'd already be shot to hell. Something doesn't add up." Carnahan suddenly paused and leaned heavily against the wall. "Hey, Doc. Help me downstairs, will you? I'm feeling pretty wobbly all of a sudden."

"Well, what did you expect, Carnahan?" growled Doctor Griffith as he slung the rifle he was carrying over his shoulder and steadied Carnahan. "Did you think Erik's magic wafer could heal a sucking chest wound in a few hours? I'm amazed that you're still alive at all! Okay, Carnahan, I've got you, let's go. One step at a time."

"Be ready for anything at any time, now, Erik," said Carnahan as Doctor Griffith helped him toward the stairs." Damn, I wish I didn't have this hole in me! I want to be in this fight. I want to . . . I want to . . . Doc, wait a second. I have to catch my breath."

Mother Catherine rushed to the top of the stairs. "Erik, something is happening. The power is off. We have no lights or power in the electrical receptacles in the shelter."

"They've probably cut the power to the convent—phone service, too, if you have a landline," said Carnahan, breathing heavily.

"No one's cell phone is working either, and we can't get any radio stations even on the battery-powered radios."

"Oh, okay, I think I know what's happening," said Carnahan. "The Resistance must have launched their big plan—hitting the regime everywhere at once where they are most vulnerable—the power grid, satellite reception, television and radio stations, electronics, vehicles, everything. And not just piecemeal like they had been doing. They've been putting this plan together for a long time. I learned about their plan almost a year ago. I've been compiling info about it as it trickled down to me, hoping to learn how deep and wide the Resistance had burrowed into the regime and critical infrastructure. None of that information got any farther than my home filing cabinet. I didn't pass any of it on up. If this is the work of the Resistance, they caught the regime flatfooted. Their timing couldn't have been better for us. This could really help us when they . . . hey, Doc!"

Carnahan slumped into Griffith's arms.

"Erik, give me a hand here," said Doctor Griffith. "I can't hold him up. I hope the stubborn s.o.b. hasn't killed himself."

Erik gathered Carnahan in his arms and carried him down to the emergency shelter as Doctor Griffith and Mother Catherine followed them down.

Chapter 18

Although Erik thought Carnahan's assumption that the helicopter incident was an aborted attack was correct, he decided to inspect the roof to ensure the helicopter had not faked the control problems as a ruse to drop targeting, incendiary, or other devices on the roof while hovering over it. Erik scanned the perimeter from each window through his night vision goggles, scrutinizing every stump, fern, shadow, or irregularity. After seeing no soldiers or police positioned around the convent, he crept out the east-facing main door, the exit least visible to anyone he may not have detected but who may have been watching, and pulled himself onto the wooden awning above the front door and crawled up onto the roof, then paused to listen. Erik then crept across the roof and searched for objects the helicopter crew may have dropped. Relieved at finding nothing, he climbed down and reentered the convent. Erik then shoved the eight hand grenades they had collected earlier into the pockets of his jacket, along with extra magazines for his rifle. Then he sat at the south window and watched as Laura watched from the west window.

Erik and Laura said little to one another as they continued their watch through the night. Almost imperceptibly, the weak light of morning crept over the convent. As Laura watched through the window, she noticed a fox stop to sniff the turned ground where she and Erik had buried the officers and then trot into the forest. There was still no sign of anyone around the perimeter. Then Bobby, carrying a food tray, walked into the room where Erik kept watch.

"I gotcha this, Erik. I gotcha some breakfast! I gotcha some for Laura, too! Where's Laura? I gotcha breakfast, Laura! Mother Caff'rn made you some sweet 'taytas and some fishes. She said you eat sweet 'taytas and fishes, and she made some. Got a thing full of water, too, so you can drink some water."

"Thank you, Bobby," said Erik, "I will take Laura's breakfast to her. Tell Mother Catherine that we appreciate this."

"Yeah, I'll tell her, but I wanna give Laura her breakfast. I wanna see Laura. I like Laura. I wanna see Laura."

"Good morning, Bobby, I am over here in this room," Laura called out, half-singing the words. "Come and say hello to me quickly, but then I want you to hurry back downstairs. I do not want you to be up here if the bad people return."

Bobby carried Laura's breakfast to her, gently sat it on a chair, and hugged her.

"You're my big sister. You're my big sister, Laura," Bobby said. "I like you. I'm your little brother, huh, Laura? Ain't I your little brother?"

Laura was surprised and, for a moment, unsure how to react. "Bobby," she said, "I would be proud to be your big sister. And I am proud to have you as my little brother. Thank you very much for bringing my breakfast. And remember, Bobby, big sisters always protect their little brothers, so I want you to go downstairs with the others now because we do not know when the bad people will return."

"But I ain't scared of them bad guys. You and Erik can sing, and they'll get scared, and I'll chase 'em away 'cause they'll be scared just like yesterday. You don't scare me when you sing, but the bad guys are scared when you sing."

UNTIL THE RESCUE SHIP ARRIVES

"It may not happen the same way today, Bobby, so if you want me to be your big sister, and if you want to be my little brother, please listen to me and go downstairs with everyone else. Mother Catherine, Sister Clare, and especially Lisa will want you to be in the shelter with them if the bad people return. If our friends downstairs become afraid, you can help them to be brave like you are. So, listen to your big sister and go downstairs now, Bobby. Will you do that?"

"But, I think Erik wants me to help him watch for bad guys. You want me to help watch, don'tya, Erik? You want me to help watch, don'tya?"

"No, Bobby. Listen to Laura and do as she asks," replied Erik from the other room. "I will come get you if I need you to help me."

"But I wanna do somethin'. I wanna fight them bad guys. I wanna do somethin'. I'm brave. I ain't scared."

Erik stepped into the room with Laura and Bobby. "There is something you can do for me, Bobby," he said, taking the rescue request launcher off his wrist. "Come here. Allow me to fasten this to your wrist. Here is how you open it. This light will tell you if the rescue ship is getting near."

"Is that a watch?" asked Bobby.

"No, it is very different from a watch. Do you see that blue light? If it begins blinking very fast, that means our rescue ship is getting near. When you see it begin blinking fast, I want you to run up here and give this back to me. But you must promise to keep this on your wrist until you give it back to me so you do not lose it. That is very important. And you must promise to take good care of it so you do not break it. Will you do that?"

"Yeah, I promise, I'm careful, and I promise if it's blinkin' fast, I'll tell you. I'll run up here and tell you if it's blinkin' fast. I won't touch nothin' on it, so I don't break it, and I'll tell you right away if it's blinkin' real fast."

"Thank you, Bobby, and if anybody asks why you have it, just tell them that you are helping me by wearing it."

"I'll tell 'em," replied Bobby. "I won't let 'em take it neither. If it's blinkin', I'll come tell you and give it back to you."

"You are a good, reliable soldier."

"Yeah, I'm a real, able soldier. And Lisa says I'm a marble, too."

"Lisa said you were a 'marvel,' Bobby," replied Laura.

"Yeah, I know. I'll watch for when that blue light starts blinkin' fast. I'll tell you, Erik, I'll tell you if it starts blinkin' fast."

After Erik clasped the rescue request launcher onto Bobby's wrist, Bobby bounded back down to the emergency shelter, excited at being given an important task. Erik returned to his post at the south window as he and Laura, who had settled again at her post at the west window, watched and quietly ate their breakfast. When they had finished, Erik walked into the room where Laura was keeping watch and told her he was moving to the east window near the convent's main entrance. Laura stood, grabbed her rifle, and said she would cover the north window.

"This planet's star is rising, my beloved," Erik whispered in the abbreviated version of their language," and although we have seen or heard nothing since the helicopter last night, I am sure they are organizing somewhere, near, but far enough away that we cannot see or hear them." We can do nothing if they attack with aircraft, but we can destroy a lone armored vehicle if we can get close enough to drop a grenade inside. Defeating two or more vehicles will be difficult but not impossible. I believe they will quietly bring their infantry through the forest and deploy them far enough outside the convent perimeter that we cannot see their movement as they surround us to prevent anyone from escaping. If they have armor, they will likely destroy the convent with their armored vehicles and then bring up their infantry to ensure that we all are dead. We can only make guesses, but that would be a good tactic for them. However, with the strange mixture of soldiers and police, as Carnahan described, and the confused command structure controlling it, they may make mistakes we can take advantage of. I must be in the forest when they arrive. I will see what they bring against us and how they deploy. I will look for vulnerabilities. If Carnahan is correct in his belief that the Resistance organization has sabotaged some of the regime's equipment and capabilities, that too may improve our chances of disrupting their attack long enough for the rescue ship to arrive. Whatever plan they have, though, we will adapt to it. We must strike them first, rob them of the initiative, force them to defend rather than attack, and keep them on the defensive as long as possible.

"You and I will scan the entire perimeter now, and if we see nothing, I will run into the forest to the east of us and scout the perimeter from within the forest. If they are not yet there, I will patrol the area until they arrive. When I believe there are enough of them in position for us to disrupt their attack, I will begin singing, and you will begin singing as soon as you hear me. If vehicle or aircraft noise doesn't smother the sound of our voices, we will at least scatter those who are on foot, create more confusion for them, and gain us more time. Our rescue ship must be near. May the All Holy One be pleased to have it arrive before the fighting begins."

"My dearest one," said Laura as she looked into his eyes, "you know that I am the one who should do this. You know that, even as gifted and capable as you are, I am faster than you and can outmaneuver even your best moves because I am lighter and nimbler. I will do this."

Erik reached toward her, stroked her face, and then hugged her. "What you say is true. But no, you will not go, and I do not need to explain why, do I?"

Still carrying her rifle, Laura hugged him tightly with her free arm. "No," she replied, "I know why. At this moment, I hate it, but I understand why."

She fully understood that his love for her, their family's honor, and his personal honor and self-respect compelled him to forbid her from performing a dangerous task for which he was physically capable. Not only was it a matter of personal integrity, but it was also woven into the many precepts contained within the "Traditions of the Warrior Brotherhood" that Erik and every young male of their race learned, letter and spirit, as solemnly taught, upheld, and handed on from father to son for many generations. As the young males progressed from childhood to young adulthood, they learned and lived according to these traditions long before their fathers presented them to the Council of Patriarchs to take the "Oath of Faith, Honor, and Courage." Nor would Laura allow herself to shame Erik and their family by dishonoring the "Traditions of the Sword and Shield Sisterhood," whose young female members also pledged fidelity to the "Oath of Faith, Honor, and Courage." Laura knew that deliberately weakening another's resolve to uphold their pledge was as severe a betrayal of the oath as failing to uphold it oneself. Their traditions required self-discipline and sacrifice, but doing so also made hard decisions clearer and easier to accept, and all knew that upholding their traditions was the mortar that held together their way of life.

Father Hughes walked into the room with Buster. "Do you think I could take Buster outside for a few minutes? It's been hours since he's had a chance to go out."

Erik scanned the edge of the forest again. "Father, you can try it, but stay on the east side, no more than a few strides from the door, and make him do his business quickly. We will watch for any movement around the perimeter. If we call out to you, run back inside whether Buster has finished or not."

Erik adjusted the night vision goggles for daylight enhancement and scanned the tree line around the perimeter from inside the convent house. Patiently, he adjusted the depth of field on the goggles to see more deeply into the forest with as much clarity and detail as possible. He noticed no movement. If the enemy was out there, Erik thought, they were exercising excellent discipline in their deployment.

Father Hughes gripped Buster's leash and grew nervous as Buster sniffed and wandered. "Come on, Buster Boy. We can't dally today," whispered Father Hughes.

When Buster finally finished, Father Hughes tugged on his leash, and they began to walk back to the house. Buster suddenly stopped and stared out toward the open field on the south side.

"What do you see, boy? What do you hear? Ah, I see it now. But you heard it before you saw it, didn't you?"

He pulled the reluctant Buster back toward the house. Laura was already at the door, hurrying them in.

"A small drone, Laura, to the south," said Father Hughes.

"Yes, Erik and I just saw it, too. It almost certainly saw you, but that would not reveal anything useful to them other than that you may have noticed their drone. It is unarmed but is probably gathering last-moment intelligence before they attack."

"I'm going back downstairs to offer mass while we still have a bit of time," said Father Hughes. "By the way, Bobby is downstairs, sitting in a corner by himself and not allowing anything to distract him from watching for the lights to change on the device you gave him. He's barely said a word. He just stares at the blue lights, waiting and ready to dash upstairs to let you know if they start blinking faster. For all our sakes, I pray that your rescue ship arrives soon—today—now!"

"Keep praying, Father. It should be very near by now," Laura replied.

"Oh, I almost forgot to tell you," said Father Hughes. "Major Carnahan has been lying in his cot and listening to a portable radio that can pick up shortwave radio transmissions. He heard a local ham radio operator say that the police blocked all of the roads in this area because of a chemical spill. Well, I think we know the real reason the roads are closed, don't we? And I think we also know it has nothing to do with a chemical spill. They have this area surrounded and cut off because they don't want civilians in the way when they attack us again. Carnahan told me that they may be having trouble planning their attack partly because they fear what you and Laura did to the last bunch who attacked us, and they aren't sure what other surprises you may have or how to plan for them. Carnahan says another worry they may have is they don't know how many of you there are—when the two of you sing, it sounds like dozens of voices to us humans. Despite all that, Carnahan still believes they will attack us today. He says they won't let this become a long standoff because that will allow too many unexpected problems to arise. Moreover, they must assume that you have help coming—which I hope will be confirmed for them very soon. Maybe they'll remain overly cautious for just a wee bit longer, just long enough for your rescue ship to get here first, eh?"

"Yes, Father, let us hope they delay for, as you say, 'just a wee bit longer,' and then we will give them many more surprises," replied Erik with a hint of a smile.

Father Hughes, amused by Erik's attempt at light-heartedness in the face of the looming dangers, winked at him and said, "I like your fighting spirit, young fellow. I think you may have an Irishman or two in your ancestry somewhere," which brought a low guttural chuckle from Erik."Okay, my friends," said Father Hughes, "I will get myself and Buster out of your way for now, but I am ready to help you anytime. Whatever you need from me, just let me know. I'll do whatever I can."

As Father Hughes led Buster down the steps to the emergency shelter, Erik and Laura moved from window to window, watching the drone crisscross the convent grounds until it finally disappeared into the heavy, gray clouds to the west. They continued moving from window to window for several more minutes, checking for movement around their perimeter.

"My dearest one, you must wait," said Laura. "I see another small drone flying over the guest cottage—look, now it is moving over the south edge of the property above the driveway. This one is not armed either, but it will see everything you do if you go outside.

"I agree," replied Erik. "I will wait a little longer, but I must get into the forest before the authorities are prepared to attack us. If drones continue flying over us, I may be able to shoot them down if there are only one or two of them flying low. We cannot time everything perfectly, but I must be out there in position to strike them first and throw them into such confusion that their attack falls to pieces. We have a difficult task, my beloved. I would much rather have you safe in our home than here, but I am also grateful to have you with me. I alone could never do the work that you and I together can do. Together, you and I may be able to rescue our friends as they have rescued us."

"Yes," replied Laura, "we will help our friends, and then, my beloved, we shall go home, home, home!"

Chapter 19

"Come on in. I've been waiting for you. You can talk in front of these gentlemen," said the square-jawed man. "They're all friends of ours. Your people are doing some impressive work considering how few they are and how big the risks they're taking."

"Thanks," replied the man dressed in oil-smudged mechanic's uniform as he walked into the room, lit only with a camping lantern hanging over the table, where the stocky, square-jawed man and two other men he didn't know were sitting. "They're all doing everything they can," he continued, "and you're right, there aren't many of them, but they're all in the right places. We and our people in the other Resistance cells caught the regime with its pants down this time, and we're pushing as hard as we can to keep the regime reacting to as many problems as we can create for them, everywhere we can, for as long as we can. Some of our people have already paid a heavy price for it. But because of their sacrifices, this regime and all the affiliated regimes in their world federation are learning a lesson about all the technology they rely on to keep everyone under their bootheels. The lesson is if everything works just right, all those complicated tools and assets can do amazing things. But if, for whatever funny reason there may be—let's say, for example, if a few components here and there in some key systems suddenly decide to stop working, all those complicated systems suddenly can't do a damned thing. Electricity stops flowing through the power lines, lights go dark, backup systems fail to back up, communication systems stop communicating, cameras go blind, and everything online goes offline. And if a few crafty little mischief makers here and there decide to transform expensive, high-tech police and military equipment into expensive, high-tech, non-functional police and military equipment, that is when the very naughty plans of very naughty people begin working very well."

The men at the table laughed, and the square-jawed man replied, "That's what we're hearing! We've been listening to shortwave reports from all over, and our disruptions are having a bigger effect than we dared to hope for. So far, we're hearing about electrical grid and communications failures occurring not only here in our region but also across this country and everywhere else in the world. Our saboteurs are hitting every weak link and target of opportunity, forcing the regime to spread their attention in a thousand different directions. Other friends of ours in other countries who have been monitoring shortwave transmissions are hearing reports like that, too, just as you say. It's affecting governments, militaries, and civilian systems across the board. We're hurting them in some countries worse than in others, but wherever it's happening, it's because our associates, outside and within the regimes, are hitting them where they know they can hurt them. Our friends in the military and law enforcement are sabotaging the systems and the equipment they use and interfering in every other way they can. So are the civilian technicians who are with us. Around here, as you can see, almost everything that uses electricity has, as they say, gone dark. So, good work, old man! Good work! Congratulations to you and all your people! You and all our other friends made this possible by helping us form the necessary contacts and relationships outside your immediate circles, which we needed to get this done. You didn't waste a minute."

UNTIL THE RESCUE SHIP ARRIVES

"I'll pass the compliments along," said the mechanic, "We all did our part in it. But now comes the hardest part—keeping the pressure on them, keeping them on the defensive until everything begins falling apart for them and coming together for us. My main concern is if we lose too many of our embedded people, we lose the initiative."

"I know, said the square-jawed man. "We need to know who's still operational and who's not as soon as possible. But I wanted to tell you before we get into other matters that our entire organization in this region realizes that our timing was perfect because of the tip your friend Carnahan gave you that you passed on to us. We wouldn't have launched the plan for several more weeks if he hadn't told you about this window of opportunity to hit the regime while its attention was focused on matters they thought were more important than hunting down those of us in the Resistance."

"Don't insult me by saying Carnahan is my friend," replied the mechanic. "I've always thought of him as a snake—especially lately. A couple of months ago, he had me rig a shut-off switch in his van so he could avoid being tracked by satellite. Who knows what scheme of his made him think that was necessary? And I don't know how he learned I had connections to the Resistance, and I don't know how long he's known, and I don't know why he didn't arrest me when he found out. Neither do I know how he learned that we were planning something big. But that's his job, so I suppose he got the info either from a mole he managed to put in place or by interrogating one of our people the old, hard way. The day he pulled me aside and told me to pass along the message to launch the plan early, I was worried that I had either just stepped into a trap or had unintentionally become the guide to lead him straight to you. But I decided to pass his message on and let you decide what to make of it. The results speak for themselves. We hit them good this time."

"We had a long discussion about Carnahan's tip before deciding to roll the dice on it," replied the square-jawed man as he lifted the coffee pot from the little propane stove. "After all, the source was Carnahan. He's pretty high on our target list, and I'm sure he knows it. But since he's known you were with us for who knows how long without arresting or questioning you, we decided to take a big chance that we could turn things to our advantage regardless of Carnahan's motive for telling us to launch the plan early. We still don't trust him, of course, and we don't yet know what his game is, so he's still on our list. But all of that aside, launching the plan when we did couldn't have worked out better. We needed a big win. Here, have a cup of coffee with us to celebrate. Enjoy it because it will be a hard-to-find commodity for a while."

"What have you heard from your people about the regime's reactions and retributions?" one of the other men at the table asked the mechanic. "They would have known almost immediately that most of this mayhem is sabotage from within. Have they arrested any of your people yet?"

"Just before I left work to come here, one of the cops who are with us told me that they shot two of our people at regional headquarters in Salem when they tried to run to avoid arrest," the mechanic replied. "I'm sure they knew they'd be shot before they ran twenty yards, but that was their way of avoiding giving up information under interrogation. The same cop also told me that a Special Security Police helicopter pilot carrying an assault team to attack a target aborted the mission before deploying the team. The pilot was another friend of ours—a young guy who joined us only a few months ago. He pretended to have control problems with the helicopter. Unfortunately, he didn't convince anybody, and as soon as they landed, the team he was carrying beat him up, interrogated him, and then shot him. I don't know if they got any damaging information from him. In addition to that story, I've heard other reports about some of our people here in the Northwest Region getting caught, but we haven't been able to confirm any details yet. We know we'll lose people, maybe even some of us here in this room before all this is over. That's just the cost of doing business. But no matter what, we have to stay on offense now. We have to keep enough of our embedded people alive and in the fight to keep the regime on the ropes."

"True enough. All the federated regimes will react like a bunch of wasps whose nest got knocked down if we allow them to sort themselves out and regroup," said the stocky, square-jawed man. "We have to keep the pressure on them, just like you say. We've staggered them, but we haven't beaten them. They still have all the muscle at their command. We have to keep hammering them and keeping them off balance until the citizens see that the regime isn't so omnipotent after all and realize that overthrowing them is possible, and this is their last chance to do it. We need to find more regime insiders brave enough to work with us, and we must make it clear to everyone that all of us together outnumber the regime many times over. When a few percentage points of citizens lose their fear and work with us, we can make the regime bleed from a million cuts and defeat them. But we have to do it before the regime reorganizes.

Another man at the table leaned forward. "One of my sources told me that the military is dealing with computer system malfunctions and electronic glitches cropping up in almost everything that isn't completely mechanical—which means just about everything except small arms. Several of my contacts told me that military communications are as crippled as civilian communications, so that part of the plan is working, too. Local television stations are down. Only a few scattered, low-power radio stations are transmitting on backup power. None of the internet, cable, or satellite systems are working—apparently, our hackers are pretty good. And since the saboteurs are our people working from the inside, they'll see that nothing gets repaired quickly. From what I've heard, it's only the clandestine shortwave and C.B. radio operators around the world, running battery-operated equipment, who are transmitting any information—and thanks to our saboteurs, the regime can't locate where those signals are coming from," he said with a chuckle."

"The downside to all this, though," replied the mechanic, "is that the hospitals and clinics will be affected because the supply chain is down. People will die. Quite a few medicines have been hard to get, but now, all medicines will be hard or impossible to find. When the trucks can't get fuel, they can't deliver medicine, food, or anything else. Food was already in short supply, but it will be impossible to find tomorrow. You can bet your last dime the regime will use food and medicine as bait and as a weapon, withholding it even when it's available and blaming us for the shortages to convince the people to turn against us. The list of coming complications is long. If these conditions linger too long or get worse, the citizens will hate us for the problems we're creating while we're trying to overthrow the regime. So, we need to win this very soon, or the citizens will decide that being a regime slave who gets a meager meal once or twice per day is better than not eating at all. We can't expect them to support us if we make them suffer too long. We must remember that before the regime grabbed power, people had grown soft and unprepared for hard times. So, Mr. and Mrs. John Q. Public will react to how their lives are now, not how they will be after we overthrow the Supreme Global Federation."

"Yes, we know all that," said the stocky, square-jawed man. "We have a few ideas that we hope will mitigate some of those problems, at least temporarily, but that's all I can tell you about that for now. One more thing," he added, "what do you know about this rumor that Carnahan is involved with space aliens? The question sounds so stupid when I hear myself say it that I'm almost too embarrassed to ask. And I wouldn't ask, except reliable, sensible sources have asked me if I know anything about it."

"I've heard that too," replied the mechanic. "Like you, I wouldn't give it a thought except that good people have told me they heard it from somebody they trust. All I know about it is that there are people higher up the chain of command than Carnahan who believe it. I did hear that two cops had an altercation with an alien on the highway by the coast, and I heard another rumor about some kind of mass hysteria breaking out among a couple of dozen cops who tried to raid a building where an alien was supposed to be hiding. But who knows how far down the gossip trail these stories have traveled? You can't put any value on any of them. Some say the increase in spot checks, roadblocks, and cops everywhere you go is part of the hunt for the alien. So, is the alien story true? Who knows? Almost anything could be true these days."

Chapter 20

After nearly an hour, the drones ceased flying over the convent grounds, so Erik prepared to dash into the forest ahead of the expected attack.

"I know you will defend our friends well, my beloved," said Erik. "If their infantry charges the convent, they will be easy targets when they reach the open ground. I will leave half of the grenades with you. You may need them, too."

"No!" replied Laura. "You will take them all. You will have a much better opportunity to use them than I will. We will not argue about this."

Suddenly, Bobby bolted into the room.

"Erik! Erik! I'm sorry, Erik! I went to sleep, but it's blinkin' real fast now! The lights are blinkin' fast! I'm sorry, Erik! I went to sleep, but they're blinkin' fast now!"

"How long were you asleep, Bobby?"

"I don't know! But it's blinkin' fast now! I'm sorry, Erik. I didn't want to go to sleep. It was a accident. I went to sleep, but I'm sorry. It was a accident. Are you mad?"

"No, Bobby, I am not angry with you. Did anyone else notice when the lights began to blink faster?"

"Hu-uh. Nobody but me was watchin'. Was I bad? Will somethin' bad happen 'cause I fell asleep, and I don't know how long it's been blinkin'?"

"Do not be upset, Bobby. I know you wanted to do a good job. The rescue ship is very close now. Good things will happen when it arrives."

"So, you ain't mad at me?"

"No, Bobby. Father Hughes told me you were focusing very hard on your task."

"Yeah, Erik, I was focusin'. I was focusin' real hard, but I fell asleep. I didn't mean to. Is the rescue thing comin' in a few minutes to kill the bad guys and take you home?"

"I do not yet know when it will arrive or what it will do, but it will do whatever is needed to help us. Give me the rescue request launcher now, Bobby, and go back downstairs with the others. Laura or I will call for you if we need your help with anything else. Thank you, my friend. You did well."

"Yeah, I did well, and I didn't mean to go to sleep. I watched it and watched it. You're really not mad?"

"No, I am not angry, Bobby. I still believe that you are a good soldier."

"Yeah, I'm a soldier. You tell me if you got another job for me. I won't go to sleep. I promise. It was a accident."

"I believe you, Bobby. Tell everyone downstairs that the rescue ship may arrive soon. And stay down there with them so we know where to find you if we need your help again."

Erik fastened the rescue request launcher onto his wrist. Suddenly, he and Laura heard singing from the emergency shelter.

"I do not know what they are singing, my beloved," said Erik, "but I think it is one of the songs they sing to the All Holy One. We should take a moment to petition him in our way, but quietly so we do not upset our friends."

Singing in low whispers, Erik and Laura offered a short, simplified version of one of their hymns as they watched the convent perimeter. When they finished their hymn, they could hear the sisters and the others continuing to sing. To Laura and Erik, the voices of the humans, even the best voices, sounded harsh, strained, and shallow, but they understood the sentiment behind those voices. This understanding generated feelings of affection in Erik and Laura toward the simple melodies of their human friends that otherwise would have grated on their more gifted ears.

Once again, Erik scanned the forest edges with the goggles, adjusting the depth of field for clarity at various distances into the forest's shadows.

"Listen! Vehicles!" shouted Laura.

Erik paused and heard the faint, barely perceptible sound of an engine to the west of the convent. "I am late, my beloved. I must hurry," Erik said. He patted his jacket pockets to assure himself that the grenades and extra magazines were secure. "We shall do as we have planned. Keep extra magazines in your pockets at all times. Remember, I love you, and I will take you back to our home. Neither of us will die on this planet. Both of us will go home. That is my promise to you, and may the All Holy One assist me in fulfilling it."

"Go now, my dearest one. Fight well and destroy the enemy. And remember, you are taking my heart with you," said Laura, using their race's traditional parting phrase to a loved one leaving for battle.

"My heart remains with you until I return," replied Erik, completing the traditional parting. He then turned and dashed out of the east door.

Erik crouched as he ran east into the forest. When he was far enough into the trees that he could no longer see the buildings or the convent grounds, he slowed his pace, patrolled silently toward the south, and then angled to the west. Erik paused and listened at irregular intervals, repeating this pattern as he patrolled. The sound of the vehicle engine emanated from somewhere in the forest ahead of him to the west. He crouched and listened. Then he heard someone shout, and someone else replied with a shout. He marveled at their lack of effort to maintain even a modicum of silence. He realized he had given them too much credit earlier when he thought they could have assembled inside the forest but were exercising good discipline. Erik was encouraged by the probability that these were low-quality troops led by an equally low-quality officer. If so, this would be a valuable gift. Erik removed the goggles from his pocket and scanned the area where the shouting had come from. As he adjusted the depth of field on the goggles, he saw movement in the gaps of the foliage and trees due west of him. Erik then pocketed the goggles and, like a hunter stalking prey, crept forward, testing each step for the feel of a twig that would snap under his weight, changing his footing when necessary. Soon, he was near enough to see glimpses through the foliage of men standing around an armored personnel carrier that had moved into place. Erik watched and listened as the man in command of the mixed collection of soldiers and Special Security Police climbed onto the roof of the armored personnel carrier and barked a few unintelligible orders. Erik noticed several men he had not previously seen rise and move to different positions nearer the forest edge bordering the open grounds of the convent. Then he heard twigs snapping and the rustling of branches as other men also shifted their positions. Eric mentally noted the general location of each and stalked toward the nearest one.

He regretted having been delayed by the drones and not entering the forest before the regime's forces arrived. Even so, he was encouraged that this attack appeared as haphazard and disorganized as the previous one and led by an unimpressive officer commanding poorly trained, poorly disciplined men thrown together piecemeal. These failings on their part made him smile. He knew that he and his beloved could throw this collection of rabble and their plan into disarray, hopefully long enough for the rescue ship to arrive. If only the rescue ship were here now, he thought. It would be nothing for it to deal with this inept assembly of humans. However, it was not yet here.

Erik knew that nothing could prevent violence now. These men surely would not treat the people in the convent mercifully even if they surrendered. Undisciplined soldiers and police are always a danger to civilians, and those who were now preparing to attack had a score to settle with the occupants of the convent, doubling the danger. These men would destroy the convent and everyone in it. Unrestrained aggression against these troops was justifiable and necessary if he hoped to prevail. Nothing he and his beloved did now would worsen their fate or the fate of their friends in the convent. He and she would create a devastating storm of shock, terror, and destruction with their voices and the captured human weapons to buy themselves more time. For a moment, he imagined how beautiful would be the sight of that gray orb, the rescue ship, if it suddenly appeared and unleashed its tiny defender orbs. The orbs would destroy these humans before they knew what had happened. How much more time must he steal from the regime to keep everyone inside the convent alive until the rescue ship landed? Could he do it? Of course, he could do it, he said to himself as he recognized the voice of doubt whispering in his ear.

Erik crawled into a slight depression behind a tree with a broad, thick trunk, only a dozen paces from where he believed the nearest soldiers had positioned themselves. He rolled onto his back, drew a full breath, and began singing with all his voices and all the volume he could generate. At once, he heard Laura's chorus of voices joining with his. Erik's low, thunderous, reverberating harmonies rumbled through the forest and over the startled men as Laura's higher range of voices surrounded them with choruses of such perfection and purity that the men, uncertain of what these strange choruses portended, began to tremble as fear settled upon them. Then, in precise unison, Erik and Laura shifted from vocalizations of indescribable beauty and broke into a dense tangle of menacing, tormented wailings that sounded like the roof of Hell had ripped open, releasing the deafening cacophony of horror rising from the damned.

Within moments, the most susceptible men began running through the forest, overcome by the guttural roars, shrieks, and torturous screaming and moaning that filled the air around them, crushing their sanity in the grip of the malevolent howls of damnation that filled the air around them.

One man leaped up and bolted past Erik, tripping, stumbling, and rising again as he tried to outrun the sense of doom that he carried with him as he ran. Another panicked trooper ran past, pleading for mercy. Yet another soldier, already emotionally incapacitated, howled nonsensical syllables as he crashed through the forest. Then Erik heard a long, agonizing scream from only yards away, followed by a single gunshot. Erik heard other men crouching around the armored personnel carrier bellowing like injured animals as they succumbed to their inner self-accusations.

Then bursts of automatic rifle fire cracked and ricocheted through the forest, followed by the thumping of the personnel carrier's heavy machine gun as the emotionally tougher men and the troopers inside the vehicle that had somewhat muffled the effects of Erik and Laura's voices desperately forced themselves to lay down suppressing fire to drown out and perhaps destroy the source of the overpowering, incapacitating vocalizations that seemed to emanate from every direction, but which they apparently believed originated somewhere in the forest around them. Small tree branches and pieces of tree bark fell on Erik, and chunks of dirt kicked up by bullets striking near him spattered him. Tumbling ricochets buzzed through the air as the torrent of projectiles ripped through the forest and lashed the undergrowth around him. The fusillade, joined now by a few more troopers who, clinging to their last threads of self-control, continued to fire their weapons in an indiscriminate arc, cutting down some of the panicking police and soldiers as efficiently as it cut down foliage and tree branches. Without pause, Erik kept singing, ignoring the fleeing men who often ran or fell dead within yards of him.

Then the firing stopped, but Erik and Laura kept singing. Soldiers and police continued to blunder through the forest in a hopeless attempt to flee from the inescapable horror of the guilt that gripped them. Then Erik realized the reason for the sudden ceasefire. He heard the engine of another vehicle.

Immediately, Erik stopped singing the tormenting tones and called out a wavering three-toned call that prompted Laura to stop singing. Erik sprang to his feet and sprinted toward the sound of the first vehicle. He ran upon the original armored vehicle behind which four men crouched. Erik fired a burst from his rifle, killing the four men. Then he jumped onto the vehicle, threw a grenade into the open turret, and dove to the ground. After the grenade detonated, Erik ran toward the second vehicle and crew, which he could now partially see through the thick foliage. He fell to the ground when the heavy machine gun from the newly arrived personnel carrier fired a blind burst in his direction, again without regard for any of their comrades who may have been in the line of fire. Erik hurled another grenade toward them, followed by another after the first grenade detonated. He then ran parallel to their right flank and maneuvered to their rear, taking advantage of their undisciplined firing to mask the noise of his sprinting through the undergrowth toward them. When Erik was at their rear, he darted from one position to another, stopping, looking, then dashing to the next position. The firing paused again, and he listened to the men's voices as they tried to assess their situation.

"Two o'clock! I hear something at two o'clock," yelled one of the men, and the heavy machine fired a burst toward their two o'clock position, followed by a volley of rifle fire toward the same area.

"Whatever, whoever that is, it's all around us, Sergeant! They're everywhere!"

"Keep your head together, damn it! All of you!"

"But what's going on? What the hell's out there? What...."

"Shut up! We're all rattled, but we're still here and still alive because we kept control of ourselves—maybe just barely, but we didn't fall apart and run like the rest of them. Everybody who cracked up and ran away is probably dead."

When's the rest of our platoon gonna get here?" someone yelled.

"How the hell should I know? You saw what it was like at HQ. They're just throwing together whoever they can find, along with whatever vehicles they can get running to send with them. I think both the lieutenant and the sergeant of the platoon we were supposed to link up with are either dead or ran away, so until somebody else shows up, it's just us with me in command of this mess. We need to know how many of us are left. But don't sound off! That'll tell whatever is out there where everybody is, too. How many can you see who can still fight?"

"Eleven, that I can see," replied one of the men after a pause. "There may be others out there hiding, though."

"Let 'em hide! Eleven of us can handle this with what we have," said the man in the turret. "This old rust bucket may only have a Ma Deuce, but .50 cal' will chew 'em up. Let's level the buildings, kill everything that runs out, and get the hell out of here, Sarge."

"I like it. But we'll wait another ten minutes and see if anybody who can still fight joins us. Then we'll blow this place to hell. Now, spread out. Make a perimeter. Crawl and keep low. Whoever or whatever attacked us is still out there, and we don't know which direction they'll be coming from. I've got a feeling we haven't killed any of them yet."

As Erik listened to the conversation, he crawled toward the men positioned around the personnel carrier. He had to destroy the vehicle and its machine gun. Rounds from its heavy machine gun would smash through the convent walls as if they were tissue paper. No one inside the building who wasn't below ground in the emergency shelter would be safe. He could now see that the vehicle was parked facing the convent. But another piece of luck for him: the rear ramp was open.

Silently, Erik rose to a crouch and crept forward until he saw five of the eleven men and was now in full view of the rear of the armored vehicle. He threw a grenade into the open rear of the personnel carrier. While the grenade was still arcing through the air, he opened fire on the five men near the vehicle and then dropped to the ground. As soon as the grenade detonated, Erik leaped up and charged the vehicle. One man, bleeding badly, tried to raise his rifle, but Erik fired three quick rounds into him, then hurled another grenade over the vehicle, landing it in front of it in case other troops were there. The grenade detonated, and Erik charged forward. No one was there. He dropped to the ground and listened. He had killed the vehicle commander and the man in the turret with a grenade and five others with his rifle, but where were the four other men they had counted? For nearly a full minute, he barely breathed, hoping to hear the faintest sound to reveal the location of the four men who were still out there and capable of fighting, but he heard nothing. He then crawled around the vehicle and paused to retrieve eight more grenades and six more magazines of ammunition from the men he had just killed, filling his pockets to the limit of their capacity. He inserted a fresh magazine into his rifle, climbed to the top of the vehicle, and after taking a moment to figure out how to open the breach to the heavy machine gun, he opened the breach, laid a grenade on it, pulled the pin and jumped to the ground and lay flat on his stomach. After the grenade exploded, Erik ran back to the first vehicle and disabled its heavy machine gun. He lay silent and listened, surprised no one had opened fire during his movement. Then, he rose to a crouch and began working his way back toward the convent to give his beloved some of the extra grenades and ammunition he had captured. Erik paralleled the edge of the forest, staying far enough inside its edge to avoid being seen by a casual glance but near enough to notice any movement in or near the open areas of the convent grounds. He chose not to hunt for the four remaining men, who, if alive, he assumed were demoralized and hiding until others arrived.

At that moment, with just himself, a rifle, and a few grenades, a meager arsenal which, so far, had sufficed, he felt grateful to the Distant Voyager Service for training them to handle some of the common weapons used by humans. As Erik crept through the undergrowth, he discovered several soldiers and Special Security Police lying dead, some from gunshot wounds, others simply from terror. He cautiously stepped over them, his eyes searching for movement as he slipped through the forest. Then he discovered two men a few yards ahead of him lying prone at the edge of the open convent grounds, their rifles shouldered and trained on the convent, ready to kill anyone who ran across the open grounds, stepped out a door, or appeared at a window. Erik aimed his rifle and made a clicking noise with his tongue. The two soldiers jolted in surprise and rolled to face whoever had caused the noise as they raised their rifles. Erik fired two short bursts. Were there now only two more soldiers hiding out there somewhere, he wondered, or were these just two among many others who were unaccounted for but still capable of fighting? Erik pocketed two grenades from one of the men he had just killed before moving on until he reached a position where, if he chose to do so, he could dash across a mere hundred yards of open ground to get back to the convent. If he retraced his steps from earlier and returned to the convent from the less-exposed east, it would require several more minutes of slow patrolling, and he might not be in a position to respond quickly if fresh regime forces appeared and attacked while he was on the eastern edge of the forest.

Erik paused at the forest's edge for several minutes, listening and watching for movement in the forest and the perimeter. He saw nothing. Erik dashed toward the convent. Immediately, rounds from a light machine gun cracked the air as they passed him. Then, several rifles opened fire. Erik fired a wild burst from his rifle toward the area from where the light machine gun tracers were coming. A burst of fire erupted from a window of the convent. Laura, his incomparable Laura, was giving him covering fire. Then, another rifle began firing from another window. "Griffith!" he said out aloud. That has to be Griffith."

Rather than leaping and tumbling as he ran, Erik raced toward the convent at full speed, returning fire as he ran. Then, a third rifle opened fire, covering Erik from another window of the convent. "Carnahan!" he said to himself. "How can he?"

His heart swelled with admiration for all of them as they laid suppressing fire on the machine gun, which was now only firing intermittently. Suddenly, two jolting blows knocked him to the ground. He rose again and ran as more rounds ripped past him, then he was knocked down again. This time, he could barely move. He struggled to his knees as bullets thumped into the dirt around him. Then he saw Laura, rifle in hand, bolt through the convent door and run, then leap, roll, and zigzag with a speed, fluidity, and grace that no human nor any other earth creature could equal. He feared for her, but he didn't try to dissuade her. He knew her too well. She, the treasure of his soul, who he had vowed to protect and bring safely home, was now racing to protect and save him. For a moment, he was so awash with love for her that he barely noticed his pain. He turned and fired to distract some of the fire away from Laura as she raced toward him, knowing she had little chance of dragging him to cover, but her resolve that they would return home together or die together was unshakeable.

Erik suddenly lost his equilibrium and fell onto his side.

"No! No!" he growled, shaking away the deadly temptation creeping over him to close his eyes. "It will not end this way!" He could not die, leaving her exposed in the open with bullets sailing past her. He had promised her they both would live and return home together. He could not fail her.

He inhaled a painful breath, forced himself to his feet, and fired another burst toward the machine gun. He stumbled toward Laura and continued to fire at the light machine gun as Laura ran toward him. Laura was within one stride of him when a bullet struck her in the side, and she fell. Erik heaved himself toward her and caught her as they both tumbled to the ground. They immediately rolled to their sides and fired a long burst toward their enemies, changed magazines, fired several more bursts, and changed magazines again.

As Griffith and Carnahan continued firing to cover them, Erik stood and pulled Laura to her feet. Defying their wounds, they tried to run, linking arms to steady one another. Another rifle round then struck Laura in the back. She gasped and clutched the sleeve of Erik's jacket as she slid to the ground. Erik dropped to the ground and rolled on top of her to protect her from being hit again. He tried to purge from his mind the fear that she was dead. As they lay there, Erik, uncertain of his own wounds, whispered to Laura his assurances that she would live and that they would return home. Laura lay silent, her eyes closed. Grief washed over him. He felt his strength and resolve bleeding away as the blood of his beloved mingled with his on the ground where they lay. He held her tightly and closed his eyes, rocking her gently in his arms. A softness settled over him, and he barely heard the continuing fusillade. It was death, gently stroking his face, inviting him to join his beloved.

Then Erik opened his eyes and roared. He stood, lifted Laura into his arms, and began staggering toward the convent. Incoming fire from the troopers and return fire from Carnahan and Griffith filled the air as Erik forced himself onward, remaining conscious only by force of will, barely staying on his feet. He bent his upper body over Laura to shield her as she lay limp in his arms as he hobbled toward the house, dragging his feet now with each step.

Suddenly, all firing from the convent ceased. Doctor Griffith and Father Hughes rushed out the east door. Griffith ran like a man thirty years his junior while Father Hughes, stiff-legged but determined to help, hustled as fast as his knees permitted.

"Give me that, Erik!" demanded Griffith as he grabbed Erik's rifle that hung around his neck and began returning fire. "Keep going!" Griffith yelled. "We ran out of ammo in the house."

"Doctor. Three magazines in my left pocket," grunted Erik, breathing heavily, "Take them."

"Give her to me, Erik," said Father Hughes as he reached to take Laura.

"No! Just keep me on my feet! Keep me from falling!"

As Doctor Griffith fired short bursts, Father Hughes positioned himself between Erik and the enemy fire, supporting Erik's left arm to help him carry Laura and wrapping his arm around Erik's waist to steady him. A rifle bullet hit Erik's back, another bullet struck Father Hughes in the thigh, and they fell to the ground. As Erik fell, he turned to land on his side with his back toward the incoming fire to protect Laura. The wounded Father Hughes rolled onto his side, shielding with his body Erik's head and back. Doctor Griffith ran to a different position to draw fire away from Erik, Laura, and Father Hughes as he fired single rounds to conserve ammunition.

During the blur and tunnel vision of action, no one noticed the dull gray sphere, barely twenty feet in diameter, silently appear on the wet grass thirty yards from the convent house. Suddenly, a flash of light erupted from the top of the orb as a stream of gray, tennis ball-sized orbs launched from the larger craft and streaked toward the enemy troopers. Rapid flashes of blue light burst from each orb, creating a long series of reports, like strings of firecrackers exploding, echoing through the forest and across the convent grounds. Scattered, narrow columns of smoke rose around the forest perimeter, accompanied by the yelps and screams of dying men. Then, in less than two minutes, there was only silence and the smell of smoke. The orbs then flew to the northwest, where, in the distance, muffled cracking and popping indicated that the orbs had discovered the anticipated reinforcements. After only a few minutes, the orbs returned, swarmed briefly around the convent, and then hovered in a stationary perimeter above the trees around the convent grounds.

Aware now of the rescue ship, Erik struggled to his knees. The wounded Father Hughes rolled himself to a sitting position and tried to steady Erik as he attempted to stand while holding Laura in his arms.

"Stay put, Gerald, I'll help him," said Doctor Griffith. "Erik, let me take her for you."

"No! No! I will carry her. Just help me to my feet!" barked Erik.

"You're hit bad, young man, let me . . . ."

"No!" growled Erik. Then, with a deep gurgling groan, bleeding and breathing heavily but still cradling Laura, Erik rose to his feet and shuffled toward the rescue ship.

Bobby ran out of the convent. Lisa, Sister Clare, Mother Catherine, and all the sisters dashed out the door behind Bobby to stop him, but he outran them.

UNTIL THE RESCUE SHIP ARRIVES

Bobby ran up to Erik. "You're hurt, Erik! I'll help. I'll carry her, Erik! I'm strong! The big ball thing is here! Don't die, Erik. Let me help you! Oh, Laura! You're my big sister! Don't die, Laura! Don't die!! The big ball thing! It's here, Laura! Oh, Laura! Don't die! Don't die, Erik! Please! It's here now! It's here! Please, please, let me help!"

"No . . . go back, Bobby . . . go back to . . . to . . . ." Erik couldn't finish the sentence. He could barely breathe as he plodded toward the rescue ship.

"Please, Erik! You're hurt bad, Erik. I don't want you to die! You're my big brother, Erik! You're my big brother! Let me help! Please, please, let me carry Laura!"

Doctor Griffith gently grabbed Bobby by the arm. "Leave him alone, Bobby. He wants to do this himself."

Bobby tried to pull free of Doctor Griffith and reached for Erik. "Let me carry Laura! I'm a good soldier! I'll help you carry her! Don't die, Erik! Please! Please!"

Erik didn't reply, saving the last of his energy to carry his beloved to the rescue ship.

Bobby slumped to his knees. "I'm sorry I went to sleep, Erik," he cried. "I'm sorry I didn't see the lights cuz I was sleepin'! Please, Erik, I didn't mean to fall asleep! Don't die, Erik! Don't die, Laura!"

Erik said nothing as he stared at Laura's face and plodded toward the rescue ship.

Lisa grabbed Bobby, hugged him, and, with difficulty, pulled him up from the ground. "Come on, Bobby, my sweet. Leave Erik alone. You might cause him to drop Laura. You don't want him to do that, do you?"

"Huh-uh, I don't want him to drop Laura. She'll die, and he'll die, just like Mama and Daddy. I don't want nobody to die no more. Nobody. I don't want Erik dead. I don't want Laura dead. I don't want Daddy and Mama dead. I don't want nobody dead no more. No more, no more, no more!"

Lisa gently embraced Bobby as he wept, gently swaying with him as if she were rocking and soothing a baby. "Oh, Bobby, my precious little Bobby, I know you miss your mama and daddy, sweetheart, but I'll be your mama if you want me to be. I'll be your mama."

Mother Catherine, Sister Clare, and the other sisters gathered around Erik and Laura, following them closely, ready to catch them if they fell, and whispering prayers as they followed them.

As Erik carried Laura toward the ship, Doctor Griffith felt Laura's wrist for a pulse and tried to lift her eyelids to look at her pupils. Erik shoved him aside with his shoulder.

"She lives! Do not touch her!" Erik growled.

"I think she's gone, Erik. I felt . . . ."

"No! She lives! We are going home! We . . . we are . . . going home."

"Erik, please," implored Sister Clare, "we all love Laura. Let us help you carry her."

"No! My beloved lives! I will carry her home. I . . . I . . . ."

Erik, soaked with his and Laura's blood, halted, swayed, and, for a moment, looked as if he were about to die while holding Laura in his arms.

"Look! There is our home!" he said as he lifted his head, his eyelids fluttering, blood trickling from the corners of his mouth. "There is our home! Do you see? I am taking her . . . home. I promised . . . I would take her . . . home."

Erik attempted to sing something in their language but coughed blood. Then he spat, grimaced, lifted Laura higher, pressed his cheek to hers, and shuffled toward the rescue ship. Everyone pressed in as closely as they dared, their arms instinctively half-extended, ready to catch Erik if he fell as he carried Laura. No one dared to say anything more to him, not knowing how he would react in his pain and his rapidly clouding mind.

UNTIL THE RESCUE SHIP ARRIVES

A door noiselessly opened on the rescue ship. Everyone halted as a slender robot ran out of the spacecraft toward Erik. The robot was dull gray, as was the rescue ship. It had four tentacle-like arms, each with a five-fingered hand, walked on two legs, and had no head, only a slight hump between its shoulders where a head would otherwise be. It sang a short, intricate phrase to Erik, who then allowed it to take Laura into its two lower arms. It then wrapped its two remaining arms around Erik, who collapsed in its embrace. As it held Erik and Laura, it turned toward the group of humans who were staring in awe.

"You are safe. You have nothing to fear now," it said in a clear, calm, human-sounding voice. "You are under our protection. Wait here. I will return. I have some things to say to you." It then carried Erik and Laura into the rescue ship.

As they waited, they watched the small defender orbs individually circling, flying away, returning, without any pattern, each one going in a different direction but always several remaining in the air around the convent grounds. The orbs made no sound as they flew, not even a rush of air. They were like round, gray spirits gliding silently through the material world around them.

Everyone gathered around Father Hughes as Doctor Griffith knelt beside him and applied a hasty bandage around his leg wound.

"Mother Catherine, sisters, let us offer a prayer for our friends," Father Hughes said as he sat on the ground and made the Sign of the Cross, "In nomine Patris, et Filii, et Spiritus Sancti...."

When they finished praying, Father Hughes turned away from the group and buried his face in his hands. Sister Clare stepped toward Father Hughes, but Mother Catherine gently stopped her.

"No, Sister," whispered Mother Catherine as she leaned close to Sister Clare. "I'll speak to him. He and I have known one another for many years. I know how to talk to him."

Mother Catherine leaned over, placed her hand on Doctor Griffith's shoulder, and said, "Doctor, maybe you should check on Major Carnahan. He's still all alone, sitting inside by the window, you know."

Doctor Griffith looked up at her and, understanding her intention, turned again toward Father Hughes and said, "Mother Catherine is right, Gerald. I should check on Carnahan. He exerted himself way more than he should have. I'll be back in a few minutes to check on you. When that robot returns, I'll ask him if he'll do something to help you and Carnahan while he's here."

As Doctor Griffith walked away, Mother Catherine placed her hand on Father Hughes's shoulder. "Father, I was very unfair to you during our conversation in my office. I was wrong, terribly wrong, to suggest that you are responsible for all that has happened. All the fault rests on the prideful regime, behaving as tyrants always behave, bringing evil upon people and, ultimately, upon themselves. You did a loving thing, Father. If you had not brought Laura and Erik here, who knows what they would have suffered at the hands of those devils? And all of those men lying dead now out there in the forest—it is their superiors' blind obedience to evil orders that killed them. Their blood is on the hands of their leaders, not yours, Father."

Father Hughes sat silently, his face still buried in his hands.

"Where, Father," Mother Catherine continued, "where along the way during all of this could you have done anything that would have brought a better outcome? You know you did the right thing, and we both know you would do it again, even if it cost you your life. Perhaps you forgot something you told me just a few hours ago. Do you remember? You reminded me of our history. You reminded me that, through the centuries, our convents and monasteries have sometimes served as refuges to hide people from those who abused their authority. Sometimes, the consequences of helping others were horrible, but our predecessors certainly would do it all again, just as you would, because it was the right and moral thing to do. So, give yourself some credit instead of blame, Father. Let me suggest this: Over the years, you have heard confessions covering every conceivable sin, and sometimes what you heard weren't sins at all but merely someone judging himself too harshly. Think of the advice and encouragement you gave to them. Give yourself that same advice, that same reviving encouragement."

Father Hughes lifted his head and looked up at Mother Catherine. "I'm alright, Mother. Really. I'm alright. I was just a bit overwhelmed for a moment, that's all. I'm alright, though. Thank you, my dear friend. Go on, now, and help keep the others calm. I'll wait here until Paul returns to finish doing whatever he's going to do for my wound."

The fifteen minutes they waited outside the rescue ship seemed like hours, but finally, the door opened, and the robot walked out to them. The sisters covered their mouths, some hid their faces in their hands, and others clutched the arm of the person nearest them, dreading the news they expected the robot to tell them.

"Everyone, please listen," the robot began. "Your two friends, whom you have named Erik and Laura, are alive. They have severe wounds, but they are much stronger than you humans. Our medical and surgical capabilities will heal them. To help them heal, I will keep them unconscious as I treat their wounds during the voyage back to our world. Shortly before I landed this spaceship, I received a message that Erik had transmitted to me with the details of their experiences during this voyage and their time spent among you. He told me about all of you. You have earned the gratitude of our entire race. I am a machine, but I speak for those who built me. Our people will never forget your love, courage, and sacrifices. We would not have expected this from your people, but you have taught us that we still have much to learn about your race. I assure you that Erik and Laura will always carry you in their hearts. I know this because

Erik said so in his message. He and Laura will dearly miss all of you. This voyage is their last. They will now return to their village and their family. They will heal and become strong and healthy again. It will, however, be difficult for them to live the quiet, private life they hope to live because they will now be historical figures in our world. Their names and their experiences among you here on this planet will be written into the history of our race, and your names will be remembered alongside theirs for as long as our world exists.

"We will be leaving you soon," the robot continued, "but we are not leaving you to the mercy of your enemies. As you have learned from Erik and Laura, we detest tyrants. You have seen the small orbs flying all around you. Each of you here will have one of these orbs assigned to you as your protector to watch over you wherever you go. You may not always see it, but it will always be with you. Nothing in this world can harm you as long as your protector remains on this planet with you. You have seen an example of what these devices can do. If an entire army of soldiers tried to abduct you, they would be dead in moments. However, they can also protect you with non-lethal means. The orbs are intelligent. They know when lethal force is necessary and when it is not. The orbs will understand you when you speak to them. You can tell them anything you want them to know, whatever that may be. If necessary, they can remain here with you for slightly more than five of your years before they will need to return to our world to replenish their power supply. When the time comes for them to return to our world, your orb will hover near your face and flash red five times. That is the signal telling you it is leaving.

"Meanwhile, your world will experience some hardships because the orbs not serving as your protectors will selectively destroy much of the technological and military assets of the tyrants. When possible, during these attacks, they will spare the lives of your enemies, but sparing their lives is a secondary concern. Many of their people will die. Unfortunately, the same technologies that help the tyrants enslave you intertwine with the infrastructure that provides your necessary goods and services. It is impossible to destroy your oppressors' advantages over you without causing you hardship. We will try to limit these difficulties as much as possible, but at least for a while, your lives will not be easy.

"During these disruptions, the tyrants will be weakened. Your resistance organizations can defeat them if they take advantage of this opportunity. As we stand here, some of the several hundred orbs I have deployed are already attacking various targets. The orbs will carry out these attacks throughout the world, night and day, wherever necessary, until you overthrow the Supreme Global Federation, as it calls itself, or until the orbs must return home. We will provide you the opportunity to reclaim your freedom. Use this time well. Remember how this tyranny became possible. It is up to you to ensure it can never be possible again. I have told you what the orbs will do. You will do the rest. Your people will do the fighting. Victory must be your gift to yourselves. Only then will you value and defend it as vigorously as you must. But in the limited ways I have described, we will help you. We owe you our help because you helped our people, knowing it could bring grave danger upon you. We admire courage and those who make sacrifices to help others. We sympathize with desperate, righteous causes, and we believe every desperate, righteous cause deserves at least one ally. Now, do your part. Ensure that your resistance organizations attack and remain on offense until you prevail. You will not have another opportunity like this."

"But we don't know anyone in the Resistance," replied Mother Catherine.

"I do!"

Everyone turned to see who had spoken. Doctor Griffith had pushed Carnahan in a wheelchair to where the group had gathered.

"I saw this thing folded up in the corner of the emergency shelter," Carnahan said, pointing to the wheelchair," so I had Doc get it out and chauffer me up here. As I said, I know a few people in the Resistance. They don't like me much right now because I was the man who hunted them, but I think I can charm them enough to make them listen to me. The disruptions you mention are exactly what the Resistance has been trying to do, but their efforts have only been of limited, temporary effectiveness. So, you can believe they'll make full use of your help when they learn what's going on. You bet they will."

"You are Thomas Carnahan," said the robot, "I will treat for your wounds. After treatment, you will walk back to the house feeling strong and breathing normally. In seven or eight days, you will be healthier than you have ever been before."

Then, the robot turned toward Father Hughes. "You are the priest, Father Hughes, who saved Laura from dying on the beach. I will treat your wound. You will walk out of our spacecraft without assistance, and in two days, your wounds will be merely red marks on your leg."

"Will this treatment fix my bad knees, too?" Father Hughes asked.

"I will heal your knees, too,' replied the robot.

"Mister, I don't know what to call you," said Doctor Griffith," but may I see what these treatments are, how you do them, and how they work? I'm a doctor. I'd like to see what you do if you don't mind."

"You are Doctor Griffith," said the robot."Yes, you may watch. You will not understand everything you see, and I will not try to explain all of it, but you may watch the procedures. Erik also told me to give you our supply of nutritional wafers, which have been helpful to Carnahan. They are not difficult to manufacture. They will be beneficial to your race and will save the lives of many of your people. Father Hughes, Thomas Carnahan, I will now carry both of you into the spacecraft. Doctor Griffith, please follow us."

"Mister robot! Mister robot!" yelled Bobby as he pulled away from Lisa and pushed his way to the front of the group. "You better make Laura and Erik all better. You make 'em all good and better, 'cause Laura is my big sister, and Erik is my big brother, and I'm their little brother, and I'm sayin' you, you, you make 'em all better. You don't let 'em die. You make 'em all better. You just better do that."

"You are Bobby, yes?"

"Yeah, I'm Bobby, and I'll tell one of those flying ball things to blow you up if you don't make Laura and Erik all better."

"Bobby, the orbs would not do that, but you do not need to worry about Erik and Laura. They will live, and they will be strong and happy. Do you do you enjoy movies, Bobby?" the robot asked.

"Yeah, why?"

"Would you like Laura and Erik to send one of those orbs back from our world to show you something even better than a movie that will prove they are healthy and happy?"

"Yeah, I wanna see a movie showin' 'em all healthy and happy. Don't you forget to tell 'em to do that. And don't play a trick on me. I'll tell one of them flying ball things to blow you up if you trick me."

"I am a machine, Bobby. I do not forget, and I do not play tricks. Before this month is over, you will have your proof. One of the orbs will come back to visit you. It will find you wherever you are because your protector orb will tell it where you are. It will bring a special message for you and everyone here. You will like the news it brings you, I promise you."

"Okay, mister robot. Tell that ball thing to come right back here with a movie showin' Erik and Laura all healthy and stuff. I'll be here."

As the robot turned to carry Carnahan and Father Hughes toward the rescue ship, one of the sisters whispered to Sister Clare, "I wonder why that robot didn't offer to do something to, you know, fix Bobby?"

Lisa, who had been standing behind her, replied, "Sister, how can you, of all people, say such a thing? How could you not understand? Look at that beautiful, sweet boy! Look at him! If you knew and loved him like I do, you would understand that Bobby doesn't need to be 'fixed,' as you put it. He is not broken! Do you hear me? People like Bobby are here to fix the rest of us—to use your thoughtless term—by teaching us something about loving others!"

Lisa took Bobby by the arm. "Come on, my dear son, let's go back to the house."

"But Lisa, I ain't your son. My mama's in Heaven."

"I know, Bobby, I know. That's just my heart talking instead of my head. But I love you as if you were my son. Sometimes, I feel as if you really are my son."

"How does your heart do that, Lisa? How do you make your heart talk."

"Never mind, sweetheart. People just say things in funny ways sometimes."

Epilogue

The man standing behind him removed the handcuffs from Carnahan's wrists and yanked the pillowcase off his head.

"Have a seat, Major," said the stocky, square-jawed man sitting at a battered table before him.

Carnahan looked around the room. It was a boiler room of an old building he assumed was somewhere in Portland, although he couldn't be sure because of the long, deliberately circuitous route his escorts drove to get there. But to Carnahan, its location didn't matter. What mattered was that they had taken him here for this meeting rather than killing him on the spot. He knew that meant they had at least believed enough in the plausibility of his having changed allegiances to hear what he had to say.

"You can call me Alfred," said the man.

"Why not call you by your real name? I know who you are."

"Yes, I suppose you do, but here you will call me Alfred because the others in this room don't know my real name, and they don't know each other's real name. If you call any of us by our real name—even if it accidentally slips out of your mouth—you'll never utter another word. So, let's get down to business, Carnahan. I received word that you've turned traitor to the regime, went into hiding, and now want to put your talents to work with us. We have confirmed that your name has joined the names of our people on the regime's list and that you're a wanted man. But that could be part of a deception, couldn't it? So that doesn't count for much with us. We've also heard something about you pulling a jailbreak for a prisoner as your last official act as Commander of the Special Security Police. If that story is true and not part of a deception, it could be a mark in your favor with us, and you know it. Unfortunately, we can't confirm what happened to the prisoner. We know he was last seen in your custody, but he's not the only prisoner who disappeared while in the custody of your fine organization, is he? And there's the fairy tale that's going around, and getting more detailed each time I hear it, about you getting involved with space aliens at a convent, slaughtering and scattering combined elements of the Special Security Police and National Guard. Space aliens—that's a really good one, Carnahan. Leaving the space alien aspect aside for the moment, one of our sources did confirm that thirty-two cops and guardsmen were killed or missing after an event that occurred at a convent not far from here, and thirty-two more were killed a mile or two from there. But there are no living witnesses to confirm who attacked them. We know it wasn't the work of our people because we don't yet have the capability to do that. But that doesn't prove Martians have joined our cause. Oh, I almost forgot to mention, I also heard that you got shot in the chest sometime during all that, but here you are, moving around like a teenager. Do you think we may need just a little help believing your story, Carnahan? If not, I want to make it crystal clear to you. We need a lot of help believing your story. So now, I give you the podium. Make us believe you. Throw out the fairy tales and tell us your story. The real story. The whole story. Convince us. Do I even need to tell you how much your continued good health depends on you making believers out of us?"

Carnahan leaned forward and smiled. "I'm not too surprised that you've heard all of that, Alfred, because I'm the one who made sure that the news got to you. I know who talks to the people who talk to you. So, here I am, Alfred. I come to you unarmed, full of trust and confidence in your wisdom and sense of fair play. After today, we'll be on the same side, best buddies, comrades in arms, probably drinkin' buddies by the time this little pow-wow is over, right?"

The other three men laughed, but Alfred clenched his jaw and leaned toward Carnahan.

"Go ahead and play the comedian, Carnahan, but I haven't forgotten the faces of my friends who have disappeared or are dead—disappeared or dead because of you and your thug cops doing the dirty work of the scum that you answer to. Now, here you are, all sassy and brassy, and I am supposed to shake your hand, believe your fantasy stories, and welcome you into our fold with a hug and a kiss because you have so much outstanding inside knowledge to offer us. Well, I don't buy it, Carnahan! Oh, I know that something happened up there at that convent. I don't know what, but something did happen up there—that much is verified. But I say the rest of it is crap! I say that the story about you breaking a prisoner out of custody and turning traitor to the regime is crap! I say your making some kind of alliance with space people against the regime is a pile of crap! I say your getting shot in the chest and getting miraculously healed by your Martian friends is an even bigger pile of crap! I say you thought that if you cooked up a story that was so stupid even a little kid wouldn't believe it, we'd think that it must be true because you'd never dare try to sell us such an idiotic story unless it was true!

"Well, here's my warning to you, Major Thomas Carnahan: you may not make it out of this room alive. You have ten minutes to convince me beyond a speck of a doubt that every word of your story is gospel truth, or in ten minutes and two seconds, I will put a bullet right between your eyes, and they'll be scooping your corpse off a street in Portland or fishing it out of the Willamette River tomorrow. The clock starts now, funny boy!"

"Sounds fair to me, Alfred. First, allow me to stand and show you my wounds."

"Go ahead, Carnahan, do whatever you need to do. The clock's ticking."

Carnahan stood and pulled off his shirt. "What do you see, Alfred?"

I see your ten minutes and my patience wasting away, Carnahan."

Carnahan turned around and showed his bare back. "What do you see now, Alfred."

"I see a dead man, Carnahan. You'd better do something to persuade me to give you the rest of that ten minutes because I'm ready to pop you right now."

Carnahan buttoned his shirt and sat down. "You couldn't see anything because my wound completely healed in seven days because of the treatment I received on the alien ship. There's something else that you can't see. I can't see it right now either, but hovering somewhere in this room is a tennis ball-sized orb that follows me everywhere, and it will continue to follow me everywhere for some time to come. It is my protector. It is one of the many alien orbs that destroyed our attackers at the convent. Each of us at the convent has one of these orbs assigned to us as a bodyguard for a certain period of time. Many more of these orbs were assigned to carry out attacks against the regime's assets, here in this region and around the world, to help us get the upper hand on the Supreme Global Federation, so we'd better take advantage of the help these orbs provide us. You've probably wondered who the freelance saboteurs are who have been helping to cripple the regime everywhere in the world. Well, Alfred, it's not the work of freelance saboteurs. It's the work of the orbs. They are tilting the odds in our favor by surgically attacking the regime and leveling the playing field for us—actually, giving us a bit of an advantage. To prove that this and all of the other elements of my story are true, I invite you to participate in a little demonstration. I am asking my protector to spare your lives, but I'm telling it to knock all of you on your butts if any of you make the slightest move to harm me. So, if it is proof you're looking for, Alfred, I ask you, pretty please, with sugar on it, pull a weapon and kill me—just like you said you would. Even better, all of you, all of you at once, pull your weapons and commence firing. I'll just sit here until you do. Forget the clock, boys. Just kill me now."

The other men sat still, but Alfred stood and pulled a pistol from his waistband. Instantly, a blinding blue flash filled the room, knocking Alfred to the floor and hurling the others out of their chairs. Carnahan walked around the table, grabbed Alfred under his armpits, and lifted the dazed and disoriented man into his chair.

"So, do you believe me yet, Alfred? It's all right, old boy. You don't have to answer right now. Just sit there and collect your scrambled wits for a minute. When your brain clears up and you can remember who you are and where you are, we'll get down to business. I have a list of names for you—names of regime big shots, cops, and soldiers with innocent blood on their hands and plans for paying each of them a surprise visit. I have the locations of secret warehouses where they've been hoarding food and medicine to create shortages. I have the locations of small, secret prisons where the regime is holding people they haven't yet decided to execute and who need us to rescue them. These are ordinary citizens, patriotic former politicians, bishops, priests, other clergy, and even a few Resistance members—and that's just the beginning.

"How are you feeling now, Alfred? It looks like your eyes are starting to focus a little bit again. So, did I pass the job interview? How about it, Alfred, do you believe me yet?"

BOBBY WIPED THE SMUDGES from the front door window on the guest cottage. Suddenly, a gray orb appeared just above his head and began changing colors, something his protector orb had never done.

"Are you that flyin' ball thing from Erik and Laura? Did you bring a movie from Erik and Laura? The robot told me that you...."

Bobby stopped talking as faint blue rings of light emanated from the orb and surrounded him. Then Erik and Laura appeared in front of Bobby.

"Hello, Bobby," said Laura. "We are not really here even though we look real. What you see is part of the movie the robot told you we would make for you. Erik and I are feeling very well. We are completely healed of our wounds, just as the robot told you we would be. I wish we were there with you so I could give my little brother a big hug. Erik wants to say hello to you, too."

"Hello, Bobby, my little brother. As Laura said, we are very healthy and strong now. I am sure that you are healthy and strong, too. As your big brother, I ask you to continue being a good soldier by helping the sisters at the convent and doing your duty as well as you can. Whatever you do, Bobby, do it the best that you can. That is how other people will know you are a young man they can always depend on. And especially, Bobby, be sure to do your best for Lisa. The robot told me about the loving things he heard Lisa say about you when all of you were gathered near the rescue ship. While we were there with you, I saw how much Lisa loved you. She loves you as if she were your true mother. Lisa regards you as her son even more deeply than you regard Laura and me as your big sister and big brother. Lisa would happily adopt you and become what your people call your foster mother. Laura and I think it would make you happy, too, Bobby. Do you love Lisa enough to think of her as your mother? Think about that idea, Bobby. Lisa loves you very much, and we believe she will do whatever is necessary to adopt you as her son if you want her to do that.

"This part of our message you are watching now, Bobby, is only for you. No one else will see or hear it unless you want the orb to show it to someone," said Erik, "but Laura and I also have another message to show everyone else there at the convent to let them know how grateful we are for everything you did for us. We will also show everyone our home and our village so you can see what our world looks like. You will also meet some of our relatives and friends. No one on your planet has seen these things, and no one except you and our other friends at the convent ever will see these things. So please, Bobby, go now and tell everyone we have a message for them. Tell Father Hughes, Doctor Griffith, Carnahan, Lisa, Mother Catherine, Sister Clare, and all other sisters. Gather everyone together so that all of you can watch the message. The special orb that brought this message to you will stay with you for several days, if necessary, until you can watch it together as a family. It will be much more enjoyable that way. And all of you are family now.

"We must end this part of the movie now, Bobby," Laura said. "We miss you, and we are proud to have you as our little brother. We will never forget you, Bobby. Goodbye for now."

The blue rings disappeared, and the orb ceased changing colors as it hovered. Bobby stood quietly for several minutes. Then, he finished cleaning the window and set his bucket of cleaning materials on the ground.

"Okay, ball thing, you follow me," Bobby commanded the orb, then ran toward the convent house. "Mother Caff'rn!" he yelled. "Mother Caff'rn! It's here! The Laura and Erik movie! It's here! Call everybody so they can see it!"

Mother Catherine heard Bobby yelling and rushed out the door. "Bobby! What's wrong?"

"Call everybody, Mother Caff'rn! The Laura and Erik movie is here! The ball thing is here with the Laura and Erik movie! You're s'posa call everybody, and we're all s'posa watch it together! Laura and Erik said we gotta watch it together like a fam'ly. They said we was a fam'ly, and they want us to watch it together like a fam'ly. Call everybody! Call Father Hughes, and call that doctor guy, and call Sister Clare, and call that cop guy, and call all the sisters! Oh, and, and, and call Lisa! I mean . . . call . . . call Mama. Call Mama Lisa. Yeah, 'specially call Mama Lisa!"

The End

Also by D. E. Miller

The Road and Other Liars
Until The Rescue Ship Arrives

Milton Keynes UK
Ingram Content Group UK Ltd.
UKHW042003281024
450365UK00003B/143